G000138835

Playing Mercy

Matthew David Scott was born in Manchester. After studying in Sheffield he lived in Edinburgh before settling in Cardiff where he teaches English.

Playing Mercy *is a mighty and moving hymn to belonging, pride and growth. Only a man unafraid to write from within his own culture could produce, without any sentimentality, such a passionately-convicted work. If you feel yourself playing host to the demon of judgementalism, then read* Playing Mercy. *Matt Scott loves his characters and the world that produced them, and the rest of us should, too.*
        Niall Griffiths

Playing Mercy

Matthew David Scott

Parthian
The Old Surgery
Napier Street
Cardigan
SA43 1ED

www.parthianbooks.co.uk

First published in 2005
© Matthew David Scott 2005
All Rights Reserved

ISBN 1-902638-55-7

Editor: Gwen Davies

Cover design by Marc Jennings
Printed and bound by Dinefwr Press, Llandybïe, Wales
Typeset by type@lloydrobson.com

Parthian is an independent publisher which works with
the support of the Arts Council of Wales and the Welsh
Books Council

British Library Cataloguing in Publication Data
A cataloguing record for this book is available from the
British Library

For Catherine 'Kitty' Draper

Thanks to: Mum, Dad and Claire; the Scott and Draper families; the Boys in Manchester and all the Sheffield lot; the gang at the Woodside WMC; friends in London, Swansea, Cardiff, Atlanta and anywhere else you might have ended up; Gwen, Dominic, Richard and all at Parthian; lloyd robson and Marc Jennings; Jeremy at Red Handed *and George at* Blowback; *Alan for the photo and all at Slung Low Theatre Company; Alex Mercer; Drooghi Clothing in Cardiff; Studd Menswear in Manchester; special thanks to Niall for all the support; and finally, always, Jo.*

Friday 7th November 2003

08.30

Chris is looking for Keeley. He stands against the wall of the science block and gazes down the school driveway. Youngsters are scaling the tarmac – some fractions of slow-moving gangs, others singular and hurried. Chris seems indifferent, unaware that just over the driveway's horizon, oozing down the main road in front of the school, a whole world goes on without him. Chris is looking for Keeley.

The science block is a squat tartrazine orange annex to the main school building. It seems difficult to refer to it as an extension, more a cheap prosthetic limb. Professional photographs in the school's prospectus dangle it as 'contemporary' and 'well-resourced' but the only function it serves at the moment is gaudy backdrop for the blue of Chris' jacket and the silver of his tight-fitting cap.

Chris' cap crowns his shaved scalp at an angle made more obtuse by the degree to which he tilts his head in order to keep watch. He looks out through shatterproof blue eyes balanced on his lower lids. Dark, full eyebrows bracket an upturned nose – sloped due to genetics rather than his stance – and his lips are pursed as if about to spit. Chris has the ruddy complexion of someone who has lived his entire life on a cold and windy day.

Over to Chris' right, two boys are playing pennies against the grey wall of the main school building. They have both pitched one pound coins almost flush with the wall. A third boy walks up to the kerb and all three dog each other like hip hop video dice throwers. Boy number three balances his pound coin between his index finger and thumb; squats, stands, stoops, and pitches. All imagine the coin in super-slow motion as it follows its trajectory, perhaps even a shimmering edge as it eclipses the low November sun before it lands photo finish close to the other two coins. This will be a hard one to call and all three stand back with folded arms, sigh foggy thoughts into the air, and suck their teeth. Chris of course isn't bothered by such peripheral events. Instead he hollows out the pocket of his jacket and takes out some chewing gum. The incline of the driveway, like the break of an escalator's wave, is still showing no signs of delivering Keeley.

Barbara stares across the Food Court. She isn't looking for anything. She is sat at one of the yellow plastic tables at which all manner of limp snacks and weak beverages are served daily. Not citrus yellow, not sunshine yellow, but luminous battery-egg yolk yellow. She is waiting for the end of her shift.

The Food Court is on the top floor of the Archer Indoor Shopping Centre and has been Barbara's to clean for the last three years. Right now the place is spotless: the tables, the flooring and the worktops transfigure under the strip lighting. Once upon a time Barbara would have taken pride in this sacrosanct cleanliness but today, as with most days now, she simply sparks another Lambert & Butler.

Barbara first took the job because she had to. Not because she was broke – even though she's not rich by any stretch of the imagination – but because in her whole life Barbara had 'never looked a gift horse in the mouth'. The job had been her younger sister Jean's, but Jean had fallen pregnant again and so had to be replaced. Given her recent loss, the whole family thought that it was the perfect opportunity to take everything off Barbara's mind.

The night before her first day she hardly slept at all. She hadn't had a job since she was seventeen when David had begun to show, and despite cleaning up other people's shit ever since, she couldn't be sure if she did it properly – whether it stood up to the scrutiny of the experts. The anxiety of such a personal inspection had her set off for that first day, with morning yet to shake off the habit of night. She made her way past what was to become David's Garage, swept below the bowling green, scaled the ramp of the multistory car park, and faced up to the automatic double doors. She stood outside them for a while, half trying to compose herself, half trying to figure out why they hadn't opened at her customary sesame. The security guard on duty slid the doors manually and invited her in for her first day.

Today is the day. Chris has been watching Keeley for a few weeks now, seriously researching her for at least the last three days; today he is going to make his move.

There is no evidence of such ambition in his posture by the science block wall. His hands are clasped behind his back, an arc of space between his shoulder blades and the base of his spine. One boot stanchions the wall, the other planted firmly on the concrete and covered lazily by a black rucksack. The only movement comes from Chris' mouth as he moulds a tasteless old tablet of chewing gum across his front teeth in an attempt to squeeze out any remnants of freshness.

So much is brewing in the compressed bustle of the outside world that there seems to be a certain naivety to Chris' focus. At this time of the morning the main road beyond the crest of the driveway brings lives to a standstill. It pumps like a swollen vein through these northern suburbs of the city while districts flex and junctions twitch at the cells that are coursing towards the metropolitan heart. Chris thinks nothing of this. Instead he looks out to the sun and then, blinking away the green and blue footprints left by its glare, notices a silhouette form before him.

The sun seems to have a personal vendetta against Billy. He waits outside the Garage for David to arrive while trying in vain to dodge its beams and eat one of the sandwiches his wife Beth had left in the fridge. She'd gone to bed by the time he got home and his head now feels a lot worse for that fact. The sandwich isn't going down well. It is his favourite – rubbery cheddar and tangy pickle – but every mouthful seems to sit hot on his lungs. Billy is experienced enough to know that he must eat something or he will feel shit all morning.

The Garage overlooks a daycare centre for the elderly where Billy and his friends used to hang out when they were younger. Some of Billy's first sexual experiences took place behind that building and although today's youngsters follow in the footsteps of Billy and his friends, Billy is safe in the knowledge that his generation were the first to fully utilise the magnificent facilities of the Old Folks'. From the front, the Old Folks' gives the impression of the clean and well-designed modernity any family would want as a place for their elderly relatives to while away the days; safe from marauding teenage gangs and buggy-wielding single mothers. However, the beautiful paradox of that design is that as the elderly leave the inside of the building at dusk, the youngsters colonise the building's exterior. The very youngsters who make up the marauding gangs, the very youngsters on the road to becoming the next buggy-wielders. But Billy and his friends got there first.

Leaned against the Garage door, nostalgia almost bringing a dry smile to his lips, Billy's reverie is broken by the reality that the notion of Billy and his friends is a fantasy. Anyone from around here could tell you that Billy and his friends are in fact David and his friends. As if to illustrate this fact, David is now Billy's boss, the owner of the Garage and the reason Billy has arrived to work early today. He wants to make the right impression. He wants half the day off. It's bound to work of course. How long has he known David? They're like brothers.

The same rays of sun that doggedly search out Billy catch Marie in their crosshairs, waking her up with a headache and a sore back. She groans as she gropes the windowsill for a drink, cleaving the curtains and allowing the sun to streak in. Eventually she locates her drink next to the old music box she was given as a young child. Her mother never forgets to leave a drink for her daughter on the windowsill above her bed. When Marie was young she used to sweat a great deal in her sleep and so Barbara has always left her a drink for the night and salted her meals well. Marie is glad this morning, if not grateful.

As she looks out of the curtains to curse the sun personally, Marie stretches and turns to the mirror. She never took off last night's make-up before she went to bed and the eye shadow that once complemented the blue of her eyes has instead formed crispy silver lines across her eyelids. Her eyebrows are smudged and mascara is flecked above her painted cheekbones; the natural rotund rosiness of her face is covered with an orange foundation that gives her a Sunny Delight glow. A large spot that had erupted without warning last night on her high forehead is still concealed by sludge while another has forced its way through on her babyish chin. Her patchy red lips have a weird white gunk collected in the corners. She looks up her nose and pulls at the end of it before it bounces back into its naturally-upturned position. Despite them both being her brothers, she looks more like Chris than David. She looks nothing like their mother.

Marie picks up her clothes from the floor and takes them through to the bathroom to put in the linen basket before collecting her phone from its charger on the way back. That is something she never forgets to do before bed.

The house feels occupied even though she knows nobody will be in. Then it makes sense – Squire, the dog. Marie can hear him excited behind the living room door at the smell of last night's perfume as she heads downstairs. She walks through the kitchen and into the living room to be molested by the grey muscle of Squire. After a few pats, tummy tickles and the smell of this morning's breath, he calms down and goes to his basket. The short grey hairs on the sofa give away the fact that he is only doing this for show.

Adept at multitasking, Marie gathers three remote controls from the floor by the settee, and puts on Box through the stereo whilst checking for messages on her phone. She smiles at one and quickly erases it before turning up the volume and heading back into the kitchen.

In an eye that looks nothing like her daughter's, Barbara feels a tear form. The tear is not caused by sorrow, or by the blue-grey double helix of smoke ascending from the cigarette she is still finishing. It is not caused by the fumes from the strong detergent she has to use. It is a collection of the thoughts she saves for the future. Ignoring the kitchen staff now arriving, she retreats into the memory of that first day.

The security guard led Barbara to the storage room at

the back of the Food Court. The Archer Centre looked monstrous under the livid glare of the fluorescent lighting – its pyramidal skylights like angry teenage blackheads. The guard opened a heavy door and took Barbara into the guts of the building. In here was an entirely different world, a world of riveted chipboard, sawdust, builders' scribbles and litter. The storage room lay at the end of this intestinal corridor and within, she found the cleaning trolley that still drags her around today – a mutant creation of dented metal tubing, scratched plastic surfaces, a space for bucket and cleaning products underneath and sides housing rowlocks for the mop and brush. The storage room was detailed with unbranded detergent bottles, unlabelled boxes of disposable gloves busting at their stapled seams and rolls of black bin liners spewed out like destroyed videotape. The security guard gave Barbara her instructions for the day and then headed on to be spewed back up into the shopping centre whilst playing with the keys in his pocket. Exactly the same happened every morning since.

The story was identical for Chris. Despite hope springing from the momentary blindness caused by the sun's footsteps, the silhouette that took shape before him was not that of Keeley, but that of just another customer. It is one of the boys who were playing pennies. The Third Boy. While the other boys sucked their teeth and sighed solutions, the Third Boy simply used his reputation to take charge of the situation and picked up what were now *his* winnings. A simple look let the other players know that an executive decision had been made and they had to stand and watch as any sense of justice faded into the air like their breath. The Third Boy simply smiled as he put three brand new pound coins into his pocket.

David drops his keys into his pocket as he climbs out of his second hand BMW and steps out across the entrance of the Garage.

'Billy, you look like shit.'

Billy struggles to eat another bite of his sandwich and nods. It's true; Billy doesn't look his usual self. Usually he is tanned, green eyed and centre parted. Today his wet but unwashed hair sticks to his head, his green eyes simmer red and his tan looks dangerously jaundiced. David looks his usual self: classical.

'What's up, shat the bed or something?'

Billy smiles weakly as he gives his answer: 'You know me, Dave: true professional. Work-a-fucking-holic. Much on today?'

'Nah. Fuck all really.'

'Shit. Half day then?'

David stops and looks straight at Billy. He raises an eyebrow and smiles.

'You're a rum bastard, you are!'

Billy looks at his half-eaten sandwich and tosses it out onto the pavement for the pigeons. He'll get a proper breakfast later.

Marie has another stretch and thinks about her breakfast. She is sat at the impractical large wooden kitchen table in one of the chairs that aren't jammed against the magnolia wall. She plods over to one of the fitted cupboards where she finds some Nutella and a packet of Ryvita. She puts back the Ryvita and then, after scooping out a dollop with her finger, the Nutella too. As she places the jar back, sucking the spread from her finger, she notices a box of two hundred duty-free Lambert & Butler cigarettes on top of the cupboard. She takes a chair from the dining table and stands on it to check the box. Luckily the box is already open so she takes a packet and gets down off the chair.

She undresses the cellophane from the packet of cigarettes, flips the lid and plucks the silver flap before collecting a lighter from the top of the fridge and heading to the back door. Standing on the backdoor step, Marie lights the cigarette and blows blue smoke out across the little yard. Her cold breath makes it seem as if she is exhaling much more than she inhaled.

Autumn has really hit town. The orange-brown leaves cover dog turds on the new block paving like nature's own practical joker. November means birthdays: Chris', David's then hers. It is Chris' birthday on Sunday, which means it will be hers in less than three weeks. She thinks about what she wants. Money. She better start getting the same amount of money as Chris soon. She'll be fourteen after all.

Being just fourteen, the Third Boy's reputation means nothing to Chris as he tentatively steps towards him. Chris raises his head slowly so that the Third Boy is looking straight into the barrel of his nose, and invites him to speak.

Although he was bigger and tougher than his competitors,

he is smaller and more suppliant in the presence of Chris but still attempts bravado in his approach: 'Got any cigs?'

Rather like the shop assistants of the city's more upmarket boutiques, Chris reacts with annoyance at the question, despite this being his job. He sells cigarettes in school. His brother David has a friend called Graham who gets them for him and splits the profits. Graham is well known amongst the townsfolk and knowledge that Chris is selling Graham's cigs in school means that Chris is the only person selling cigs in school. Full stop. The price is more of a question mark.

'Who's asking?'

'Erm – me.'

'Has "me" got any cash?'

'Yeah.'

'Right, well I've got some cigs. Fifty a go.'

'Fifty a go! It was thirty yesterday.'

It is true, yesterday was thirty pence per cigarette and in fact for the rest of the day it will probably still be thirty pence. But the Third Boy has pissed Chris off by distracting him from his watch and the Third Boy can see the strain in the warped plastic of Chris' eyes. As way of an apology he takes out one of the one-pound coins he has just minted.

'I'll have two, then. Please.'

Barbara's cigarette has whispered past the manufacturer's stamp. She looks back out across the Food Court.

Already ruin is setting in. The footsteps of the kitchen staff are leaving ectoplasmic trails on the wet floor, the perforated edge of a wage slip trails across a worktop like dead skin, and coffee has collected around the edge of an ashtray on another yellow table. The tear is stillborn in Barbara's eye. She puts out the cigarette and decides she has more important things to cry over.

There is still no sign of Keeley.

11.05

Graham. 'Golden Graham'. That's how he's known around these parts but never to his face. He is so called because he wears a lot of the stuff, absolutely loads of the stuff: two chains – one of which is at least three inches thick, the other thinner but carrying a cross that would shame the most ascetic Christian. A heavy sleeper in his left ear. Wedding, sovereign and signet rings dotted about his digits as well as another tasteful article bearing the simple legend 'G' on each middle finger. A fat gold bracelet on his right wrist looks anorexic next to the watch that adorns his right. One canine and two incisors are luxuriously capped.

He leaves his council house, locking the heavy steel door, and heads out into the street, patting the white Sierra Cosworth on his driveway like a well-loved pet. The sun has not climbed much higher than it had been in the early morning but its light bounces off the newly resurfaced tarmac like a cry between mountains.

The local authority laid the tarmac in a fanfare of publicity a couple of weeks ago. The Council Leader, the Mayor, and the Chair of the Residents' Association shone creamy smiles in the local press as years of pressure finally paid off. Nobody else was really bothered. In fact, most residents could do without the local authority getting involved in their affairs. So far it has meant speed bumps that stop the Hail and Ride buses coming anymore, CCTV scaring off door-to-door meat and perfume sellers, and this bloody tarmac reflecting the sun into everyone's eyes as they try to nod hellos to Graham.

They all say hello to Graham, and in return for this show of neighbourly respect, Graham reciprocates with a nod, a wink and a burnished smile. This smile is more important to them than that of any elected representative – a smile that tightens Graham's ice-blue eyes, stretches the nostrils of his fountain-pen nose and reveals boyish dimples. Despite the scar dissecting his left cheek it's a winning smile.

Marie isn't smiling. She sits on the settee, legs bent under her behind at ninety degrees, elbow denting the cushioned arm, and head slumped into her palm like a heavy hinge. She looks uncomfortable and unhappy but it is all for show as Barbara has just arrived back from her after-work errands.

'Are you okay, darling?'

The heavy bags Barbara carries bear no weight in Marie's

conscience. She heard her mum's footsteps – footsteps she has come to recognise like the signature she can forge so well – a good thirty seconds before the key hit the door. This perfect pitch comes from practice. Marie can distinguish the footsteps of the everyday passer-by from her mother and brothers with ease. As this was her mother, there was no panic. Barbara can be convinced of anything by her children, a weakness born solely of love but a weakness to exploit nonetheless. Marie quite rightly believes she could get away with murder. It would be different if her dad were still around.

'Yeah.'

Curling an arm so that one of the shopping bags slides down into the crook of her elbow, Barbara presses the back of her hand to Marie's forehead.

'You are a bit hot, love. Would you like a nice drink? I've bought some cream soda.'

Marie tries not to answer straight away although she desperately wants to. Instead, she raises her arm and mimics her mother's concern.

Chris, Zeb and Snowman have their forearms on the banister, their chins on their forearms and their arses stuck in the air. The stairs in the art block are where they hang out at break and so that is where we find them: leaning on the banister, looking out across the yard.

The yard is far from busy – most pupils preferring to spend their break-times fighting their way to the vending machines – but still the boys stare out across it like fishermen watching the horizon for an impending storm.

Their speech mirrors this. The words themselves are light and insignificant but they hide every fear that they wish they could express, a fear of what happens next. What is waiting for them once the safety net of five periods a day, five days a week is taken away at the end of this, their final year in school? What are they going to fill time with once they have to marshal their own lives? It is a fear they will never speak of, one they will actively hide but every word they mumble is dense with it, each phoneme a stone skipping across the ominously still water before it disappears forever. Snowman throws first.

'My mum's fucking gutted. Never seen her like it.'

A sigh precedes Chris' reply.

'Yeah.'

Chris' reply sinks beneath the surface a few feet before Snowman throws again.

'Bound to be. I suppose.'

Plop.

When they lose focus on the concrete, the boys accidentally catch their reflections in the window. Snowman is the tallest, decked out in Manchester United training top and blue cap with earflaps. His trousers would skirt dangerously above his brown Rockport boots if they were not tucked into dark blue Donnay socks. Snowman looks like a bit of a joke but it isn't his sartorial elegance that Snowman is notorious for. Snowman is notorious for going further than anyone else before thinking about it. He is pure entertainment. But not today. His grandmother died last week and his mother and father have taken it badly. Well, he thinks they must have but a steady glaze of alcohol has replaced any real emotion in their eyes for as long as he can remember. His grandmother looked after him, bought him his clothes, gave him a KitKat to eat at on his way to school every day.

'Frank isn't happy either.'

Zeb's comment is cast out into the water. Snowman bites as usual.

'Frank?'

'Kish's Frank. The shop.'

'Oh. Right. How come?'

Zeb reels him in with the complacent stretch and yawn an easy catch deserves. 'He hasn't sold a KitKat since.'

Snowman barely reacts. He accepts that there are too many reasons why this was meant to happen. Zeb just sinks back into his earlier position. They are bored and scared, desperate for something – anything – to happen. Chris is still looking for Keeley. Or rather, he has sent Kish to look for Keeley.

It's always Kish who gets the dirty jobs. He blunders his away along the humanities corridor, his huge frame clipping the posters on the wall, posters of people he doesn't recognise trying to coax him to read. It is break-time and as a Year Eleven he isn't meant to be in this section of the school. He very quietly tells the teacher on duty that he is on his way to the library.

After being allowed to pass, he stops at a vending machine where Year Sevens are clamouring for chocolate and sweets. This depresses him greatly. He has a bag full of chocolate he should be selling at this very moment. He takes a bar from his bag – Galaxy Ripple – and tears off the wrapper before putting the whole lot into his mouth. A whole bar he could have just made a profit on instead of being on his way to see Chantelle, Keeley's best friend.

Chantelle always ends up doing the dirty work. She stands outside the girls' toilet checking out the new ringtones she downloaded for her mobile phone last night. They all sound the same. The smell of smoke is walking tall in the corridor as some Year Nines cough their way through some of Chris' wares in the cubicles over her left shoulder. Chris. It's been obvious all week that something was going to happen on the Chris front but you know what boys are like. Trust Keeley to stay home today. The dirty work is dirty enough without having to do it *all* on your own.

Kish thinks the very same thing as he kills the Galaxy Ripple and discards the wrapper on the floor of the corridor; it lands silver side up.

A glittering object tempts a twenty-year-old heroin addict called Martin onto the street. He twitches his way over to Graham who feigns ignorance whilst keeping peripheral vigilance. Martin is shaking and sweating and yearning for Graham with bold desperation in his paper print eyes. He skips and hops to catch Graham's steady roll and goes into his pocket. His hand retrieves a sudden flash of silver and Graham spins around and grabs him by the wrist. Martin is holding a digital camera.
    'Whoa! Martin. You shouldn't sneak up on me like that.'

'Sorry, Graham, I've just –'

'Yeah, I can see. You hurting? I've told you, Martin. You need to stop with that shit. Look at you. How's your mum?'

'Fine, she's –'

'And the TV? How's the TV I got her?'

'Fine, Graham, fine, it's –'

'I bet she feels safer as well with *the new CCTV round here.*'

A hand is rested on Martin's shoulder. Graham fixes him with an outwardly sympathetic glare before glancing over at the camera trained on them. At last Martin understands. He puts the camera back in his pocket.

'Sorry, Graham.'

'Don't worry about it, Martin. You go home. Try to be cool and come and see me later, alright?'

'Cheers, Graham.'

'Oh, and Martin. Those antiques you brought round. Really nice, good job.'

'Cheers.'

'Cheers, Mum.'

Marie takes the glass of cold cream soda from her mother. Mmm, Cream Soda.

Cream soda on the way back from Nanna Dee-Dee's was one of Marie's oldest memories. Marie, Chris, David and Barbara would stop at Frank's Food and Booze as a reward for staying quiet and listening to Nanna Dee-Dee talk non-stop about what Nora from the greengrocer's had done that week. The boys would each get an iced Jubliee and a packet of Toffoes while Marie would get a small bottle of American cream soda. Even then the boys got more, but the clear fizz would keep Marie sweet. If only things were still so simple.

Shopping bags are left on the kitchen floor like babies on a convent doorstep as Barbara takés the drink to Marie in the front room. Marie takes the glass around the rim with her fingertips and double-jointedly swings it around to her mouth.

'I bet you're feeling better already, eh?'
Barbara looks on. She tucks her chin into her neck, smiles, and goes back into the kitchen to start packing away the shopping. The freezer door opens with an unnatural gasp and Barbara puts in the Creamy Chicken Kievs. Marie is still on the settee, watching Box while her mother attempts to converse through shouts and repetitions.

'It's going to the dogs, that Archer Centre, you know?'
'What?'
'It's going to the dogs. The Archer Centre.'
'What, Squire?'
'No. The Archer Centre.'
'Yeah?'

Box is playing more of the same, and Marie loves it. She sings along before remembering herself and letting out a little cough. The front room is nice. Really nice. Well, nicer than school. David redecorated a few months ago. The walls are painted peach with a green leaf-patterned wallpaper dado cutting them in two. The floors are easy-fix laminate and the marshmallow three-piece suite bakes in front of the natural-look fire. In the corner is a huge entertainment system: video, DVD, PS2, N64, Nicam Digital Stereo Widescreen TV. Two huge speakers are fixed to the wall either side of a pine-framed mirror that sits above the fireplace while two more on stands flank the settee. On the mantelpiece are school photos of David, Chris and Marie, as well as a picture of their little cousins Jenny and Paul in their christening gowns. Although it isn't his birthday until Sunday, Chris has two birthday cards up. The first is from his Uncle Patrick, all the way from Australia, and is a simple print of an Aboriginal painting. He always posts one early to make sure it gets there in time. Their father's older brother, he moved away to Australia when he was eighteen. The rumour goes that it is because he is gay. Next to that is a huge 'Happy Birthday to a Special Brother' card from David. David can't hold onto surprises; he gave Chris his present – a Stone Island jumper – nearly a week and a half ago. But that's David.

Leaning on the bonnet of a recent re-spray and looking over at Billy: 'This mean you're not out tonight then?'

'Eh? Oh. No. I'm feeling all right now. I'll be out. For a bit.'

'What's up, then? You've got a face like a smacked arse.'

Billy wipes his greasy hands and looks at David. 'Just thinking about my mum. You know, with Nanna dying and everything.'

'Shit, yeah.'

'Yeah. Snowman hasn't taken it well either.'

''Course.'

David looks at the ground. All morning Billy has been trying to put a brave face on it, blaming his mood on a hangover, when all along he was grieving. Worrying and grieving. David can't believe he didn't see through it earlier.

'Tell you what, mate. That half-day. It's yours if you want it. We haven't got a lot on anyway.'

'Nah, I –'

'You'll do as you're fucking told. I'm the boss round here.'

Billy tries his best to balance pleasure, grief and gratitude in the look on his face.

'Cheers, Dave.'

'I know what it's like. Remember? Clear up here and you can fuck off to see your mum. Don't. Wasn't long ago I was in the same boat. Not long ago at all.'

1994. That was the last time Graham had been arrested and it was a fact that he was fiercely proud and protective of.

He was fourteen and working for a local entrepreneur on the auctions, collecting the money that punters had handed over in exchange for dubious electrical goods. One day a rival entrepreneur turned up looking to put Graham's boss out of business. Graham got on the end of a double-bladed Stanley knife, Someone Else got on the end of a crowbar and when the police arrived, only Graham and the Someone Else were left. Neither entrepreneur came forward, both protégés went down; the Someone Else got two years in prison (he had previous, apparently; Graham's seen him since – nice bloke) while Graham got six months in a young offenders' institute and the scar. He kept his mouth shut so that his boss might see fit to reward him on his release. He'd seen *Goodfellas*; he knew the score. Only when he came out, his boss had given his old job to another fourteen-year-old and couldn't be seen fraternising with Graham after everything that had happened. Come on now, you've got to understand. It's nothing personal.

Graham will admit freely that he was young and stupid but he hasn't been arrested since and his old boss pissed off some city centre boys and met a loud and headless end a few years ago. 1994. That's a long time.

Chris checks his watch. It seems like an age has passed since he asked Kish to do his bidding. He looks at Zeb. Maybe he should have sent Zeb. Yeah, Zeb is quick. But so is his mouth. A gob on legs, David calls him. He is short and skinny, his head so much bigger than his body that his neck looks like snapping. Perhaps it is only those incredibly large ears acting as some kind of counterbalance that prevent this from happening. Chris can never fathom why all the girls fancy Zeb.

No he was right to send Kish. Kish is reliable.

Kish can see Chantelle outside the girls' toilets. They are disgusting, stink of smoke, and have those bins for –. Eugh. Kish doesn't even want to think about that. What he sees in front of him is repellent enough.

Look at the state of her. She must be about fourteen stone but still wears a skirt that looks like it has been sprayed onto the top of her thighs. At least she doesn't have fake tan like the rest of them. She's mixed race and works her weekends at a tanning salon. She wears a Carbrini hooded top but the pockets around her midriff only draw attention to her massive gut. Her left hand is buried deep within one pocket, her right hand still dancing across the buttons of her phone despite being hampered by a fist full of cheap gold. She's got big tits.

So has Kish.

Look at him! The fucking big bear. Every time that Chantelle sees Kish she laughs. He is just like a cartoon character, everything is round and lumpy. He must be over six feet tall but he is at least five feet wide. His trousers are tucked into the top of his socks and his baseball cap is just a little too tight – tapering his upper and lower extremities like a spinning top in a massive red jacket. Still, as he gets closer, his light brown skin; his shaved eyebrow; the border around his hair, his deep brown eyes.

That toffee-coloured skin; her green eyes like maps of the world; the stud above her top lip, her top lip!

She's pretty fit.

He's pretty cute.

'Alright, Chan.'

'Alright, Kish.'

'Listen, Chan. I've got a favour to ask.'

Chantelle's phone shuts with a snap.

Marie finishes her cream soda and puts it on the floor with a quiet click. In the kitchen, Barbara is putting away the tins. She smiles as she puts away the macaroni cheese, remembering that it was the only thing that David would eat as a child. Chris' fetish was rice pudding and Marie's oxtail soup.

'I've got some oxtail for you here, love. Do you want some?'

'Oh, I don't know, Mum.'

Of course Marie is already licking her lips at the prospect but has to remain in character. She knows exactly what her mother's response will be, so much so that she mouths along to the words like a song on Box.

'You still have to eat love, and soup's the perfect thing. Got to keep your fluids up.'

Barbara knows Marie's response so well she has already poured the soup.

'Go on then, Mum. If you say.'

Squire, sensing a feed, trots expectantly around the back yard.

Graham struts triumphantly down the road. He looks over at the Red Lion and smiles. It found another supplier of under the counter cigarettes a few months ago. Until Graham found out. It now has no under-the-counter cigarettes. Turning right at the Red Lion, Graham walks up past Kwik Save and across the main road to Frank's Food and Booze.

The main road is now almost clear and is easily trampled by the crepe-soled shoes of Graham. Working up from the shoes – the latest Nicholas Deakins – Graham wears blue ankle socks; navy blue Henri Lloyd brushed denims with the band of his grey jockey shorts licking above the waist; a light blue crew-necked CP Company sweater, and a threequarter-length black DKNY leather jacket. Underneath his black Armani Jeans baseball cap, his blonde hair has been harvested as a number one crop, the only giveaway to his colouring being the three-day stubble that dresses his face. He smells of L'Eau D'Issey.

Graham uses his fingertips to prod open the shop door before stopping and surveying this small part of his kingdom. Frank's Food and Booze is a typical corner shop trying its best to compete with the supermarket on the other side of the road. The strip lighting is on, the fridges are full of wafer-thin meat and there are at least eight feet of soft porn on the top shelf of the magazine rack.

Graham picks up a *Daily Star* and an *Exchange and Mart* before heading to the counter to see Frank himself. Frank swipes the paper over the infra-red sensor on his till.

'*BEEP*!'

Barbara reaches into the microwave to collect Marie's soup. She lifts the kitchen roll from the top of the bowl, and drops it into the pedal bin. She then takes a dishtowel and cups it beneath the bowl before placing the bowl onto a tray. Squire is scratching on the door outside and although Barbara tries to ignore him, it is as if the door was made of slate and the noise is unbearable. She goes around to the back door and opens it, Squire bounding in and jumping up to Barbara's knees.

'Get down you, I know, I know.'

She looks out across the yard and spots a cigarette butt on the block paving. Just next to her foot on the step is a small black stain and some loose strands of tobacco where the cigarette had been put out. It is fairly fresh, so it couldn't be her or David so that leaves Chris or....

It must be Chris. She knew him selling cigs would end up in him smoking them. She strides out across the yard to pick up the butt and spots Mr Buckley next door through the slats in the fence.

'Morning, Barbara.'

'Morning, Mr Buckley. Police said anything yet?'

'No. Apart from it's very unlikely I'll see any of it again.'

'Little bastards, eh? Steal from their own mothers, some of them would.'

'Not yours though eh, Barbara? A good lot, yours.'

'Yeah. They're not a bad lot. Anyway, youngest isn't too well so...'

'Only Mummy can make her better. I know. Tell her to get well soon from me.'

'Will do, Mr Buckley. Ta da.'

'Laters.'

A smiling Kish floats away from Chantelle. He's done his job well and feels the satisfaction circumnavigate his body. He looks at his watch. Not long until the end of break, he's not going to make it back to the art block in time. He wonders whether he should let Chris sweat a little, at least until dinner, but he decides that would be cruel. Kish isn't that kind of person. Not like Zeb. Kish takes out his mobile phone and stops in the corridor. He types in his message to Chris and presses send.

'*BEEP!*'

Frank scans the rest of Graham's items.

'Alright, Frank? Business still good?'

Frank's real name is Sukraj and business has really picked up since he started paying Graham one hundred pounds per week for security. He doesn't put a guard on the door and he hasn't fitted any new cameras but Graham's security has definitely worked.

'Well, you know. Can't grumble.'

'Good, good. Get rid of those cigs?'

'In a day, Graham. They all went in one day.'

'Well, Uncle Graham did say. You'll be wanting more then?'

'Yes, definitely but –'

Graham looks up from his paper for the first time since his conversation with Sukraj began. He doesn't like 'buts'. However, he is going to give Frank the benefit of the doubt.

'But?'

'The security. You know, things have really gotten quieter lately and –'

Ands. Graham could usually handle those but he really didn't like the sound of this one.

'And?'

'Well, I was wondering if I needed, to – if it was necessary for me to –'

'You want to stop with the security?'

'Yes. Yes, Graham.'

Sukraj looks at Graham's Adam's apple. It springs forward and retreats again like the trigger on a pricing gun.

The fridges hum, the strip lighting flickers.

'No problem, Frank. I'm glad things have got quieter. Not like we had a contract or anything, is it?'

Sukraj's fingers slide from the counter in relief and he looks to the ceiling before meeting Graham's eyes again.

'Thanks, Graham. I don't want you to think I didn't appreciate –'

'Shh, Frank. You know me. I'm all about the community. I didn't like to see you being singled out because, you know, that bin Laden and all that.'

Sukraj Singh is a Sikh.

'I know, Graham, I just –'

Graham doesn't *believe* in just.

'Don't worry Frank. It isn't a problem. I'll have these and a packet of blue Extra.'

Sukraj hands over the chewing gum and smiles a tight-lipped smile. He presses 'cancel' on the till.

'No, no, Graham. On the house.'

'You don't have to do that, Frank.'

'No, I insist. After all you have done for me it is the least –'

'Cheers, Frank, and if anything happens, which I *hope* it won't, you know where to get me.'

'Yes, Graham. Thank you.'

'Ta da, Frank. Take care.'

Graham walks out of the shop and tosses a chewing gum into his mouth. 'Hope'. Now that's something Graham can't get wound up about. He can only laugh when it comes to hope. He finds it ridiculous. He throws the newspaper into the bin.

The cigarette butt lies on top of a soup-stained piece of kitchen roll in the pedal bin. Barbara picks up the tray. Squire is now in the kitchen too and is scratching at the living room door but Marie finds it easier to ignore. Barbara works hard to avoid treading on him while she pushes the door handle down with her elbow. To do this whilst carrying the tray requires a great deal of skill and Barbara is pleased with the lack of fuss in her handling of the situation. As the handle gives, she pushes the door open with her right hip and walks in backwards, kicking the empty glass across the laminate flooring. It skips across the floor like a bouncing bomb and hits the skirting board by the TV. By sheer reflex, Barbara tries to stop the glass, and the bowl of oxtail soup slides off the tray, topples in mid air and spills the thick brown liquid across the floor. Backsplash hits both Barbara's ankles and the fringe on the settee. The bowl itself lands in the mess and then rolls an oxtail trail across the easy-fix laminate. Squire follows the trail and begins to lap up the mess. Barbara lets off a volley of expletives.

'BE-BEEEP, BE-BEEP!'

Chris pulls out his mobile phone and reads the message. He puts the phone back in his pocket and breathes a sigh of relief. Everything he'd been hoping for has just come true. The bell goes for the end of break.

12.55

Time is pressing Kishan up against the inside of his bedroom door. The huge cardboard box that takes his whole span to hold is forcing him to back-heel the door open and reverse out onto the landing. He hears his mother downstairs and can smell the delicious spices of his heritage creeping up them. His father is still in bed. With a late night on the taxis to come he needs his sleep but the rest of the family are in school: brother Tarampal – a carbon copy of Kish blundering around Year Nine – while sister Gurdeep reaches out towards big school from her Year Six bunker.

Kish is the eldest son and so a great responsibility falls on his broad shoulders. He is well aware of this and has been planning to take it for many years. But not in the traditional sense. Not in the sense that his parents have in mind. Kish has seen where the real kudos lies on the Estate and he is striving for something much bigger than tradition.

He makes his way slowly down the stairs, rocking from foot to foot and ducking to avoid hitting his head. Putting the box down in order to open the back door, he catches a look at himself in the mirror. He needs a haircut. He cut his hair many years ago despite his father's turban but still wears a metal band around his wrist because he reckons it looks cool. The border around his ears is growing out. Maybe he'll get Zeb's mum to do it for him tomorrow. Might even get a Nike swoosh shaved into it. Yeah, he needs a haircut but he's still feeling good.

Over his right shoulder, in his reflection, is a picture of him from Year Seven. Chubby, school tie and V-neck jumper, bum fluff moustache already beginning to show. Now it looks nothing like him as if time and change have chiselled away at the old Kish and left this man in its wake. Because Kish is really starting to feel like a man these days. He lifts the box back up. A man. It's time for Kish to start calling the shots.

Over at Snowman's grandmother's house, Zeb is calling the shots.

'Two – nil, with just under fifteen minutes to go, and Real are really showing their class now. Can Barça *somehow* find their way back into this one?'

Snowman wishes he wasn't: 'Fuck off Zeb.'

If there is one thing that Snowman takes seriously, very seriously, it is Pro Evolution Soccer on the Play Station 2. He has played many football games and they all bring with them different shades of memory – from the nostalgic rose-tinted glow of Kick Off and Sensible Soccer to hindsight's ruddy embarrassment when recalling any football game developed for the SNES. But even the ultra-satisfying two or three-day bouts of Championship Manager have never come close to this. As far as Snowman is concerned, you can stick your fucking FIFA up your arse. Pro Evolution Soccer is the closest to the real thing you can get. But reality has its dangers and right now Snowman is feeling the hurt, fear and anger of a home defeat in the biggest La Liga derby there is.

'And that's three! An exquisite pass only matched by its finish, Ronaldo coolly lifting the ball over the despairing dive of –'

'I'm telling you, Zeb, if you don't fuck off I'm going to fucking bang you!'

The sound is down and this is all the encouragement Zeb needs. He sits back and swaps a wry smile with Chris whose Real Madrid side are pounding Snowman despite him only ever playing the game when he comes here. Snowman lives at the top end of the Estate, the opposite end to Chris, and the roughest end. All around Snowman are key indicators that there is a fourth dimension to the overspill: boarded up pubs, children's play areas that fall way below European standards, and tanning salons. But although change reshapes the landscape, it leaves the silt and boulders of yesterday strewn across it like an Ice Age glacier. The house is one of those things left behind. It is a testament to the dreams of those who cleared the slums and moved their inhabitants to clean, efficient and affordable council housing. Snowman's house is of a bygone age. This is because the house – like Snowman – had been cared for by his grandmother. For her now, all tangible dimensions have imploded and this house teeters on an almost timeless event horizon. Its extremities are being slowly torn apart.

The cabinets and cupboards are a mixture of frosted glass and teak veneer. Both the settee and the two chairs that match it are enveloped in crimson faux-velvet and have sturdy mahogany-look legs. The wallpaper is beige with synthetic stripes screaming down to the skirting board at such a speed that if you follow them with your hands you can create enough friction to burn yourself on the harmless-looking brown and gold finish. The carpet itself is a sign of the covenant made between time and manufacturers in the good old days. The thick blue curtains have tiebacks, and the walls are adorned with strange and wonderful objects including a four foot-long bed warming pan. Nests of tables are scattered around the room pinning a fixed point in the grand scheme of things for tissues and coasters, photo-frames and ashtrays.

One such ashtray however has lost its way and finds itself on the floor in front of the fire – between the boys and the game. In this a spliff is occasionally flicked, its edges rolled and gently ground to remove waste as its smoke drifts towards the chimneybreast. This adds a misty focus to the photographs which stand humbly on top of the three-bar fire. The photographs are of Snowman and Billy at their first Holy Communion; both of them with bowl haircuts; white shirts with a red ribbon pinned to the front; grey shorts, grey socks and highly polished black brogues. Their hands are joined in an amen that looks more like they are playing mercy and their mouths deliver the same young attention-loving smiles. Ten years stood between these special days, but both brothers are missing exactly the same milk teeth. Both were also expelled from their Catholic primary schools before confirmation. Despite this, you can almost see the proud stare of their grandmother etched onto the images from the thousands of times she gazed upon them. You can actually see her fingerprints on the frames that haven't been cleaned since she died. Such slovenly reminders were never a part of her world, they would never have lasted that long with Nanna still around. The squalor is already setting in; the house is already making its way back from the brink of clean, unseen oblivion and into a messy, bellicose Universe. In fact Nanna's fingerprints will possibly be the only ones to grace those frames again – marks of the pride that nearly burst her heart every time she looked upon her two little angels. Now the contents of an emptied laundry basket are dumped unashamedly on one of the armchairs and the floor is sprinkled with spliff ash.

The floor of the front room is now clean and the house is once again empty apart from Marie and Squire. Even though she has just been shopping, Barbara feels so guilty for spilling her daughter's favourite meal that she has gone back into town to buy her second favourite: fish and chips. She might even get battered bits if there are any.

Marie is still watching Box, with Squire lying in his basket, a brown moustache of oxtail soup flopping over his lips. Marie is in love. She has been seeing this guy and he treats her right, buys her nice things. When her mum gets back she'll eat the whole of her fish and chips and proclaim how she feels much better. This is not to make her mother feel she has done her job well. This is a necessity. He's taking her to Don Juan's restaurant tonight.

Last night he took her to the city. Town proper. She met him in a quiet pub called the Longbow and they got a taxi into the city centre. It was the first time she'd heard the phrase 'set fare'. She liked the sound of it. They drank in some of the trendy bars on the revamped dockside before going to Club Eternity. The old lifts and machinery of the docks rusted away in the background as progress danced before them under subtle lighting. Afterwards, he shagged her behind the car park underneath a security lamp. All night he let her snort his cocaine.

Marie needs her mum to get home quickly. She needs to show her how much better she is feeling now. What is the hold up?

Impatience is David's middle name. He looks down the queue of bodies in McDonald's and wonders what they are all doing here. Obviously he knows what they are doing here – they, like him are waiting a long time for some fast food – but unlike him, very few of these people look like they have finished work early. 'Do these people not have jobs?' It's a phrase that was a favourite of his father's and is now becoming more and more a part of David's conventional artillery.

Not that David is a snob, God no, but he does have a sense of what is just and unjust, and David believes that however you earn your money – whether as a solicitor, a mechanic or a thief – you are at least *earning* that money. You are involved in some kind of *labour*. For David, these bastards in here filling their face with burgers, slowing down the pace of fast food, haven't earned the money they're spending. They've scrounged it. The only leisure time they have given up is to fill in forms and turn up to one appointment every two weeks. In fact, they probably had the forms filled in for them. At least if you're a crack dealer you are out there earning your dough.

David runs these thoughts through his head and he is soon at the front of the queue.

'Can I help you? Excuse me? Can I help you?'

'Shit. Sorry mate. Erm....'

With such griping squeezing his head free of its bitter juices, David can be forgiven for not hearing the Starless Wonder behind the counter, but his pause to form an answer is ridiculous. David has had the same thing every time he came in McDonald's for the last six years: large six chicken nugget meal and a cheeseburger. What drink would you like with that? Coke.

The response has become almost a reflex action, so much a part of his instinct that he sometimes has to stop to remember if he has actually said the words. So why the pause? The pause is for his fiancée, Tina. He is trying to decide which McFlurry she might like, and that if he bought her one, would she be pissed off that he wasn't helping her in her fat-busting crusade. She just *has* to get into the new dress she's bought for the Christening tomorrow. Perhaps an apple pie would be better.

'I'll have a,' fuck it, if she moaned he could use it as a guilt trip some other time, 'large six chicken nugget meal, a cheeseburger, and a… an apple pie.'

'What drink would you like with that?'

'Coke.'

'Anything else?'

'No thanks, Tommy love.'

Barbara counts out the change from her purse. She knows the price by heart and always pays in full, even though Old Tommy tries to give her a discount.

Old Tommy is, as his name suggests, an old man, but he has always been known as Old Tommy. This is because his chip shop has always held the virtues of what this town used to be like. He knows most of his customers by name, has seen their children grow up and take their children across the road to McDonald's, but he refuses to allow his standards to fall just to win *them* back. The place is always spotless, the fish is always fresh, the batter a recipe passed down to him by his father. He doesn't sell chicken, he doesn't sell donner, he doesn't sell pizza or curry sauce. He sells fish, chips, puddings, pies, mushy peas and the best gravy anyone has ever tasted. His batter bits are free of charge.

Old Tommy stands behind the sizzling range without so much as a bead of sweat forming below his salt white hair. This whiteness is matched by his coat and enhances the redness of his skin. There is no microwave in Old Tommy's chip shop. The only gadget visible is an old transistor radio behind him that allows him to follow the cricket score from a far-flung test match. Behind that is a small white envelope with a handwritten name on it. Barbara can't make out the name on it. She has known Old Tommy a very long time.

'You haven't got any batter bits have you, Tommy?'

''Course, love. On the chips?'

'Yes thanks. How are they doing?'

'Same old, same old. Good start, but they've lost three wickets. As soon as this fellow goes, it'll be the usual collapse. Bet your life on it.'

She pushes the change across the counter only to be met with a look from Old Tommy; a look that shines from his blue eyes and through his white wispy eyebrows like a patch of summer sky through high clouds. A look that says, 'Why do we have to do this every time?' Barbara glances back an embarrassed, 'Because it is at least one thing we can make sure never has to change,' before giving her usual reasons: 'Tommy, you can't afford to give your food away. Not with that McDonald's across the road. Those kids don't know what proper food is.'

Tommy backs down with dignity.

'The only reason they come over here now is to do what ever they do round the back of the shop. Honestly, Barbara, the things I find round the back of there. And they wonder why this Estate is going to the dogs?'

'Not mine, though, Tommy.'

'Oh no, Barbara, your lot know respect. Been brought up right, see.'

'Yeah. But it's getting harder, you know.'

'It always will. Just got to keep on trying your best.'

'I know, Tommy. Ta da now.'

'Ta da, Barbara.'

But Barbara doesn't move. Everything has followed the script so far but Tommy seems to have forgotten something.

'Oh, hang on, Barbara. At least take this can of coke on the house. Allow me that.'

Phew! For a minute there, Barbara thought she'd lost another part of her life that had been constant. She always gets a free can of coke for her pains. But that isn't the reason she comes here.

She thanks Old Tommy and heads out of the shop, the sound of his radio all that's left to keep him company.

'And it's four!'

The joypad hurtles towards Zeb's face on its deliberate trajectory. His reflexes are too quick and he dodges it, hearing it smash into the Communion pictures on top of the fire. Zeb runs out of the room laughing and heads upstairs pursued by the enraged Snowman. He truly is a terrible loser. Zeb screams as Snowman dives for his legs but Zeb's superior athletic ability and lower centre of gravity allow him to leap this lunge and crash his way into the bathroom, locking the door behind him.

Snowman never really stood a chance. Zeb is quick and slick in every way, epitomising all that his peers hold in high regard. He is one of the County's top 100m runners for his age group and will be offered professional terms with City on his sixteenth birthday after scoring 98 goals in one season for the school team. So assured is he in his prowess that he dresses as if already sponsored by the most sought-after brands for his demographic: today a grey Ecko hoodie and navy blue do-rag, his school trousers slung low, a canvas belt worn to keep them hunched above trainers that never cost less than £110. He wears a tiny diamond stud in his right nostril, his left earlobe housing two larger but less genuine-looking stones, and beneath his rag a hairstyle that owes more to the Nazca landscape than a housing estate.

He slips to the floor with his back to the door, howling with laughter while Snowman shouts and bangs. He'll give him a few minutes to cool down before he ventures out.

Chris uses Zeb and Snowman's fun and games to check the text message he felt vibrate in his pocket just before he scored his fourth goal. He takes out his phone and flicks it open with his thumb before pressing the appropriate buttons in the appropriate order like a blind person who has learnt how many steps it takes to get from their doorway to their settee. The number is unknown. He reads the message:

ware do u wont 2 meet l8r? mmb. Keeley

Keeley.

He looks at the game again. It is paused on the options page. He presses replay to watch the goal that broke the photos. All day in school, Snowman had been talking about this afternoon. Chatting on and on about how he was going to kick Chris' arse on Pro Evolution Soccer, show him what an expert looks like. When Chris refused to respond he'd even offered to be West Ham to Chris' Real Madrid before deciding that he wanted to give a real exhibition performance and so needed the skills of the Barça players. Only in the name of entertaining the fans, of course. Snowman had gone on and on and on and now, from no matter which angle Chris chooses to review the last goal, it is always scored by his team, it always sails past Snowman's goalkeeper and it always takes the tally to four – nil. Chris puts the phone in his pocket. That's what happens when you talk about something before it's happened. He might reply later.

David casts a chivalric shadow as he opens the door for a teenage girl dragging a buggy out of McDonald's. From her there is no reply. He stops a second to check out her arse and then walks out himself, over towards the doors of the Archer Centre, muttering to himself about simple courtesy.

He *hates* the Archer Centre. This too is full of work-shy soap-dodgers and people with no self-respect. It kills him that his mother cleans up their shit. His mother. The fact that Tina works here bothers him less, because working at WH Smiths – well – WH Smiths. Even the sound of it seemed more respectable. Much classier than Crazy George's, much less vulgar than Clinton Cards, more mature than McDonald's.

He strides through the automatic doors, almost beating them for pace, and down the central mall. There is nothing in here that he would like to buy. He slaloms past the clipboard soldiers, each one working for a different accident claims company and makes a right into WH Smiths. Walking upstairs to the music and video department, he spots Tina straight away. Every time he sees her, he remembers why he asked her to marry him. She is gorgeous. Even in her uniform she is fantastic looking: long bone-straight blonde hair to her shoulder blades; perfect nose; lifeboat lips, chocolate brown eyes and a body that has been given a double tick by her perfectly plucked eyebrows. Tina takes pride in her appearance and David respects that.

'Alright, babe!'

'Hiya, David. You haven't got me –. Oh, David, you know I'm on a diet!'

'So you don't want it, then?'

A pause almost as ridiculous as David's in McDonald's.

'Go on.'

Something about Tina's lack of will briefly appals David but he soon gets over it. He loves her and he is always surprising her with nice things. This is because he loves her, he is sure of this, but it seems like every time he has a romantic notion he always ends up having to ask for something in return. If that was David's intention, he could handle it. A transaction like that is common in all walks of life – I want something therefore I have to give something. But the fact that he thinks of the surprise first, only for it to be hijacked by the request later, frustrates David beyond belief.

'Baby.'

'Yeah?'

Tina sees the request looming in his downward glance.

'Oh, David. You *are* still coming to the Christening tomorrow, aren't you?'

''Course, babes.'

He'd forgotten all about that.

'And you've got the wine I asked for?'

'On my way to get it now, aren't I?'

Here goes....

'You know tonight?'

'You're not letting me down, are you?'

'No, well, God. I've got to work late at the Garage. I'm going home after this to let Mum know! We've had loads come in at the last minute and I can't turn business down, can I? How else could I put a rock like that on your finger?'

David hates using that one but that is the one he always ends up turning to. The thing is, David is Tina's prize. Her prize for being the fittest girl in school. The fittest girl in school always got to go out with the cock of the school. It was her right to have him: they were the celebrity couple. So David, in order to maintain a few aces up his sleeve had to not only be hard, but successful. Not only successful, but successful legitimately. *He* is going to buy her a house, *he* is going to pay for a holiday in Mauritius, *he* put that rock on her finger, and he's done it all with *clean* money. Not gangster money like you'd expect from the cock of the school, but clean money. Hard labour money. This town is full of ex-fittest girls in school, all stretched and saggy from kids, all looking cheap and nasty because their cocks are in prison. Tina wasn't going to have to deal with that and although David hated it, he did need to remind her of this every now and again. What hurts more though is the fact that this moral high ground has very shaky foundations. He isn't working late at all. He is going for an early evening pint with the lads. With Billy and Graham. This makes letting her down feel all the worse but there is nothing he can do about it.

Marie hopes he's still coming. He's told her not to text him, that he'll ring her later, but she's seen the way David always lets down Tina and isn't sure if that's just how it goes with older men. With younger men she's fine. With boys. But older men she isn't sure.

She sits on the toilet and imagines what it is like to be married. The reason she thinks of this is because of the awful smelling vodka shit she has just done. If you were going to marry someone you'd have to be completely unashamed, you'd have to feel comfortable with allowing your husband to know you can shit like that. Although Marie is used to the shit and smells of the body – living as she does with two brothers – she can usually hide behind their odd pride in the odours they create. This pride means that they'll even take responsibility for *her* smells if it means a hearty laugh from the other. But married, with no one else to hide behind, you'd have to...

'I'm home love! Love? I've got some batter bits as well.'

What the fuck is she thinking about! Marie shudders, stands up, wipes her arse and opens the bathroom door.

Zeb slowly opens the bathroom door once he is sure the coast is clear. This is only after he has put up with Snowman pretending to try to break down the door, shouting promises and curses, and even taking the ridiculous step of trying to simulate the sound of himself walking back down the stairs while in fact still being outside the bathroom door. Zeb responded to this particular tactic by simulating the sound of himself masturbating while calling out Snowman's mother's name, bringing Snowman out of his bluff and back to the rage Zeb knew and loved. For now though, the coast is clear and Zeb has to think of something else to keep himself occupied for the next five minutes.

He walks out onto the landing and heads towards Snowman's room. As he walks in, the overwhelming aroma of sweat and dermatological shampoo hits him. He grimaces and ventures further into the room, stepping over CD cases and what seems like every fake Manchester United shirt available on the black market. He sits down on the lower bunk of the beds that still take up the majority of the room, and has a look around.

The room is such a mess that practical joking is almost impossible. In order to play a practical joke the subject needs some kind of purity that can be defiled, some point of principle which can be exploded embarrassingly in their face. Unfortunately, the dire truth of Snowman's existence is so explicit that any simple kind of practical japery is out of the question. Quick raids on brief periods of pride are all that the novice practical joker can muster with Snowman, but for Zeb – a master practical joker – that is what makes the whole thing more exciting. Snowman is a real challenge. Toenails in the bed, sleep-administered shit moustaches, and late-night multiple pizza deliveries are just too passé when it comes to winding up the Snowman. To hit him, you have to hit hard.

Zeb gets up off the bed and heads out again to the

landing. Just as he is about to admit defeat and go back down the stairs he smells another odd smell. A smell that is odd now because of its absence from the rest of the house. The smell of Snowman's grandmother.

For a few seconds Zeb thinks this might be a step too far. But this is only for a few seconds. After these few seconds are up, he enters Snowman's dead grandmother's bedroom.

Her odour pervades every corner and Zeb is briefly spooked at the prospect of being in here. Nothing – it seems – has been touched. Even the old girl's electric blanket is still spread out across the bed. He walks over to her dresser and sits down. It is the oldest piece of furniture he has ever seen, old enough to have no plastic anywhere and drawers that don't exactly match. Out of sheer curiosity he opens one drawer. In it is a large box, matching in colour and texture to the downstairs three-piece suite. He opens it and finds the trinkets that used to give Nanna Snowman her jingle: huge brooches in gruesome, twisting designs, cameo rings, and a highly polished locket. These everyday objects of an entire life dance across Zeb's memory. Energised, he attempts to open another drawer. This time however it is locked and his attention doesn't span as far as hunting down a key so he turns to the mirror and spots the chest of drawers in the reflection. Lying on top of them among boxes of pills and some other old photos are her glasses. They are huge, brown-rimmed, tinted goggles with a mother of pearl chain attached that kept her from losing them. He tiptoes across the room and picks them up, holding them out like the skull of a dead bird before bringing them close and putting them on. He turns around

49

in the mirror. He can't see a fucking thing! He can imagine his eyes, magnified to joke shop size and he can't help but laugh out loud. Realising what he is doing, Zeb covers his mouth cartoon-like in order to stifle the sound. He takes the glasses off the bridge of his nose and they hang loosely around his neck while he opens her wardrobe.

Barbara closes the cupboard door and puts a plate on the table. She puts the can of coke next to the plate and opens up the parcel of fish and chips. The smell makes her hungry but she wants to get back into the clothes she bought last year from the catalogue and so she resists stealing a chip. She places the whole parcel on the plate before sliding the paper from underneath like a holiday camp magician. Squire has smelt the goodies and despite the treat of oxtail soup to start with, he has plenty of room for his main course.

'Go on, get out, you greedy bugger. Eat your own food and you might get some of this.'

Marie sits at the table and starts to tuck in. The chips are greasy but golden and flecked with the orange scraps of left-over batter. She looks up at her mum who looks away quickly as if having been staring at a stranger on the bus.

'Do you want a chip, Mum?'

'Oh no. I'm not keen on them any more. All this healthy eating I'm doing.'

Marie has a sip of the can of coke and shows her understanding by changing the subject.

'I'm feeling loads better now. I could probably go in for the afternoon.'

She looks at her mother. Deep in her subconscious she

recognises the kindness her daughter has just shown her and her brain is flooded with the need for reciprocation.

'No, love. There's not much point now, is there? You stay here and keep your mum company.'

Squire barks before Marie can answer and runs to the front door. Marie hears David's footsteps approaching. Barbara wonders what is going on. The doorbell goes.

Chris and Snowman look at each other. The after-ring of the doorbell is still humming. They jump up quickly, Chris wafting the ganja smoke around the room in a feeble attempt to clear the air. Meanwhile Snowman has grabbed the ashtray and run into the kitchen only to re-emerge with a No Frills air freshener. As he pshhhhts the air, the bell goes again, both boys shouting some kind of stalling noise with all the conviction of a half-three apology. When they think they may have done enough, Snowman gives Chris the nod before going to answer the door. This is when Chris notices the broken picture and the glass. He grabs the nearest thing he can find – a pair of Snowman's seen-better-days underpants from the pile of washing on the armchair – and heads over to the wreckage. But it is already too late. Someone is coming through the living room door.

Phew, it's Kish.

Kish!

'Alright, Chris? Chris? What have you got there?'

'It's the glass. The photo. Fuck it.'

Chris throws the pants to the floor and sits back in the opposite armchair. Kish is carrying the box he left home with – a box so big that it obscures even his immeasurable size. Chris uses this opportunity to draw attention away from his embarrassment.

'What the fuck is that?'

'Don't mention it, mate.'

'What?'

'No worries. You don't have to thank me for anything. I've only set you up with the girl you've been wanking over for the last year.'

Chris hadn't thanked him because this contravenes one of Chris' fundamental rules and jeopardises the affair. You don't talk about events before they are due to happen. Not directly, anyway. That just opens the crack in the armour that would allow chance to escape and destiny to fill the vacuum. The way Chris sees it, as soon as you start thinking things are going to be okay, they won't be. As soon as you start expecting things to happen, they won't. He'd never, ever wanked over Keeley.

'Oh. Yeah. Cheers.'

'You're fucking welcome. Shit. Anyway, "What the fuck are these?" These, boys, are our beer and weed money for the next few months.'

Kish walks into the front room and drops the box on the settee. This allows Snowman to re-enter his own front room – Kish had been blocking the whole doorframe. In a flash of inspiration, Snowman pretends to trip over a wire and pull out of the wall the plug that gave the Play Station 2 its power.

'Fuck!'

'Fucking hell, Snowman, the game!'

'Shit. Sorry, Chris.'

'No matter. Only a few minutes left. I'll have the win.'

'Nah, mate. Can't have the win. Match abandoned. Got to be a replay.'

'A replay? Fu –'

Kish hates computer games and has heard this argument too many times for it to be of any interest.

'Will you two shut up and have a look at this?'

Kish's interjection is met with enthusiasm by Snowman who bounds over to the box. Chris saunters over more slowly, obviously still smarting at the injustice served upon him by Snowman's trailing leg. Kish opens the box.

'Well, what do you think?'

He pulls out a beige-coloured Ralph Lauren summer jacket. Snowman and Chris look at each other. They can see how excited Kish is but are both thinking the same thing. Snowman goes first.

'Mate. Nobody wears those anymore.'

'Fuck off, it's Ralph. Everyone wears Ralph!'

Chris decides to take his turn.

'Kish. It's old. If they were Burberry it'd be different.'

'Burberry, Ralph. Fucksake lads. They were a fiver a pop!'

Both Snowman and Chris recoil from this figure. Chris knows his clothes through his brother and both know their street value. Even in bulk. Chris tries to steady the ship.

'Where are you going to sell them, Kish?'

'Pubs, school...'

'No, no, no. You can't do that.'

'Why not?'

Snowman takes the baton.

'Because of Golden Graham.'

Kish knows who Golden Graham is. Sees him as an example of all he could be one day. But even though the answer is staring him in the face, the vision of the plans he has blinds him from making any connection between Golden Graham and the current situation.

'Yeah? So?'

'Graham fences round here. No one else. Unless Graham invites you to sell them for him, you ain't selling Jack shit.' Kish looks at Chris to counter Snowman's claims, but Chris nods an affirmation. Snowman's smile confirms the new faith his friend seems to have in him. He speaks again. 'I know Graham, and you'll be lucky if he takes those off your hands for £3 a go.'

Snowman has just seen his whole afternoon restored. The game in which he was being pounded four nil by a novice has been abandoned, he has been backed up all the way on a fashion call by Chris, and he has managed to slip out just enough information about his dealings with Golden Graham to spark a little jealous curiosity. Kish however, is clinging on.

'Fuck you. I'll ask Zeb. Zeb'll tell me straight. Zeb!'

All this time, Zeb has been waiting outside the living room door to pounce. Like the deadly striker he is, his instinct told him wait, wait: the golden opportunity is yet to come, but on this cue, with Snowman's stock at its highest, he knows that now is the time to strike. He leaps through the doorframe.

'DO YOU WANT A KITKAT, LOVE?'

54

The three boys in Snowman's front room stand aghast. Zeb is stood in the doorway, dressed head to toe in Snowman's dead grandmother's clothes. He is even wearing her jewellery. Zeb can see that none of them think this is funny but it is as if his reflexes have been replaced by that of the dead woman. He can't speak, can't move, even as he sees Snowman pick the warming pan off the wall, raise it over his right shoulder and smash it straight into Zeb's left ear. Zeb crashes into the box of jackets on the settee and lies there, sparkled in a dead woman's clothes. And still, no one is laughing.

15.14

Double science last thing on a Friday is the penance that Chris and the boys have to pay for the rest of the privileges they enjoy as Year Elevens. The whole of Year Eleven has double science last thing on a Friday but how easy your time is depends upon which set you are in. The very bottom groups get the good teachers: the teachers who don't try too hard to understand where the kids are coming from and can more than handle any discipline problems thrown their way. Top groups get the teachers who can't handle discipline problems but know their subjects inside out. Real 'those who can' candidates. Middle groups get the roughest deal. They get the mediocre teachers. Teachers who aren't funny, aren't brilliant but aren't social rejects or sadists either. The teachers who are trying to *understand the kids*. The real problem with these teachers is that you never really know where you stand with them. With bottom group teachers you know that if you push too far you are going to get what is coming to you. With top group teachers you know that if you step out of line at all you are going to get what is coming to you – usually from a teacher more senior or fearsome than the teacher whose line is crossed. With mediocre teachers the grey area is so large that it is difficult to know what is coming and when, so double science, last thing on a Friday, in a middle group, is a nerve-wracking experience. Especially if you are Chris and in a class with Zeb: Zeb who needs to know where the line is as if his very existence depends upon it. As if the very definition of Zeb is flush with this line. Chris sits next to Zeb, on the line.

'Hairy arse.'

Graham is now sat on his front doorstep. He looks out at the cul-de-sac he lives in as he takes a very late lunch of milky tea and a chicken burger. He's had a busy day. One thing about those who spend their careers in alternative industries is that they are *still industrious*. The hours are long for they are almost always working. People often make the mistake of believing that these people are their own bosses. Their orders come via different lines of communication, but are orders all the same. People like Graham do not escape the cruelty of the daily grind. If it were that easy, everybody would be doing it.

Still there are perks. If there weren't, no one would be doing it and Graham enjoys some perks. Take his chicken burger. This chicken burger is from the Balti Hut, a late-night takeaway selling all kinds of greasy goods from seven o'clock in the evening. The Balti Hut is another local business that has come to him for advice on their security needs, and so, if Graham needs a chicken burger, or a large donner, or a keema nan, or a lamb bhuna, Graham can get it any time he wants. A perk. He looks at the ground where a large blob of mayonnaise has plopped onto his driveway.

Chris looks straight ahead. Zeb looks back and pretends he thinks Chris hasn't heard him.

'Hairy arse.'

This time Chris turns around to Zeb. Zeb smiles and flicks the upbeat of a nod. It is Chris' turn. The turn in question refers to a particularly childish classroom game; because of the game's juvenile nature, hilarity is brought to any classroom it is played in. The premise of the game lies along the lines of the old game Bollocks, in which one person would say 'bollocks', then the next person would have to repeat the word, only louder, until one of the players was shouting 'bollocks' so loudly that the teacher could no longer ignore it. The subtle difference in the game being played here, however is that one person says 'hairy arse', only for the other player to reply 'furry balls'. Again the volume increases with each turn. It is called Hairy Arse Furry Balls.

And it is Chris' turn. He looks at Zeb and then at the clock on the wall. If there was one night he needed to get away on time, it was tonight. He looks again at Zeb who looks back at Chris. It is his turn. It is *his turn*.

'Furry balls.'

Yes!

The buggy is turned onto the main road, jogging and jumping on the stones spilled from a truck that thundered up this way before anyone was awake. The buggy's eight wheels, joined by mini axels to the frame of the pushchair, ride the starburst shatter of another bus shelter as they take the weight of Jenny.

She is three years old but still refuses to walk anywhere. She also refuses to give up her dummy, drink from a glass, use a toilet rather than her potty, or form proper words. In fact if you have something she wants she will usually just stretch her arms out in front of her, grunt, pull a pained face, and open and close her fingers into her palms. She gets away with whatever she can, and being the youngest, this is usually quite a bit.

Zeb is relieved. After the unfortunate incident this afternoon at Snowman's house, it is important that Zeb knows he is forgiven. He can't help himself. He honestly thought that it would be okay. That they'd all see the funny side. They usually did with Snowman.

Snowman was the butt of all the jokes. When he dared Snowman to climb out of the window in French and then locked him out, only for Madame La Vielle to return to see one of her pupils pressed up against a window, perching on a ledge three stories up, they all laughed. When he told Snowman that James McKeever had told everyone that Snowman's mother had collected leftovers from the local

Sunday League football presentation buffet to feed her family – forcing Snowman to duly deck James McKeever and get suspended – they all laughed. So why when he did this, did they not laugh? Why was this, as Chris had been saying all afternoon since they got back 'Out of order'? Zeb had no idea but one thing he did know was that by joining in this game, Chris had forgiven Zeb. Things had come full circle.

'Hairy arse.'

The cul-de-sac that Graham looks out upon is ringed with grey mottled council housing. They sit in rows of six like radioactive waste encased in concrete, awaiting shipment to the deepest hole man can find. And people live in them. People hang floral baskets outside them, turf small gardens on their fronts, put up net curtains, build porches, lead windows and put imitation oak numbered signs on them. Others just sleep in them, hardly eat in them, let the gardens overgrow outside them, have broken toys and household goods littering up the tiny driveways that mock where there will never be a nice little runner parked up outside them. There doesn't seem to be anything in between exaggerated care and utter neglect. Apart from Graham's house, which has one function: impenetrability.

The door is covered with heavy steel. Security cameras stand on vandal-proof poles – wire grates protecting their lenses from stones or other foreign bodies. A police 'stinger' is padlocked across the driveway that houses his beloved car, and massive, movement triggered lamps cling to the eaves, waiting to flood neighbours' bedrooms with alien light if so much as a cat crosses the threshold.

Graham takes another bite of the burger, more mayonnaise squirting out around the sides. He wipes his mouth with the paper serviette wrapped around the polystyrene box the burger came in. As he mops up the mayo, dabbing at the grease collecting in his cracked lips, Graham smiles. He even half coughs the beginnings of a laugh but it soon stops and turns into the sigh of a man who can't believe how little he's settled for. For the right to claim his fast food whenever the fuck he wants.

Fuck! If there was one night when everything had to be perfect, one night when Chris had to get out on time, catch the bus, maybe have a walk around the Archer Centre, go home and have his dinner, get ready and then go and meet a girl who he was having the strangest feelings about – feelings he couldn't describe, never mind understand – if there was one night....

   Chris is beginning to wish he'd done what Kish and Snowman had done and played truant this afternoon. Of course they'd be found out by Monday and punished but they'd weighed up the importance of what they wanted to do this afternoon against that fact and decided that Monday was an age away anyway. Now half past three seemed an age away and the minutes were themselves filled with the dangerous shape of Zeb's game.

Kish has more than Zeb's silly games on his hands. For a start there is the not so small matter of the box of Ralph Lauren jackets that he cups underneath either side, his nose poking out over the top, his head tilted so far back that it looks as if he is sniffing rather than looking where he is going. It is fair to say that he is pissed off.

Of course most of us would find such a situation frustrating, but Kish isn't just frustrated, he is angry. He is filled with a wrath that has no consolation as it is fixed squarely upon himself and his own foolishness. But although he is angry there is a chink of light that could help avoid embarrassment. It is this hope that has him struggling down the road.

Still, Kish is angry, a mulatto rage of dented pride and disappointment. He'd counted on these jackets to pitch him into a bigger league, slap a brand new ladder before him with a brand new peak. However, these far from brand new Ralph Lauren jackets are a troublesome snake that has had him slide right back to where he started. He'd spent all of his savings on them, savings procured by a highly successful small operation that he had been running in school for a while now, and was hoping they would at least double his booty.

This smaller operation was one he had running with his Uncle Sukraj – owner of Frank's Food and Booze – and had the kind of origins that every entrepreneur wishes they could rely upon to prove their self-made manhood. A younger Kish had amassed his huge girth not through his mother's delicious cooking, or a lack of exercise, but through being the number one customer of the school vending machine. Although this hobby had him add to his size, it made sizable dents in his pocket money and as he grew older, he began to meditate on the nature of this. Kish wanted a way of adding to both sides of the scales and it was a trip to the Cash and Carry with Uncle Sukraj that inspired him. There he saw the cost of things compared to their price and realised that it was this difference that had been troubling him for some time. He spent more and more time with Sukraj, learning about the business, helping out for free on Saturdays; and Sukraj saw Kish as a natural successor, someone to carry on the family business in the absence of any sons of his own. Kish never felt in his heart that there was future in this dream, but when dreaming of his own future he always had the feeling that his Uncle would have an important part to play.

While working at the shop one Saturday, Kish saw just how much stock his Uncle discarded once the goods were out of date. Even his Cut Price Super Sale bins at the front of the shop were never completely emptied unless by Sukraj's own hand. Kish saw a way of putting an end to such waste. As he was leaving one Saturday, Kish put forward a proposal: give him the sweets, the chocolate and the soft drinks that were out of date and he would sell them in school at Cut Price Super Sale prices for Sukraj. Sukraj felt it was worth a try. He had nothing to lose and if Kish was caught, he could say he had given the goods to his nephew as a gift.

Kish went into business straight away, selling the goods out of his school bag at *just above* Cut Price Super Sale prices, but *just below* those of the vending machines. He creamed the difference off the top, gave his uncle back his initial investment – for which his uncle would treat him to £5 per week in wages – and in just under a year, Kish had not only splashed out on lavish luxuries for himself and his friends but saved up £250. £250 that would form the foundations of his future business empire.

Kish knows how perfect the story is, but it is no good starting a story like that if the next part just fizzles away as this one seems to have. At the moment Kish feels no joy at any of his past glories for all they amounted to now were fifty Ralph Lauren jackets that nobody wanted to buy. He had to rewrite his destiny.

Such luxuries are not afforded to Chris, for his immediate destiny lies in two words: 'Furry balls.'

That wasn't really loud enough but Zeb is willing to give Chris the benefit of the doubt. After all, that's what friends are for. It's all about give and take.

Paul is well aware of this. With their birthdays being four years apart, Paul is au fait with the intricacies of the relationship he has with his younger sibling Jenny – the expectations and etiquette of familial ties. Although he gets more clips around the ear, fewer sweet treats and the blame for most household accidents, he is also being prepared as the alpha male. One day he will be expected to look after all of them and so is already being armed with the respect-gaining tools he will need. He is being made well aware of how he should look – already decked out in kids' Nike, kids' Gap, kids' jewellery and kids' attitude.

He walks as tall as he can for a seven-year-old, uses his little man looks to procure praise from members of the fairer sex much older than him, but really, more than anything, he is wondering constantly what a dead end is.

'What are they, why are they called that, what terrors must lie in them?' Paul just doesn't know, but ever since he heard his mother talking about them, he has built a detailed picture of how he imagines a dead end. A road disappearing into a strange wilderness; a purple-tinged mist sighing around short hillocks and tufts of wild grasses, cloaked figures tending to the earth, taking slow looks over their shoulders while the howls of wolves and low growls of stranded big cats whip around on the wind.

This image knocks the confidence from him for a minute and he grabs hold of his mother's hand a little tighter, quickening his step to keep up with her. The very idea of a dead end scares him to death.

Zeb's greatest fear is losing his friends. It is a strange one for someone so popular, someone with the credibility that he has, but it is this fear that cancels out that of the unavoidable trouble that is to come.

For this game can only end in trouble. Of course the glory of a few minutes notorious hilarity has something to do with it, but it is mostly this fear that drives Zeb on. While Chris is playing with him he is standing alongside him. This is solidarity. A solidarity he missed two weeks ago when he was beaten up on the way back from Snowman's house.

The boys had been having a smoke and Zeb threw a whitey and had to go home earlier than the rest. They were in the middle of an important tournament of Pro Evolution Soccer and so he couldn't expect any of them to leave that to keep him company.

As he walked home, the loneliness of not having anyone next to him to talk to, not having anyone to take the piss out of, was palpable, as if the very state of being alone hurt to touch. At first he blamed it on the weed, on his paranoia, but the feeling wouldn't go away. If you'd have asked him to say how loneliness felt before that experience he'd have said 'cold', but feeling it there, *actually feeling it*: it was red hot. Hotter than embarrassment, more searing than any anger. But this scorching loneliness was cosy compared to the company that awaited him.

On the other side of the street, outside Frank's Food and Booze, were a group of boys. He recognised most of them, but knew one of them by name. Spoonhead. He knew Spoonhead's face and name by association rather than reputation. Or rather Spoonhead had a reputation by association, and that's how Zeb knew him. Spoonhead's older brother, Cod-Eye, was famous around the Estate. Not as famous as Golden Graham, but definitely as famous as Chris' brother David. In fact he was David's counterpart, the cock of David's year but in the Catholic school that Billy and Snowman never made it to. Cod-Eye's reputation had grown since leaving school as body after broken body after crossing his path was found in gutters, shop doorways and car parks. The problem here was that unlike Chris who accepts his place and uses the kudos earned for him by David to his advantage, Spoonhead has ambition. Spoonhead wants a reputation of his own.

So he shouted across the street to Zeb, who quite rightly carried on walking. So Spoonhead shouted again, and again, and again, until Zeb could no longer ignore him.

And for this recognition, Zeb found himself in trouble.

'Hairy arse.'

So he's avoided trouble since 1994, so he is the main man on the Estate when it comes to fencing stolen goods, so he's a natural when it comes to harnessing the burgling habits of the smackheads and the destructive rage of the youth, but what can Graham actually claim to be?

Once he had just wanted to have what he has now. A nice house, a steady living, and respect on the Estate. But as he looks at the mayonnaise stuck fast to the tarmac in a viscous gloop, it reminds him of himself. Stuck. He hasn't spread through the channels of the street like the grease that runs the cracks of his broken lips. He has stayed in his safe little corner of the street while others – others who were younger than him, not as good as him – have played leapfrog and taken the streets by force. Graham is gripped by a strong sense of shame, strong enough to give him the taste and pop of acid at the back of his throat, but it is this shame that has led him to reassess his options. Graham has definitely become complacent. Not complacent enough to get caught, but complacent enough to believe he was content. This is the boy genius of the Estate's underworld! A boy whom the older heads would look on with pride that the game still had glamour; and fear that he would one day usurp them. But the game changed and Graham stayed with what he'd learned from the old school. A new breed sprang up around him, a new breed that were his age but not of his age. He'd taken the route of proper apprentice, served his time in the time-honoured fashion.

They passed him by without him even noticing. These were the once-upon-a-time car takers, robbers and the hash dealers. And now, because they'd been on the fast track course of criminality, they'd left him in the cold. Well, not for long, because Graham has big things in the pipeline, because Graham has got major capital to invest and a belly full of envy. The taste at the back of the throat, the burn in the top of the ribs. Graham needs these things. He needs the pain of want again and at last he's got it back.

Chris doesn't need this. He really doesn't need any of this. He needs to catch the bus! The thought of such impatience to catch the bus just a couple of years ago would be unthinkable but since he'd made Year Eleven the bus home has become less of a thing to fear and more of a right to claim.

When Chris was younger the bus was a true gauntlet to run: digs, cigs put out on your back, kept on past your stop, a mad kid at the back using deodorant to try to set fire to the seat, girls beating the mad kid down viciously, their hairspray making them the most likely innocent victim of his pyromania, the same girls recognising you for who your brother was and being embarrassingly nice in the vain belief that this would be passed on to him – the big prize. All of this concentrated into a two-minute period. Being a young kid was torture. You had to learn everything the hard way, no one told you anything really. Growing up was all fear and questions.

'Furry balls.'

If Paul was right about dead ends, they must lie somewhere behind them for the speed his mother is walking at suggests they are running from something absolutely terrifying. Her quick steps are definitely not the walk of someone rushing to get somewhere. He squeezes her hand, hands that look older than they are, bloated: the skin on her ruddy fingers hanging over rings like a belly over a belt. Following her hand up her tracksuit-covered arm we reach her neck. It too is dressed in gold, one of these pieces holding her name as if she might forget it – Jean. The reason she may forget is because Jean is deceitful, and like any liar, it is the important things that she forgets. It is the *truth* in her life that slips down the side of the settee. Her most recent deceit lay around her neck and covered her name. It was a faked whiplash claim for a bus she climbed on after it had crashed, and the collar – suffered for the last few months – which has recently paid up and paid off some of her catalogue debts. Whereas her neck speaks of deceit, like any successful deceiver, her face whispers a humble truth. She has red hair, short and over tussled, chipmunk cheeks peppered with freckles and full lips that you would swear could not have room for lies. But lying is her life, and just as her daughter instinctively stretches her arms and flexes her fingers, Jean is only happy when her hands are palms up and her eyes are pleading innocence.

Zeb is at his happiest now. The pain of the kicking he got from Spoonhead and his mates, the ignominy of Snowman's pan smashing him across the face – none of this matters as long as Chris sticks with Zeb now.

The clock is ticking on and they seem to be timing this perfectly, drawing out the ultimate in watching-through-fingers-hilarity from their classmates. Zeb is pleased. He'll ride this wave of notoriety all the way to another hour of security. Already the giggles have cracked through the silence, snatching breaths in a mixture of sighed appreciation and muffled disgust. That is the beauty of this game. It isn't the act itself but the chain reaction it kicks off that brings about the inevitable.

'HAIRY ARSE!'

Jean's game is mercy, playing mercy. She is far from ashamed of this. Just as with Graham, it is a full time job and she is working every hour of the day. Be it the lifted soul of a pair of Paul's trainers nullifying a six month old catalogue debt, or calling on relatives as they are about to begin preparing a meal, Jean plays commodities better than any City trader. She keeps a check on all the ups and downs of the market and unlike those who play with stocks and bonds, she can play with a much more powerful emotion than greed. Jean can make you feel that you should be ashamed for whatever you have because she doesn't have it. And like the best professionals she doesn't allow sentimentality or her personal life interfere with business. That is why once a week she makes this journey to her older sister Barbara – always around this time – as she knows that being a good home-maker, Barbara is already preparing dinner. Jean is well aware that in seeing her niece and nephew wonder at someone preparing fresh ingredients – chopping an onion, dicing some chicken breast – Barbara will not be able to resist offering them a place at the table.

What Graham really resents is never having been offered a place at the table. His rightful place. He has never been given his dues. But what he has going for him is experience. The reckless mistakes he has made in the small time are now being made by those who have rushed headlong into the big time, only if you make them in the big time the consequences are BIG. There has been a purge on the Estate recently. The police have really been cracking down, so certain figures on the Estate are going to be out of action for a while. Quite a while. Graham will take full advantage of this. But just as he has let others make the mistakes that will make him, he will have others take the risks that could bring him down.

Graham looks out across his driveway and sees one of these 'others' approach. He finishes chewing his chicken burger, stands, pulling his trousers up and adjusting his belt, and greets him as he greets anyone who is a number of years his junior. 'Alright, hairy arse?'

Sniggers have already started around the classroom at what is happening and they'll be talking about this till at least next Tuesday but Chris' mind is so completely on the evening to come that even these sniggers take a twisted meaning. They know, don't they! They know about tonight, about Keeley, and they're laughing about it. Chris is ready for the obvious questions; the scent of fresh gossip is irresistible to the girls in his year. He can already hear what will be said: 'Do you like her?'; 'She's dead nice, Keeley'; 'I'm telling you, Chris, you better not fuck her about'; 'I think you look dead good together', 'Are you going to see her again?' – all before he has even 'seen' her once.

But that isn't what they are laughing at, is it? They're laughing at the inescapable conclusion of this game. Chris can't quite believe what he is thinking. He thinks he might be losing his mind for he knows that the noises around him have absolutely nothing to do with Keeley. That he alone has brought that particular train of thought to these tracks frightens him. He runs from this fear and back to the game at hand with such recklessness that he takes it just too far.

'Furry Balls!'

The room collapses in hysterics, the teacher coolly promises retribution and Chris hangs his head at his lack of self-control. Zeb understands completely. They'll take their punishment together.

15.50

Zeb is still laughing as the bus pulls up. Chris tries to look interested but his heart isn't in it. They've just been on the end of one of the most inept bollockings they have ever been party to, which for Zeb was a clear signal of who was really in charge in the classroom but for Chris was a complete waste of valuable time. Mr Ingham, the science teacher, gave them the stony glare and sharp command in front of the class but on his own seemed to lose enthusiasm for the task. He sat himself upon the desk where the two boys were sat, flicked one leg over the other, and tried the 'let's look at this sensibly' routine. The boys looked around the class, took in the Periodic Table of Elements, then sighed just loud enough to make his nostrils flair and almost lose control. When he had finished his lecture, Zeb even had the cheek to ask whether they could go home yet.

This meant another five minutes of them 'not understanding that there had to be consequences to their actions', that he was 'giving them choices and they were giving him none'. Nobody learnt their lesson. Still, missing the school bus meant that a far superior standard of public transport awaited them at the bus stop.

Straight away it is clear to Chris that this journey is not meant for them. This bus puffs out its chest and hisses a warning as the doors open – a far cry from the resigned sigh and slumped trunk of the school bus. The clientele also differs in the extreme. Instead of the torture gauntlet of the walk to the back seat is a pretty line of part-time workers and the elderly, some kids from the college up the road looking down on those just one year and a uniform beneath them and, of course, the ubiquitous young mother – her trolley parked in the space provided on these new luxury vehicles, her toddler squeezing a flaccid Gregg's sausage roll into its mouth.

As the Boys take their seats, Chris feels something hum in his pocket. He angles inside his jacket and pulls out his phone – the 'Message Received' screen illuminated. Zeb is still making noises, his mouth flapping shapes, his hands jabbing imaginary buttons but none of these signals are reaching Chris' brain and being transformed into anything sensible. Instead Chris presses his 'Read' button and the message appears:

wot time do u want 2 meet? xxxK

Keeley.

He looks up from the message, allowing the tiniest of smiles to appear at the most extreme corner of his mouth. The impression of the words on his eyes is projected onto the back of the seat in front like school bus graffiti.

'Is it Keeley? Is it? Is it Keeley?'

For some reason, Zeb's vibrations have suddenly started to register and he is excited.

'Well? Is it?'

'Yeah.'

'What does she want?'

'What time we're meeting.'

Chris' proto-smile turns into a lop-sided crease as he says this for it is one of those necessary evils that hamper his plans to not even think – never mind speak! – about the night to come.

'Well?'

'Like I'd tell you?'

'What?!'

Zeb's astonishment is delivered with less verity than rhetoric. He was hoping to catch Chris off guard with that one so that he might think of a ploy to scupper his plans – but deep down Zeb knows that he can't pull a fast one on Chris. Zeb has long held Chris in high regard and not just because of who his brother is, but because. Well, because.

He remembers the first time they met, on a cross-country run in first year. It was one of those winter's mornings when you'd swear it should be hotter with a sun so bright hampering every wayward look. The cross-country was a long, long race. Even at the age of fifteen it seemed to be continents wide but at the age of eleven and twelve it seemed as if the sun itself was the finishing line. Zeb was flagging, sprinting always being his game rather than the long haul, and as usual he had flown out of the blocks indestructible, forgetting that this one wouldn't be over in a hundred metres. Chris was plodding, quite happy to roll in midway down the race, quite aware that it wasn't really important, quite oblivious to the veneration his attitude was raising in the scrawny light-brown boy next to him. Zeb felt the instant need to strike up conversation with the young Chris and noticed he was wearing a pair of Air Max 97 on cross-country. The same pair Zeb was wearing. That was enough.

Chris bolts from his seat and heads for the front of the bus, disturbing Zeb's reminiscence. They've arrived in the town centre bus station and are arcing around the long circular road that leads to the alighting stops. The driver maintains a speed which keeps the less confident in their seats while the likes of Zeb and Chris get up to surf the chassis – the bus a centrifuge separating the haves from the have-nots like platelets from plasma.

The town centre looks very different to the pictures that grace the local pubs: the black and white images of a pretty market town, a cobbler, a butcher, a time before the Estate, before the Archer Centre. The Archer Centre is only a few years younger than the Estate and clashes its grey concrete with plastic indigo facades. As Zeb and Chris walk through the automatic doors and traverse the waxed floor, they are flanked by the kind of businesses that will never make a pub wall: Crazy George's Discount Home Store, Stolen From Ivor, Wilkinson's and lines of shops selling greetings cards. The security guards pick up on them immediately, whispering serious messages into their walkie-talkies, unaware that their blue and silver uniforms do not strike fear into the hearts of the youth, just derision. Zeb and Chris have no time for the guards today but although time is tight, both parties will play out the drama they play every Friday when it is time for this particular stage in their journey home.

'Let's go to WH Smiths.'

'No, I'm already late.'

Every weekend starts for Zeb with a close look at the woman of his dreams. Tina. He'd seen Tina around since he was eleven or twelve and even though he knew she was destined for David, never gave up on his obsession. All he needs is one close look per week to keep him believing and Chris is the St Peter at the gates.

Chris, on the other hand, doesn't care for Tina. To him she is a big mouth and a pair of tits. He thinks his brother has more to him than a girl like Tina. Besides, Zeb always makes Chris look stupid whenever they go in to see her. It always looked as if Chris was the one with the crush, the one who was desperate to speak.

'I'm going to get a milkshake from Maccy Dees and then –'

'Ah come on, man. Just for a minute?'

Chris looks back at Zeb, and Zeb looks at Chris. Both have their eyebrows raised and their heads tilted downwards – one in the 'puppy dog' plea of the child, and one in the 'just this once' pliability of the parent. At this moment, more than any, it is difficult to believe they are the same age.

'Five minutes.'

They walk into WH Smiths, their discussion leading to a flurry of excitement in the radio communication between Archer Centre security staff and the security staff hired especially – well they are the premier store in this particular shopping centre – by WH Smiths. The boys flick quickly through a couple of magazines – *FHM* for Zeb, *Source* for Chris – and then head upstairs to the music and video department where Tina works. As they climb the stairs, Chris can already see Tina, tits rested on folded arms that rest on the counter. Pop music is blaring from the in-house sound system and Tina is watching the TV suspended from the ceiling. It is playing the highlights of a recent reality TV show that has just been released 'uncut' on VHS and DVD. The TV is on mute and so the recently Z-listed bounce around the screen to the unforgettable sound of the latest winner of a televised talent contest. Tina watches, looking uninterested in sound or vision, but concentrating solely on grinding the chewing gum in the back of her jaw. Chris has made his mind up – a camel. She looks like a mutant camel with the humps in the wrong places.

After a disingenuous look through chart CDs, Chris and Zeb head over to the counter. Tina grins as she sees them approach.

'Hello boys?'

Chris hates it when she says this and looks like that. It makes him feel sick and he speaks to save gagging.

'Hiya, Tina. Erm, are you coming around tonight?'

'No, your David's working late at the Garage. Got to keep me in the style I've become a customer to.'

Chris winces at this malapropism and waits for Zeb to speak. To speak? Zeb's lips are sealed. The only sounds are strange mong murmurings that seem to come from beneath his eyebrows.

'Mnhhhaemnnngg.'

Chris waits in the awkward silence before a genuine customer comes to the rescue. At this point he drags Zeb towards the exit, only for Zeb to pull back and lead them to a rack of posters by the blank VHS cassettes. Chris doesn't want a scene and so follows Zeb but is determined not to speak to him. They flick through the glass-fronted, metal-framed posters, counting down the seconds with the familiar faces of Dido, Jennifer Lopez and an Alien with a spliff. Already bored, Chris notices that Zeb is elbowing him below the ribs and making noises out of the side of his mouth. He tries to ignore him but soon the twitching and moaning become more embarrassing than the coded task that is being asked of him, and so Chris goes back over to the counter where Tina is bending down to change a CD. Her skirt tightens over her hips, the red brow of her thong raised above the waistband. Zeb's made his mind up – a goddess. She's a fucking goddess.

'Chris! You shouldn't sneak up on a girl like that!'

'Sorry, erm; you know Zeb, don't you?'

'Yeah, course I know Zeb.'

Silence again. All those times Chris had wished for such silence from Zeb now sneak up behind him and kick him up the arse.

'Right, we best be going, see you over the weekend then, yeah?'

'Yeah. See you, Chris, see you, Zeb.'

'Mnhhheamnnnng.'

'Oh, and Chris, tell your David not to forget the wine for the christening.'

After putting in such a pathetic performance it would be reasonable to think that Zeb would be at the very least subdued, if not shamed into silence, but Zeb is a creature that defies belief – sometimes his own – and so it should come as no surprise that as they leave the Archer Centre, Zeb offers his assessment of their meeting with Tina not so much with youthful optimism but pure bullshit.

'She wants it off me, mate, I am telling you, she want it off me in the biggest of ways!'

Chris is too used to these kinds of outbursts to take much notice, but the phone vibrating in his pocket has him surrender completely to matters that are yet to come. This makes him feel uneasy, uneasy to the point that he doesn't even check what the message is, because he knows whom it is from. He simply carries on walking towards McDonald's.

Zeb meanwhile carries on talking: oaths of what he'll do to Tina, in-depth analysis of what she really wants, insightful criticism of what she is missing in her life, acknowledgement that if David heard what he was saying he would probably not only beat him to a pulp but make him take out a full page advert in the paper renouncing his views, a full page advert with a picture, a photo, probably the one his mum took of him when he was on the toilet when they stayed in a caravan on holiday in north Wales. Yes, he knows all this, but even so, even though he knows the consequences he –.

Even Chris is shocked when Zeb stops talking. For Zeb to stop talking now means that he hasn't chosen silence, but has been shut up. Something serious has shut Zeb up. And it is serious. Sat in McDonald's is Spoonhead.

Zeb looks over at him and Spoonhead looks down. He is dressed in his school uniform: a blue sweater, white polo shirt, black trousers and black Rockport shoes. His backpack is by his feet and his cream jacket hangs on the back of his chair. A matching cap is tightened fast to his head, a head narrower at the crown than the chin, much like a teardrop, but in the eyes of his peers more like a spoon. Zeb takes a seat directly opposite Spoonhead but next to the door while Chris goes to buy two strawberry milkshakes.

At the counter, Chris decides to look at his message as it suddenly seems a lot less serious than the premonitions this current situation inspires in Chris' foresight. He presses 'read' and once again it is from Keeley. She is repeating her request of where and when and Chris remembers that the close proximity of Zeb had prevented him from dealing with her request earlier. He smiles as he thinks of how he'd forgotten this, smiles at the strength of emotion he feels for this girl he has only ever spoken to through looks and rumours. His feelings are almost threatening to take over him – to jump him on the way home. They are so varied, so indefinite in their purpose while certain in their origin that they seem as infinite, beautiful and baffling as the fractions of a circle with Keeley at its centre and Chris jogging the circumference. He presses reply, types in the place – outside McDonalds – and the time – half seven – before pressing send. He wonders if he should have put the three

Xs on the end but before this thought can drag him too far, two strawberry milkshakes appear.

Arriving back at the table, Zeb takes the milkshake from Chris without looking at him. Zeb's eyes are firmly fixed upon Spoonhead, his fingers almost puncturing the white paper tumbler.

Spoonhead looks back with flicked glances and pretend stretches of his arms to snatch hidden peeks at Zeb. He translates these glimpses into how Zeb must be feeling. Each rub of Spoonhead's eyes or stroke of his nose seems to enhance the rage building up in Zeb's face. The hot anger at the humiliation Zeb suffered at *his* hands and the hands of *his* friends, the excited blush of imminent retribution. Spoonhead decides that things are not going to get any better and so he makes a move, takes the inevitable now before this wrath grows too great.

Zeb meanwhile, in struggling to suck the thick milkshake through the flimsy straw, feels his face turning bright red. When he sees Spoonhead make his move, the surprise causes him to inhale a snotty gloop of his milkshake and so he blinks the instruction to Chris to move out and follow while he holds off the splutter until Spoonhead has left. Couldn't possibly allow him to witness that. This business is all about appearances.

Propelled by the gravity of Zeb's look, Chris starts after Spoonhead, sliding into the slipstream of his growing fear up the road between McDonald's and the Trouble and Strife pub. He looks left to check his walk in the large pub window, just to make sure it has the right mix of menace and coolness. He wipes his face from his right ear, down over his top lip and grips his chin, all in slow motion, before pulling on the end of his nose and glancing over his right shoulder to see Zeb. Zeb's mouth is now wiped clean as he jogs up behind Chris and matches him stride for stride.

The whole scene leaves Chris' immediate consciousness and veers below him as if he is watching it from above like the Aboriginal view of the landscape on the card his Uncle Patrick sent him. This image bristles across Chris' memory, reminding him of the pigeons he watched as a youngster as they swooped like a single section of a kaleidoscope constantly on the turn. The pigeons belonged to his next-door neighbour Mr Buckley and every time Chris feels a sense of synchronicity, he is reminded of their poise, intelligence and ability to constantly surprise him. Chris hasn't always had this respect for Mr Buckley's pigeons. For a long time they were merely a source of amusement as Chris would sneak into Mr Buckley's yard while he was out and climb on top of the pigeon shed. Once on top, he would jump up and down, sending the pigeons into a panicked frenzy, an insane rhythm beating itself out inside the shed as they crashed around, trying to escape. This chaos pleased Chris greatly but one day he experienced the consequences of his actions – the true essence of mayhem – and everything changed.

A few weeks after Chris' eleventh birthday he waited for Mr Buckley to head into town for his Saturday shopping before he went out into the yard, climbed over the fence and onto the pigeon shed. He began to jump, dancing to the thunder of the terror below, when without warning he crashed through the roof and into the shed itself. The pain of the rough pitch edges catching his hips and elbows couldn't reveal itself, hidden as it was by the terrifying scene around him. The pigeons darted – striking Chris in their frantic, unreasonable trajectories. Feathers and the smell of bird shit formed an insecure blanket around him and in this blind, raw and wild anarchy, Chris himself felt like one of the pigeons and kicked open the flimsy door in order to escape. As he leapt the fence and ran back in through his back door, Chris saw the pigeons flee into the sky like a cloud of pure order.

He waited the whole day in his room for Mr Buckley to return. He felt guilty. He knew Mr Buckley was unmarried, knew he didn't really have any friends – just a young nephew who sometimes came to visit – and so he felt like those pigeons may have been Mr Buckley's only friends. It hurt Chris to think that he'd made someone feel alone. Chaos is the naïve aim of youth, its full wrath something that the young cannot find any fear for; but loneliness, from the deep distance of the dark before sleep, to the endless sentry standing in the wait for a parent's return, was something all children could imagine and so understand.

After what seemed like a week, Mr Buckley's front door opened and Chris ran into his mother's room to spy on Mr Buckley's back yard from the window. Mr Buckley walked out, looked at his shed, shook his head and walked back inside.

Chris felt the spicy orange feeling that guilt gave him inside his chest. Then he heard something like the maracas they used in music lessons. He looked out of the window again and saw Mr Buckley with a scoop and some seeds. He shook the scoop and from gutters, trees, car parks and hedges, the pigeons all flew back, one by one, and into the shed – a more gentle rhythm bidding them to return. When Mr Buckley was sure the homecoming was complete, he locked up the door and from behind the shed pulled out a blue tarpaulin that he tossed across the hole in the roof like a winter duvet. He then tucked the pigeons in with a brick each corner and went back inside. Chris couldn't believe his eyes, that these creatures whose terror and relief he had himself felt, had been coaxed back by Mr Buckley with such ease.

The next day, Mr Buckley began to fix the shed and Chris went around to ask if he could help. Mr Buckley obviously knew what was going on but never said a thing. Chris became a regular visitor to Mr Buckley and he taught him all about his pigeons, Chris soon knowing most of their names by sight. He was taught how to tag their ankles, check their wings for health, he was even sometimes allowed to call them in from exercise with the seeds and shovel. But when he became old enough to know that pigeons weren't that cool, he stopped. Mr Buckley understood and still always has a hello for Chris.

By now the trio have turned left along the dirt track that leads behind the bowling green. The bowling green belongs to a private club and stands some fifty feet above the road, almost as high as the multistorey car park. Two female OAPs are on their final end: one with two woods close to the jack but no blocker, the other stood at the mat with only one option. She checks her line, dips with a hand on her left thigh and fires the wood down the centre of the green. Its speed cancels out its bias and sends it crashing into the jack to void the end. They collect their bowls and the jack from the gutter at the edge of the green before moving over to the pavilion to discuss their next match.

They are completely unaware of the three figures tagging along the broken chicken wire fence that is meant to keep their place of solace and recreation secure.

Spoonhead drops to his left and grabs a fencepost that is lying on the floor. He is now facing both Chris and Zeb, the post gripped at the bottom with his left hand, the top end resting on his right.

'Fucking come on then. You going to do anything, or just fucking follow me?'

Zeb steps away from Chris. This is his favourite part of any fight – the verbals.

'Oh, right. Had a bad day, is it?'

'What?'

'Well, you seem a bit tense. You know. A bit upset.'

'Fuck off.'

'Yep. You definitely need to see someone. Get some help. Get on them tablets your mum takes.'

A glance and smile at Chris who dutifully grins back at Zeb.

'What? What the f –'

'Deaf as well? Ears are probably still ringing after listening to your mum *scream* all night while I –'

Zeb puts his hands in front of him, one on top of the other, and begins to mime long, deep and pleasurable thrusts.

'Right. Let's go. Come on, let's have it here and now.'

'If that's what you really want.'

'Yeah.'

'You are sure, now?'

'Fucking right!'

'It's just... well... I'm giving you choices here, and you're giving me none.'

An in-joke, the ultimate show of solidarity. Now Zeb is ready. 'Okay. Put the post down and let's go. One on one.'

Spoonhead thrusts his eyebrows towards Chris and then back to Zeb.

'What about him?'

He knows Chris through his brother and has a little empathy for him. He is also sure that just like him, Chris wants a reputation of his own and sees this as a good an opportunity as any. Of course Chris wants nothing of the sort.

'Nothing to do with me, Spoonhead. I swear. You put the post down and you and Zeb can go one on one.'

It looks as if Spoonhead is about to give in. He squats down – slowly placing the post on the floor. Then he stands up straight and bolts.

The two OAPs are still sat in the pavilion, continuing their small talk, when Spoonhead comes charging down towards them. His backpack jumps from side to side as he launches himself across the bowling green but of course he has chosen the least suitable option by far; Zeb is twice as quick as most people at a jog. The OAPs see Zeb, or rather a flash of boy catching up with Spoonhead quickly, toying with him as he zig-zags as if avoiding a bullet. They feel a rush of adrenalin as he reaches the far side of the bowling green and trips Spoonhead deftly. Finally they grimace with phantom pain as the poor boy crashes into the gutter at the edge of the green.

They look up from their seats in the pavilion and then at each other. The pause in action has them wondering, asking questions, trying to work out just what will happen next when *SMACK*! They see Zeb's foot crash down into Spoonhead's face, not once, not twice, but continually. They wince with every blow but are transfixed by the action until Zeb reaches into his back pocket and pulls out a knife. The OAPs cover their eyes as they see him raise the knife above his head and start to swing towards Spoonhead. They gasp but through the gaps in their fingers they see Chris arriving at the last minute to grab Zeb and pull him away, Zeb still kicking and flailing in his frenzy. They sigh with dubious relief as Chris leads Zeb away but just as they are settling again in their seats to discuss the action they jump at a terrifying sound exploding from within the tiny frame of Zeb.

'YOUFUCKINGCUNTIFYOUEVERFUCKWITHME AGAINIWILLFUCKINGKILLYOU!'

They hold their hearts and try to hide their excitement while shaking their heads at such dreadful language. On a bowling green, of all places.

16.20

Countdown is doing nothing for Billy. Even with the new set, the new camera angle that offers a full body shot of Carol Vorderman during the letters game: nothing.

Whenever he gets home before his wife Beth, Billy always scours the house for some kind of titillating material in a desperate attempt to find something to masturbate over. He's already been through all the newspapers and magazines, but page three and airbrushed soap stars just don't do it for him – too fake. The chances of him actually doing what he wants to do to those type of girls is highly unlikely and Billy is a puritan when it comes to wanking – he likes to keep it real.

He's gone through all the videos since he came home, all the cable channels, and even had his binoculars out on the offchance of seeing the fortysomething permatan woman from across the road doing the ironing in her front room. At this rate, he is going to have to resort to his imagination.

Permatan Woman is called Sue. She lives at number eight, directly opposite Billy at number seven, on this new, exclusive housing estate. The houses come in three different designs: Silence, Serenity and Solace; Billy's house being the latter, although straight up Consolation would be more fitting. Silence offers three bedrooms, a large kitchen, bathroom and en-suite shower, two reception rooms and garage. Serenity misses out on the en-suite. Solace has to comfort itself with even less: a kitchen/diner, no garage and two bedrooms. They'd bought it as first-time buyers with hopes of a family, and now, with baby Joey already two, are growing out of it. Beth is envious of the space those in Serenity enjoy, and hates the fact that the estate is planned so that all three designs fill each cul-de-sac and remind her of her standing behind the façade of variety. Curved avenues lead to these cul-de-sacs from the road that acts as a spine to the estate's nervous system. And the residents have a right to be nervous. They average a burglary or car theft a week, despite the price they pay for such exclusivity, and bemoan the fact that the black shiny tarmac driveways, white timber porches and russet brickwork don't intimidate those from that other grey Estate venturing in and taking whatever they want. Billy's house however never gets touched, and he likes being close to his mates.

Sue is in her late forties, wobbly and orange, with huge black hair, a wrinkled neck and massive, floppy tits.

Although several stones overweight, she does the house-work in a tiny nightie that skirts her wilting arse, usually with the light on and always with the curtains open. For a long time, Billy had built an elaborate fantasy about fixing her car as a foreigner, only to be invited in to quench her sexual thirst and end up (as all of Billy's sexual fantasies do) covered in his hot, sticky semen. However, last summer, Beth had managed to get them invited over for a barbeque, and Billy was so horrified at the high resolution closeup shots that his fantasy was completely ruined. If he imagines her feasting on his trunk-like penis, he can't help noticing the bleached hair, sweeping his shaft with her top lip. Likewise, doing her from behind over the breakfast bar is a nightmare of gory varicose veins making her arse cheeks look like the eyes of an old drunk. Sue on top is unimaginable. Still, even the pixilated view from across the road would manage to satisfy him now, but she must be on the sunbed so Billy lays full stretch on the settee and flicks through the cable channels once more.

Marie is flicking through pages and pages of digital TV. The front door opens and Chris momentarily blocks the infra-red beam as he flashes through the front room, breaking her trance and spurring her into reaching for her mobile phone. Barbara hears only the rustling of Chris' jacket as he slices through the tobacco smoke in the kitchen and by the time she has taken the teacup from her lips and put it on the side, she has to shout up the stairs to catch his attention.

'Did you have a good day, love?'

Chris has already pissed, flushed and hit his bedroom by the time the words reach him. He wishes that the lock David had put on the outside to stop his mother going though his things while he was out was in fact on the inside, like normal people have it, so that he could lock himself in here for a while and not have to face the first of what he was sure would become a series of interrogations by the time the weekend was over.

He sits on the edge of his bed and looks out towards David's. Both beds are immaculately made and the room smells of Mr Sheen and Pot Pourri air freshener. To his left, the new stereo that David recently bought sits in grey glory save for a mark left on the LCD from a removed sticker. Beneath the stereo is the unit which houses the tapes and CDs. David has a large collection of CDs, stacked neatly and in alphabetic order. Chris' collection comprises purely of tapes, all taped from other people, but none taped without his express request. He, like the rest of his friends, listens to the radio, to the bootleg tapes from garage nights and other events, but Chris would synthesise these hit and miss collections into a definitive list of songs that he could borrow from other people and then put onto tape. It isn't that he is trying to cheat the system or even that he's a skinflint, he just doesn't see the point of paying for something that isn't exactly what he wants. Making the tapes is a creative process in itself – a labour of love. He ducks down and picks one up. It doesn't matter which, for they are all perfect in his eyes – they are all exactly what he wants – and puts it in the stereo before pressing the play button.

'Yeah, fine.'

Barbara doesn't like the music Chris listens to. Not in the way that ordinary parents dislike their kid's music, because she actually listens to his and takes notice. It isn't the shock of the bad language that leaps from the speakers nor is it the actual sound of the music. Barbara doesn't like Chris' music because someone is always getting hurt. None of the songs he listens to seem to have a happy ending.

She walks back into the kitchen, ducks into the cupboard to take out some onions, places them on the side, and picks up her cup of tea again. It is the fourth she has had since her sister Jean arrived forty minutes or so ago with her kids in tow. Barbara is making Chris' favourite tonight, chicken curry, and she hasn't got enough to feed Jean and the kids as well. She is aware however, that when David arrives home and sees them there he will refuse to stay, which means his share can go to the kids and she can feign some excuse for giving her share to Jean. She looks at Jean with screensaver eyes and lets most of what she is saying wash over her, her head nodding every now and again with the steady tide of Jean's words.

Jean is reaching into Barbara's Lambert & Butler packet for the fourth cigarette she has ponced off her since she arrived. She talks of her shame at taking the cigarettes, at having her sister know she can't even afford Mayfairs, that even Lamberts are luxury at the moment. Barbara looks at the new clothes her niece and nephew wear and thanks God that at least *they* don't have to go without. She takes a draining sip and puts down her empty teacup.

A cup of tea sits beneath Billy on the laminated floor by the settee, dead cold and forgotten. The floor itself is a relic of pride in Beth's mind since she found out David has just had it put in his mother's house. Billy hasn't told her about the other ways in which their front room has influenced David. The walls are painted peach with a green leaf-patterned wallpaper border cutting them in two and the marshmallow three-piece suite bakes in front of the natural-look fire. On the walls hang Matisse prints, one upside-down, and the ceiling is artexed to within an inch of its existence. It has been this way since they bought it some four years ago and every viewing of a home-makeover show makes Beth hide behind her scatter cushions in shame. She is forever planning new rooms, new themes, cutting ideas from magazines and bringing home catalogues from Habitat and the new Ikea. She rationalises the non-realisation of these fantasies in the bigger dream of a new house altogether. Maybe Silence, at a push Serenity.

On the fireplace are photographs of Billy and Beth on their wedding day. Billy looks at them and remembers the day fondly. The marriage took place in St Stephen's Church, June 2001. It seemed like the right thing to do with Joey on the way. The ceremony wasn't Catholic because Billy's family are Catholic and it meant his parents wouldn't come. David was the best man and making David the best man meant that the stag night was incredible.

With the wedding taking place on the Sunday, David suggested a Friday night event. He'd planned a night out in the city centre: chain bars and then the usual end of night leerathon at Club Eternity. Nothing special there. But he'd also planned a little surprise. Rather than tie Billy to a lamppost or hire a strip-o-gram, David decided that they should instead go to a brothel and Billy was very keen on the idea.

He pictures walking in the black door and into the foyer of the brothel: a pine-panelled room, a large mirror on the wall and a larger black woman behind the desk. At the time they arrived, she was on the phone to someone. Billy can still remember the details as if it was a script: 'Well, my name's Candi, I'm twenty-six and I've got delicious toffee-coloured skin. Are you ready to fuck? Yeah, that's right, baby, tanned all year round, and shiny too when I'm covered in baby oil... like now. I'm already wet 'cause I can tell by your voice that it's massive. I can't wait for you to fuck me hard, I'm ready for you to slap your big prick between my massive tits. Ooh, I'm playing with myself now, I can feel it. Mmm it's sooo big, pull out when you're going to cum: I want to be covered in it. That's it, mmm, oh, there's loads of it. Hurry up and come back and fuck me again, don't keep me waiting. Well then, what can I do for you boys?'

They approached the desk and were given the price list but David had already sorted it out and Billy was shown the girls he could choose from. There was Paris: a massive blonde woman, about thirty-six in a cheap red negligee and suspender set. Next to her was Strawberry: slim and about the same age, in a PVC dress and boots. She had ginger hair. At the back was a black girl, late twenties, wearing a wonder bra and a thong. She was called Kaya and Billy chose her. She was beautiful and lead Billy up the stairs to the basic room.

The room really was basic. A single bed, a TV playing porn in the corner, talc, tissues, condoms and lubricants, the smell of a hospital waiting room, the creak of a condemned building, a full-length mirror along the left-hand wall. As Billy got undressed, Kaya began to explain the procedure. It was fifteen minutes massage and fifteen minutes of sex, extra if he didn't want to use a condom. As he was getting married, Billy thought he better use one. He lay down on the bed and Kaya spent fifteen minutes rubbing talc on his back, smoking a fag and coughing. After this, she spent a minute or so lubing herself, putting a johnny on him and coughing. Then she spent a couple of minutes blowing him between coughing. Finally, she spent ten minutes on her back, faking orgasm and coughing. Having still not come, Billy was blamed by Kaya for having had too much to drink so he had a wank just to prove that the customer was always right.

As far as Billy was aware, the big day went well, but the experience of the city's vice industry had destroyed yet another of his favourite fantasies.

Graham imagined all sorts of terrible things when he heard the door go and as he looks through the spy-hole thanks God it is just David. Something has just gone down, something he doesn't want David to know about just yet, and he feels for the first time in years the rush of starting out in a new game where the dangers are shiny and unpredictable. He grabs an oily cloth housing a heavy object and puts it in the inside pocket of his jacket. He opens his door and steps outside before shutting it behind him.

'Alright, Dave, you got off early then?'

'Yeah, not much on today.'

'Must be great being your own boss eh?'

They both laugh. An in-joke. David is wondering why he hasn't been invited in.

'Just caught me on the way out, to be honest, Dave.'

'Where you off?'

'Sunbeds. Do you fancy it?'

'Yeah. Why not?'

That explains it.

Graham steps out and starts to unlock the police stinger from his driveway. David stops him and offers to take them both in his car. They both get in, neither putting on their seatbelts, then David revs the engine and they drive off.

'Still sounding good, the old girl then.'

'Fucking timeless this one, mate. Gave her tune up at the beginning of the week.'

'Things been that slow?'

'Yeah. Don't know what's up, to be honest with you. Just seems to have stopped recently.'

'Right. Well, you know –'

'Yeah. No offence Graham, but, you now how it is. Why I want to do this right.'

'None taken, mate. None taken. Just want you to know it's there if you want it.'

'I know, mate. Tantasia?'

'Yep.'

The two jump out of the car and leave the doors unlocked at Graham's request. His mate needs some pampering and he is going to show him a good time. David hates Tantasia. He doesn't understand why blokes go on sunbeds, not straight blokes anyway. They walk into the sunbed parlour and up to the reception. Graham has recently bought the place, hoping to use it as a front to clean some of the extra money he'll have coming in soon, and so he walks the shop floor not with his usual local celebrity confidence, but with the assured poise of an owner.

'Hello girls.'

The girls in question are Tammy, Toni and their younger sister Chantelle. Tammi and Toni are identical twins that didn't quite complete their Health and Beauty GNVQ at college but still managed to find jobs at Tantasia, the Estate's premier beauty salon. Chantelle has been here since she got home from school. Keeley didn't want to be with anyone as she prepared herself for her meeting with Chris.

This isn't to say that Tantasia is just somewhere to fill time. Chantelle often helps out her beautiful older sisters and dreams of growing up to be just like them. Unfortunately this is impossible. Tammi and Toni are Caramac-skinned with straightened dark hair, Tammi's streaked with blonde and Toni's striped in pillar-box red. They both stand five two and have the slight figures of the models used on club flyers. Their smiles are even and framed with lips that perch below slim, straight, small noses, themselves dissecting almond-shaped eyes and hanging onto sharp eyebrows. Apart from their hair, they differ in only one other way. Toni does all the speaking.

'Hello Graham.'

'You know David, yeah?'

''Course we do, hello David.'

'Hello girls.'

'You still with Tina?'

'Yeah. Still with Tina.'

'Ahh. I knew you two would stay together, you just matched.'

Toni's affection hides a deep hatred of Tina, the only girl bar Tammi in school to come anywhere near her in the beauty stakes (although in real terms, it is only the size of Tina's tits that beat her main contenders). Chantelle on the other hand is just shocked at the familiarity with which her sister conducts herself in the presence not only of Golden Graham but also the demi-God that is David Carty. She wants the high life her sisters enjoy more than ever.

'Listen girls. We need a good pampering this afternoon. Big night ahead and all that, so we'll have two sunbeds and a manicure if that's alright.'

Just saying the word manicure feels luxurious to Graham, and he turns around to David with a satisfied grin as he removes his gold for safekeeping with the twins. Toni opens the safe and puts Graham's gold inside. David thinks it all sounds a bit queer as he takes off his Rolex and gives it to Chantelle.

'You make sure you take good care of that now, darling. It's worth more than all that fake shit of his put together.'

David and Graham both laugh at another of their oldest gags. As Tammi takes David over to one of the tanning rooms, Graham goes into the inside pocket of his jacket and pulls out the oily-clothed parcel. He gives it to Toni with a wink and clocks her arse as she bends down to put it in the safe. Chantelle turns red and looks out of the window.

Billy gets up to have another look out of the window and knocks the cold tea across the floor. Cursing, he goes into the kitchen for some super absorbent, extra strong kitchen towel and notices the calendar magnetised to the fridge. The words 'Chris' Birthday' are written in the slot for Sunday as Beth is obsessed with sending birthday cards to everyone she knows so that she can moan at Billy when they forget Joey's. The kitchen is one room Beth is still proud of. The fridge is Smeg and all the appliances bar the hidden washer/dryer are stainless steel, from the Toshiba microwave to the DeLonghi coffee maker. The kitchen units are a darkly-varnished pine and the surfaces slate-look Formica. A Jamie Oliver cookbook is open on a metal holder and some chicken has defrosted on a plate by the transparent kettle. Billy grabs some kitchen towel and goes back into the front room to mop up. He does so quickly and is actually impressed just how absorbent and strong the kitchen towel really is before tossing it into the small bin by the PC.

He looks longingly at the computer. The internet is out of bounds. Beth works in an IT department and is, compared to Billy, a computer whiz. For a while he used the internet to fulfil his needs with frightening regularity. Thumbnail galleries, Web communities and Google's image search could be utilised in his pursuit of the perfect onanistic kick, but even though he deleted his cache, cleaned up his history, binned his cookies, Beth knows places in that computer that he can't understand or access, and can crawl around his electronic subconscious before presenting him with damning evidence about the kind of man he is.

Billy is ashamed of the man he is, but feels that if this is who he is, he'll just have to live with it. He loves Beth, he adores young Joey, but he can't help wanting more. He stopped having sex with Beth shortly after Joey was born, and remembers being surprised at how young he was for such a thing to happen. He understood that separate beds and a low sex drive were something to fear in old age, but the realisation that it could affect him at such a young age, and in just the third year of his marriage, was something that shocked him to the core. Even more shocking to him is that the situation is entirely balanced and reciprocal. Beth rarely felt energetic enough nowadays, after working the six – three shift at the call centre and picking up Joey from her mother's, and cooking dinner, and watching some home improvement shows and reading a few magazines. She is too bushed for sex. Billy understands this. He is particularly understanding because he doesn't want to have sex with her either. Beth is a professional woman, wears smart clothes to work, has a swipecard to get into the office, drives a Mondeo, earns seventeen thousand pounds a year – how can this turn him on? How can he possibly think he could get away with what he wants to with a woman like that? No. When she was in school, where they met, and she had the permed hair, fake tan on her legs and her name on her jewellery, she never stopped turning him on. But since then, since the good exam results and the access course, she's become a completely different woman altogether. Billy feels this change in her has changed him into the man he is now.

Paul has changed into an Intergalactic Space Ranger with a nose-mounted death ray, blasting the space slime that is threatening to envelop the whole universe and smother all known life. He stands above the toilet on tiptoes, his lower garments bunched around his ankles and his bare arse clenched to force the piss out of his willy with greater force as he attempts to rid the bowl of the clinging Toilet Duck.

He finishes and pulls the chain, rushing to pull up his trousers and get out of the bathroom before the plastic handle on the cistern returns to its horizontal position and triggers the bomb that Paul has left there to kill off any possibly-surviving slime molecules. He leaps out of the bathroom door in slow motion and falls to the ground, covering his head. As the debris falls about him, he gets up, dusts himself down and walks downstairs to the kitchen, another successful mission completed.

Walking into the kitchen he sees his mother finishing another cigarette and taking another from the packet. He walks over to his Auntie Barbara who is chopping onions and crying. He wonders what's wrong with her. Is she sad that Marie has stayed in the other room, alone, playing with her phone? Is she sad that Chris has stayed upstairs looking at his new shoes, taking them in and out of their box? (Paul had been on a secret spy mission before he zapped the slime, a spy mission all over the house. He'd looked in strange cupboards with quilted hot tubes in them, he'd seen the dog in the garden wanting to come in but being ignored, and he'd seen the photographs on the fireplace, one taking his interest in particular, the one with Aunty Barbara and the man he didn't know.) He looks up at his Aunty Barbara and she looks back at him.

'Oh darling, it's just the onions. Tell you what, why don't you, your sister and your mummy stay for some dinner, eh?'

Yes, this sorrow had something to do with him, the man that he didn't know in the photograph.

Billy picks up the other photograph on the fireplace, that of his son. It wasn't the arrival of Joey that changed things for Billy and Beth. She changed when opportunity arrived. Joey is just pure joy. Beth named him after the character from *Friends*, and Billy doesn't mind this. Joey is his favourite character too. Besides, when he *looks* at Joey, he sees pure Billy. Joey is his father's spitting image. The same round face, the same green eyes, Billy has even insisted on his son having the same hairstyle as him. This concession was made at the request that Beth should be the one to dress him.

Every minute he spends with his son brings ecstasy to Billy's life. He plays Play Station with him, buys him every new shirt his favourite football team brings out, points out pretty girls when they go to feed ducks in the park, and tells him things to say that will make Billy's friends laugh. He loves his son more than anything and so agrees with Beth when she insists that he sees nothing of Billy's parents.

Graham and David see nothing through their bottle green goggles as they lie naked under the all over glare of the ultra-violet lamps. David still feels at odds with Graham's earlier request. It isn't so much the idea of a manicure, but the assurance and arrogance with which the request was made. It reminds him of how Graham hijacked David's plans for Billy's stag night a couple of years back and how David felt sick at the thought of visiting a whorehouse. Still, he lies on the sunbed next to Graham while they sort out their plans for the evening.

'Well, I don't know about Billy. He looked rough as fuck in work today.'

'Yeah?'

'Yeah. Well, you should know. He was out with you wasn't he?'

'Well, yeah, but he left me in the Strife about eight. His gran isn't it?'

'Yeah. Anyway. He was rough, so I doubt he'll be up for it.'

'I'll text him later and see. What about you, are you having it?'

'Too right mate, wouldn't mind starting early, actually.'

'Yeah?'

'Yeah.'

'Right. I might have some of that as well. Meet in the Strife at six?'

'Six sounds good.'

David looks in reflex for his Rolex and remembers where he is.

'What time is it now?'

'About half four.'

'Right. Better give that manicure a miss then. Got to have my tea yet.'

'You sure?'

'Yeah. Don't want to be bolting my tea before I go out. Like to take my time, enjoy it.'

Time is creeping on and Billy's erection hasn't gone away. He knows that Beth will soon be on her way home from her mother's, after talking about whatever they talk about there everyday. In the past, he has actually masturbated over Beth's mother, but that was for a fleeting time before they'd actually met. He has another look out of the window and resigns himself to the fact that it is going to have to be eyes closed for this wank.

He trudges up the stairs and heads into the master bedroom. Beth hates this room. She hates it so much, that she sometimes wakes Joey in the night so that he'll be scared and ask her to join him in his bed. This is the one room that came from her past. It is the bedroom she dreamed of as a schoolgirl.

The wardrobes are fitted and white, with powder blue trim and handles. The carpet is navy blue to match the curtains, which have baby pink tiebacks. The wallpaper is sky blue, with a cloud patterned pastel pink border that matches the lampshades. The bedclothes match everything else. It is Billy's favourite room.

The room faces the front of the house, and so the street, but Billy doesn't draw the curtains as he lies on the bed, for the bed is just lower than the windowsill and he can't be seen from the outside. He has checked. He has also checked that the mirror on the white dressing table by the far wall keeps his image inside the room, but hasn't noticed the change in its angle as Beth left it in makeup position in her morning rush. Billy undoes his trousers and takes a tissue from the square box on the bedside table. He squeezes the tissue in his left hand, his penis in his right and as usual smiles at his impressive size. He then closes his eyes and tries a few fantasies.

Being a puritan, Billy's wank fantasies are linear and have a complete narrative, setting and mood. He has created thousands but has lost thousands in contact with actual reality and overuse. He tries a few old ones. Nothing. He tries a few he has been working on, customers at the Garage, girls he has seen out, but their vital details are too changeable and insecure in his memory for any real chance of success. After a couple of minutes of minor frustration, Billy decides to resort to what has become his only successful fantasy for the last six months or so.

It is about Beth, the Younger Beth, and him, the Younger Billy. They are in Maths, sat at the back, her letting him write his name on her bare legs. She is in uniform, a short black skirt, her shirt untucked, a gold chain with her name on it resting below a tie that has been shortened, the long end tucked into her shirt and visible in between her legs when he sneaks glances whilst writing. This image freezes in his mind as things start to happen at last, the first few pulses of a probable satisfaction tightening in his groin. The action cuts to the hill behind the school. They have decided not to go to science and instead are kissing, open mouthed and sloppily on the hill. The view is of them both and shot from below, so that he can see up her skirt as his fingers test her patience, and she pulls just too hard on his foreskin. Billy is now engaged so thoroughly in his imagination that he doesn't hear his mobile phone beep downstairs with an incoming message.

Slowly, Younger Beth gets up. Younger Billy lies back, a smile creeping across his face as she takes his penis into her mouth and begins to suck on it. She is slow and sure, concentrating on avoiding her brace, and worried about gagging. He can almost hear her recite in her mind the advice picked up from *More* magazine on how to do this successfully. In an all too brief time, she stops and sits next to him. He is still erect, throbbing and looks at her. A question burns in his mind but he is unsure of the etiquette. He half asks and she raises her eyebrows as if to prompt him. He takes this as the signal and pops the question.

'Do you mind if I finish myself off?'

She shakes her head and he smiles. He looks at her, as he does it, and as his face tightens and he is about to come, he hears her ask the question that had been smouldering behind her eyebrows.

'Billy? Billy? Are you home?'

That isn't right! That isn't the question. That's Older Beth. She's home! Billy pulls his pants up quickly, but it is too late, the first burst has made it out before he could cover his cock and spurts onto the navy carpet. He falls to the floor to wipe it with the tissue still gripped in his hand,

and curses its inferior absorption and strength compared to the kitchen towel. He can already hear her coming up the stairs behind the hands and legs sprint of Joey. Billy manages to pull up his trousers and put the tissue in his pocket as Joey runs into the room and jumps into his arms. He catches his child and swings him round to face the window so that Beth won't see that his trousers are undone and his erection pumping in his damp pants. Out of the window, he's sure he sees Sue with a pair of binoculars duck away in her tiny nightie before Beth's image takes up its reflection in the glass.

'Where were you last night?'

Billy's jockey shorts are full of his hot, sticky, semen.

16.55

Toni bites into a towel over the headrest of one of the chairs in the Nails and Beauty 'room' of Tantasia. This 'room', is in fact a simple partition in the reception area open at both ends and crooked into a flimsy trapezium so that customers may have privacy if they want it during procedures. Behind this partition is a chair, much like a barber's station, bolted to the floor and upholstered in brown leatherette. A table sits east of this chair with beauty products of every description – from acrylic nails to hot wax – littered about it. A less impressive chair, clothed in a blue-grey material that offers no pretentious disguise to its man-made origins, more in keeping with that of a call centre operative, squats to the left of the leatherette emperor, its supporting S-bend cowering under the weight of Graham's right knee and shin. He remains dressed as he was before. His shoes still on over black ankle socks, the right hanging from the chair, the left fulcrumed to the floor, pivoting in rhythm with the thrusts pumping from his bare band of groin and arse. This band is fashioned at the lower perimeter by the waistband of the brushed denims stretching around the top of his thighs, the upper formed by the light blue crew-necked sweater that has been pulled up over his flat stomach to just below the rib cage. Graham's balls hang angrily, swinging and scraping over the elastic of his grey jockeys while his leather jacket and baseball cap hang embarrassed on the hatstand opposite Tammi and Chantelle. All try their best to ignore the noises coming from the other side of the shaking divide. They can smell L'Eau D'Issey.

Toni has both hands on the shoulders of the chair, her head still buried in the towel on the headrest. A glow of sweat has formed on her hairline and the crease where her buttocks join her thighs. Her knickers are pulled just below this join, their clinical whiteness accentuating her lineless tan and complementing her white beautician's get up. This get up is got up over her hips, the press studs open to the belly button, allowing Graham to cup one of her small breasts in his left hand while his other grips her right hip tightly. She has tucked her chin into her neck, creasing it into a faux double. As Graham's thrusts become more violent, his snorts and grunts more audible, she opens her throat, stretches her nose ceilingward, and frees herself from the muffling towel in the irrational scream of orgasm: 'wwhhoOOROMmmAHEEEEEEEUHUHUHUHUHUHUH WHOAWHOAWHAWHA!'

Chantelle glows red and sends Keeley a text message:

wear u meetin him?

Marie sits looking at the screen of her mobile phone, willing it for a reply to the message she sent earlier. The blue glow of the screen fades to grey after a certain length of inactivity but Marie hits her cancel button at each fading, just to keep the light on as if this makes time stand still. She is sat at the head of the kitchen table, which has been moved away from the wall in order to accommodate Jean, Paul and Jenny. The three of them tuck hungrily into their dinners, Jean taking a chance to hmm and ah her compliments to Barbara in between mouthfuls of curry and rice.

Barbara, at the head of the table, looks across at Marie, her nostrils flaring as they let out the rage swelling up inside her in safe, steady emissions. She can't believe she has been duped again, can't believe that she has allowed herself to fall victim to other people's distress when none fall victim to her own.

She wants to take this anger out on Marie, use her unsociability at the table to form one exclamatory breath that she can push from the floor of her bubbling guts and out across the table. But she knows this would be hypocritical, as Marie's coldness is something she envies, something she wishes she could allow herself to hide in sometimes. And so Barbara continues to vent her frustration through her pulsing nostrils.

Chris is sat at the far side of the table and he feels his frustration about to be unleashed. He is pinned against the fridge freezer due to the new position of the table, the seat to his left free for David when he arrives home. Chris' rage has many sources but is flowing into the one boiling sea of this room. He is upset that Spoonhead should have showed up today, of all days, and left Zeb with the only option he had – retribution. He is annoyed that Jean has managed to wangle her way into another free meal, despite the fact he sees her in and out of the Saturn Amusement Arcade, transforming her Benefit into twenty pence pieces every day. Every day except Friday, when she bums another meal off his mother.

He is irritated that he will have to listen to the rantings and ravings of David when he discovers Jean is here, especially as these are going to be aimed much later on at his mother and never at Jean directly at the time. He doesn't see why his honest and worthy brother who isn't scared to say anything to anyone should keep his lips tightly sealed whenever Jean actually occupies the situation that so incenses him. More than Tina nagging, more than Chris nicking his aftershave, more than Billy not pulling his weight in work. Instead, Chris knows that this whole army of David's rage will be directed towards his mother and his mother's willingness to let it happen.

That his brother is so willing to take out his dissatisfaction on his mother irritates Chris. But Chris is far more annoyed by the fact that he is about to do exactly the same thing.

'How many times do I have to tell you about curry on a Friday?'

'What, love?'

'Curry. On a Friday. How many times do I have to say

don't make me curry on a Friday?'

'But curry's your favourite, son.'

This is true. Chris loves his mum's curry. It is completely homemade, no jars, no frozen stuff, just fresh ingredients blended expertly together by his mother. It beats the take-aways from the Balti Hut that David brings home every time. She originally got the recipe from Kish's mum, but since then she has added her own flavours, zapped out some of the old ones, and crafted a meal that each member of the family agrees is the highlight of their culinary week. Barbara pointing this out to Chris only makes him more ashamed and this gives birth to bastard anger.

'Yeah, but it stinks Mum!'

'Don't be daft.'

'I'm not being daft. Every Friday I go out with my mates and every Friday I'm stinking like a Paki.'

'Christopher, I will not have you using that kind of language in this house. What would Kish say if he heard you talking like that?'

Chris decides not to point out to his mother that Kish uses the word Paki more than anyone he knows, instead returning to his earlier point.

'Yeah, but I'm still going to stink!'

'Well, your friends aren't going to mind. It isn't like you'll be kissing them or anything, is it?'

Chris glows red at this suggestion. He can't say anything about Keeley and so feels defenceless. Unfortunately for Chris, Marie has felt the red glow of her brother and finds it more appealing than the disappointing blue of her phone. Now she too has a target for her bile.

113

'I don't know, Mum. You'd think they were queer, the way him and his mates go on.'

'At least I'm not a fucking slut.'

'Right,' Barbara now senses a legitimate target for *her* rage. Not even when Jack was alive was a curse uttered at the dinner table and Chris' outburst has had him cross an important boundary. It's an excuse, but one that all parties will see as valid. 'Get upstairs! I don't even want to look at someone who can say such horrible things at the dinner table. And to your sister as well.'

'She called me queer!'

'You called me a slut!'

'Well you are, you fat slag –'

'Fat? You cheeky cunt –'

'Right! That's it. Both of you. Upstairs. I will not have these youngsters listening to this filth. Go on. Go on.'

Chris and Marie look at each other before Chris takes the lead upstairs. Paul and Jenny sit, mouths hardly chewing as they get the food into their stomachs as quickly as possible. Jean puts a hand of empathy onto Barbara's and Barbara feels the rust of shame corrode her face.

David parks up his car and checks his face in the rear view mirror of the Beemer. He is worried that any operation Graham has a hand in could only be flouting regulations, and the red spread of his cheeks fills him with hypochondria that only those who know him closest would recognise. Already this year he has feared colon cancer at the after effects of a burst pile, testicular torsion at a vigorous suck from Tina and mental illness after a heavy night on the charlie. That this is his normal complexion doesn't even cross his mind. For him, it is the flush of a coming fever, possibly a strange and flourishing disease introduced by the asylum seekers that have moved in up the road.

He takes his mobile phone and pulls the hands-free set from his ear before tossing them into his glove compartment. He picks up the newspaper – a crumpled copy of the *Daily Mail* – from the passenger seat and steps out of his car, folding it beneath his arm. He then changes his mind and rolls it into his back pocket as this is how he sees the workingman should store his read. He walks over to the back gate of the house, glaring a warning to the kids playing football in the street that they should stay away from his car, and reaches over the panelling to flick the latch. As he walks into the yard, he smells curry and half curses that he will smell tonight when he meets the boys. Squire, leaping up to his knees and yelping a hearty hello, interrupts this thought. David picks up the dog and talks some dog talk, 'Hello Squirey-wirey, how are you? How are you? What have you got on your face, eh? What have you got on your face?'

Once he's down again, Squire runs around David's legs, anxious that he should be let into the house after being tantalised for well over forty-five minutes by the strange and wonderful smells emanating from inside; hopeful for leftovers. Squire trots behind David as he opens the door and steps into the small vestibule before the kitchen. David stops. Squire looks confused and runs at the kitchen door, looking up at David in eager anticipation that this is just a cruel game and the door will be opened. David on the other hand can hear Jean's voice, can make out the shape of a buggy through the frosted glass of the door and feels rage take up arms inside his chest. The fear of what he might unleash if he is forced to confront his enemy has him about-turn, head back through the back door and out of the gate. He fills the screen of his mobile a lurid green.

'There's a text message on your phone.'

Beth nods her head towards the fridge where Billy's phone sits charging. The message is from earlier, ignored in his sprint for orgasm. He gets up, and squeezes his way around the foldout kitchen table to check the phone.

'It's from Graham. Wants to know if I'm out tonight.'

'And are you?'

Billy deletes the message, puts the phone on the table and squeezes back into his seat, looking up at Beth. He told her he was out with Graham last night, down in the city centre at some new bar a friend of a friend of Graham's has a bit of money in. He knows the 'see his mates once a week' line won't work here but he has a back-up plan.

'No. No, not tonight. We're going to do a ghost shift at the Garage – me and David. Clear up the backlog. I've only come home for a bite to eat before I go back.'

He places another piece of chicken into his mouth and crunches through the green pepper that had sneaked onto the fork alongside it. Tonight was a chicken stir-fry, something quick and simple for Beth to knock up before she went to the gym. Billy thought it was perverse that she chose Friday of all the nights of the week to go to the gym, knowing full well that Friday was usually his one night a week out with the boys. Beth looks at him with the same face she always did at this time on a Friday.

'Well. What are we going to do about Joey? I suppose I'll just have to ask my mother to look after him *again*?'

Billy hates it when she uses the word *mother*.

'We can ask mine.'

He allows himself a little smile at this suggestion knowing full well how outrageous it is. The crease of his eyes as he smiles melts something inside Beth, and she smiles back. Billy takes a victorious swig of his water and swivels some noodles onto his fork. He has overcome the earlier disappointment of his dampened ejaculation with the knowledge that things still have some kind of order. He looks at Beth and remembers why he loves her, not in a word, a phrase or an image but in a pure feeling, a feeling in his chest just north of loneliness. This love spreads west to where Joey is sat with a bowl full of noodles and veg, the noodles chopped into manageable lengths for his plastic spoon/fork to despatch into his already messy mouth. Beth feels the same. Something in that smile of Billy's takes her back to a time when she trusted him, when she wrote things about him in her diary that didn't embarrass her the way they do when she reads over them now. Perhaps she should trust him, perhaps she has done too much recently to exclude him, and seeing his happiness at being able to help, she takes an unprecedented step.

'Yeah. Okay. Drop him off at your mother's just after dinner.'

Billy's face drops. He can't quite believe what he is hearing. In all their time together, he has completely agreed with Beth's evaluation of his parents and now the final source of stability in who he thought she was has been completely vanquished. He really has no idea who she is anymore.

'But tell them I'll be over to pick him up at seven and to let him wait by the gate. I'm not going inside.'

Phew! Perhaps there is still a little something to hold onto. Before Billy can give an answer, his mobile phone flashes and beeps further communication. He winces at Beth as she picks up the phone to see whom the message is from. She doesn't have the audacity to check the message itself, just the sender. She looks across at Billy with warmth.

'It's David. Must be checking up on you. Go on.'

Billy is very, very confused.

Snowman walks into his house and ignores the cries of his mother as he takes the stairs in twos. He turns right and into his room, the cold fresh air in his nostrils cleansing them enough for him to notice the smell for the first time. He opens a window and then sits the cardboard box under his arm on the bed. He opens the box and looks inside. He feels like he is in a film and so does what they do in the films – opens one of the polythene bags and dips a wetted pinkie into the powder. He pulls out his finger and takes a taste. His face creases at the chemical sourness before snapping back into faux appreciation, just as it did on his first taste of beer. He closes the box back up and moves a bundle of clothes from the floor to reveal a poorly-laid blue carpet. He lifts the edge of the carpet at one of its inexplicable midfloor joins and then lifts a floorboard. Below it is black and dusty, and for a second he cannot decide whether to put the box there after being told how much its contents are worth. This moment of uncertainty allows him to notice the numbness spreading through his tongue and he begins to bite it in curiosity. He catches a glimpse of himself in an upturned CD on the floor, his tongue flapping out over his bottom lip and his top teeth chomping down, cheeks fattened by his gurning and eyes looking puzzled. The shock of seeing himself behaving in such a way makes up his mind and he puts the box beneath the floorboards before covering them with carpet and clothes. He checks his pupils in the CD and heads downstairs. He walks into the kitchen and sits at the table. His mother and father are sat there, both greasy haired and fat.

Mother Snowman has no teeth and the lower part of her face looks like it has imploded. Her eyes are blue but half-lidded through drunkenness, with lank dog-coloured hair framing her creased and blood-burst face. She is wearing a Guinness Pure Genius T-shirt, stained and worn thin at the armpits. Her lower half – kitted in black leggings and cheap trainers – is thankfully hidden by the table. Father Snowman looks no better. His head is large and bloated, a few strands of hair glued to his barren pate by booze-induced sweat. His eyes are dark and ringed with folded skin like a chameleon. His tiny pug nose is made unimportant by the simian mouth that bulges over one of his many chins. He is also wearing a T-shirt, his featuring cartoon pigs in a multitude of sexual positions and the legend Makin' Bacon emblazoned across the top. They are tucking into the leftovers from the funeral spread put on free of charge for Snowman's grandmother's wake at the local pub. Father Snowman is dipping mini sausage rolls into ketchup while Mother Snowman waves a ham sandwich in Snowman's face. The scene before him calms him and makes him feel completely sure that he is doing the right thing.

'Go on, love. Ham, or there's some of them cheeses and pickled onions on sticks you like.'

'Cheers, Mum; I think I'm going to get a Maccy Dees later.'

Snowman goes to the sink, grabs a cup, washes it out and fills it with tap water before heading back into the front room. He feels content, that his life has some real direction for the first time. He feels ambitious, can picture himself in the latest clothes, clothes that Chris and Zeb wear, driving an old Beemer like David, shagging the kind of girls he sees Graham talking to and having a nice house like Billy to chill in and play Pro Evolution Soccer. He settles back with happy thoughts, relaxed, comfortable, when the front door crashes open and causes him to leap from his chair. He's only had the stuff an hour! He can't believe he is being busted already. The door to the living room swings open and he stands panic stricken, awaiting his fate.

'Beth'll be here at seven. Don't let Mum and Dad anywhere near him. Here's a twenty.'

Billy crushes the twenty-pound note into Snowman's hand and gives him a look of brotherly threat. Snowman stands, mouth wide open as Billy heads back out of the door, and then looks down at Joey. He has no idea why this has just happened. He picks the child up and heads upstairs.

'Come on you, let's play on the computer, eh?'

'Come on you! You've not touched that yet.'

Zeb's mother is doing her makeup and trying to urge Zeb into action on his Alphabites, eggs and beans. She is wearing a dressing gown with a thong beneath as she coats her eyelashes with thick black mascara. She is on her way to work, Zeb isn't sure where – a bar or something – and despite her frantic rushing, she looks incredible. She is a soft brown and has spiral curled hair to just below her jaw line. Her lips hang beneath a pointed Arabic nose, her whole face having an Asiatic look. Although she has recently turned thirty, her body is firm and shows no sign of the young pregnancy that has had her living a life without the support of her parents since she was fifteen. She has no lines of regret, no sagging remorse, but neither has she laughter creases.

'Zeb! Get that eaten. Your egg won't stay dippy forever.'

This warning snaps Zeb out of his inactivity and he stabs an Alphabite with his fork, plunging it into his fried egg, the pussy yellow spilling out like a burst pimple and congealing as it mixes with bean juice. He sighs relief at this sight. There is nothing he abhors more than a hard yolk.

Zeb'd been risking the consistency of his egg due to a savoured memory. He has been playing over the afternoon's events in his mind again, basking in the glory of his revenge on Spoonhead, adding twists and flourishes that didn't happen but would become fact through the retelling. Redrafting the dialogue to make himself sound even more quick and witty than he knew he was. Again he drifts into recollection. He can feel the air rushing past his face as he caught Spoonhead with such ease, he feels his leg reach out in slow motion to trip him, his consciousness leaving his body and spinning around the scene in *Matrix*-style frames as Spoonhead tumbles into the gutter. The action cuts to Spoonhead's point of view, looking up at Zeb, his frame seeming giant from this angle, a wry smile creeping across his face, perhaps even a drag on a cigarette. Then a nonchalant flick of the finished cig before Spoonhead's repentant face, pleading mercy, and the shot reverts to Zeb's point of view. Cut once more, this time to Chris, jogging up behind, stopping, watching half in reverence and half in anticipation, an age-like ticking of the seconds before super-slow motion takes over as Zeb pays Spoonhead his violent dues.

Zeb's concentration is broken by his phone beeping on the tabletop. A text message from Kish. He remembers his food and he looks down at this egg. The yellow yolk has darkened and become hard. Zeb sighs with disappointment and picks up his mobile phone to check Kish's message.

Kish sits at a table in McDonald's, his box of jackets sat on the floor next to him. He puts his phone on the table and begins to eat his meal. The first task is to remove the gherkins from his 99p Double Cheeseburger. He completes this task and wraps the unwanted pickles in the same paper serviette that he uses to wipe the relish from his fingers. He takes two bites of his burger, surveying the room slowly, trying to grab a glimpse of someone wearing a similar jacket to those in his box. Kish is disappointed. A plethora of baseball caps, tracksuits, workwear, school uniforms and parkas surround him. The only jacket nearing the style of his booty is a Burberry number, the collar turned up and the ubiquitous check giving the only clue to its being. This smarts even more when he remembers what the boys had said about Burberry.

As he sweeps the room he finishes the second bite of his burger and opens the small tub of barbeque sauce. Into this he dunks a pinch-full of fries and rams them into his mouth. The tangy sauce is penetrated by the saltiness of the fries and has him reaching for a sip of Diet Coke. He opens his box of six chicken nuggets and picks the roundest one to dunk first. He counts them, as he always does, and works out the order in which they will be eaten. Those with a protruding mini digit will be saved till last so that he might hold them as he would a drumstick – for some reason this makes them taste better.

Chewing on a round nugget, he looks out of the large window that flanks the restaurant and sees David head into the Trouble and Strife pub whilst punching the numbers of his mobile phone. He wonders if David is about to speak to Graham and whether he should ask Chris to get David to put a good word in for him. He is hoping that Graham will take pity on him as a young entrepreneur and take the jackets off his hands at the same price he paid for them. He hopes that Graham will see the ambition in him and see a little of himself in Kish's eyes before offering a hand, a generous piece of advice and finally the ultimate solution to his predicament – cash. This is his hope.

For now though, he picks up his burger for another bite and his phone goes. It is a message from Zeb. He wipes his fingers on another paper serviette and presses 'read'. Before he reads on, he sees another familiar face head into the pub, this time Billy. He wonders whether he will need Zeb's help carrying the box over to Graham's after all. Is a struggle up to Graham's going to be worth it if David and his boys are meeting up in the Trouble and Strife?

He decides that if Graham is in the pub he will not give in to his plea for help. For Graham to give in there would weaken his position in front of his friends. This could not possibly happen. Urgency rushes through his veins; he will have to get to Graham's house with the jackets before Graham sets off for the pub. He reads the message on his phone and smiles at Zeb's affirmative answer. The food he has left puts some perspective on the necessities of the given situation. He smiles as he stands up, puts his phone in his pocket and picks up the box, leaving the food behind. His priorities are changing.

Chantelle is half way through texting Keeley when Graham and Toni reappear from behind the Nails and Beauty partition. Both look quietly smug and have sweat on their foreheads. Tammi stands up and fetches Graham's cap and jacket for him. Toni heads to the toilet and Graham winks a 'thanks', the tiniest flash of gold glinting from between his lips. He then approaches the counter to Chantelle.

'You got my stuff, darling?'

Chantelle blushes at his request and takes his things

from the safe, just as she had done earlier for David with his Rolex. She picks up the gold and puts it on the counter where Graham puts it back on, piece by piece. She grabs the oily bag but Graham raises his hand, signalling to her to keep it in the safe.

'With service like this we're going to have a very successful business here, Tammi.'

Tammi nods a reply, the slight hint of disgust shading her look as Graham finally slides his arms into his jacket and mounts his cap. She looks uncomfortable as Graham gives her a friendly peck on the cheek.

'Well, see you soon. Take care, girls. Say goodbye to your sister for me.'

Graham wafts out of the door and Chantelle is shocked when Tammi speaks.

'Cunt. Don't let shit like that impress you, Chan. It's all fake, like his gold.'

Chantelle smiles, half promising, half confused, and returns to the message she was typing for Keeley.

u gotta b l8. b l8. dont let him think hes got u. chan.

'I'm telling you, Chan. You've got to be strong with wankers like that about.'

Chantelle presses send.

18.45

After spending a brief time laying on his bed and swearing oaths against his sister, Spoonhead, Jean, and even David, Chris gave up on solitary rage and decided to make better use of his time by getting ready for his meeting with Keeley. In his decision to eradicate any thought of upcoming events, he had stripped himself of any of the joy that the most important news of the day should have brought him. All day he had worried, waited, bit nails and peaked his cap in a release of some of the pressure built up inside him. But now, with their meeting only half a game of football away, he allows himself a smile.

As always, Chris' toilette begins by brushing his teeth. Chris spends a good ten minutes brushing his teeth and so in the morning rush would do them in the shower. Tonight, with the special events of the evening starting to unfold in his imagination, he stands in front of the bathroom mirror and brushes to the soundtrack of one of his tapes.

The tape itself is playing in a small brown cassette player that sits by the toilet. Its lead reaches out under the bathroom door to the wall socket that Marie had charged her phone in last night. It is an old piece of equipment bought for David on his ninth birthday and is covered in stickers covering the full history of the family's musical youth. The Stone Roses fade quietly next to a bright red Usher logo, a stencilled Nas insignia fights for space with a high resolution Robbie Williams while Trevor Nelson sits happily next to John Lennon. Jammed between the toilet and the cassette player is an old slipper; dog chewed and sweat rotted. This decrepit old piece of footwear is essential to the playing of Chris' tape. Being old, worn and battered in moments of frustration, the cassette player has many quirks and tics – one of which is that the door can no longer be closed properly. This door houses the cassette itself and so if it cannot close with the tape heads, the tape cannot play. However, some time ago, David realised that if the tape door could be held in place by jamming a third party between itself and the wall, it would play perfectly. And so the slipper found new use, was able to flourish well beyond its natural life, as an auxiliary part of the cassette player. This eureka moment was particularly important to Chris, for up until that point, if he wanted to listen to his music while getting ready in the bathroom, he had to hear a muffled bass-heavy impression of his beloved tunes seeping around the bathroom door and radiating through the walls like ghosts. Now Chris can hear his tapes as they were meant to be heard: loud and clear. Get ready as he is meant to get ready: with the bathroom door locked.

He is already a good seven minutes into his brushing and so is on the penultimate leg – his tongue. He brushes vigorously, sometimes causing blood to mingle with the white froth of the toothpaste. He often retches as the brush goes a little too far toward the back of his throat and every time this happens he has the same thought: 'How can girls suck dicks?' He spits out the waste of his brushing into the bowl and turns the tap on. He gargles a mouthful of water, followed by a mouthful of mouthwash, and then half a mouthful of water helped around his gums and tongue by his brush. The rinsing makes him gag too.

The shower has been running throughout his dental extravaganza and is now absolutely scalding hot, spraying his whole body the windy colour of his cheeks. He grabs the Head and Shoulders shampoo from the side of the bath and squeezes out far too much for his almost bald head. This extravagance is motivated by fear, the fear of ending up like Snowman.

Snowman is not called Snowman for nothing. It is because of his terrible dandruff that can only be remedied by a foul-smelling, prescription-only, dermatological shampoo. Snowman always stank of this on a Friday night and a Monday morning and Chris has decided that despite having no dandruff problems he will hit his scalp with a pre-emptive strike.

After rinsing his head, Chris moves onto the rest of his body, picking up his sister's poof ball sponge and emptying some of the Lynx shower gel Tina got him for Christmas onto it. He has already used up the Lynx shower gel his mother got him, as well as the ones his sister got him, his Aunt Jean 'got' him and Kish's mum got him. He squooshes the sponge into a lather and then washes his body: armpits first, chest then shoulders, arms then neck. He perches on one leg, the heat of the shower making him look like a lost flamingo as he scrubs the bottom of his feet, the inside of his thighs, the crack of his arse. He rinses the sponge, puts it back on the side of the bath and turns his attention to his face. For this he uses some of his brother's L'Eau D'Issey face wash. He washes his face carefully with his fingertips following the contours of his cheekbones, down the ski jump of his nose, across his high forehead and behind his tiny ears.

Once his face is rinsed he begins the final part of his shower – his cock. He rolls back his foreskin and using an index finger and some of the remaining suds caught over the top of his ears, washes the end of his dick. He curves his finger around the bottom of the head, taking particular care. He pulls his foreskin back into place and climbs out of the shower to dry, catching a good look at himself in the full-length mirror opposite the sink. His cock washing has him slightly aroused and gives an impressive girth and weight to his penis. He admires it for a second or two, wishing that it could always be this size even though he knows from the comparative glances around the school showers that he is far from small. Not as big as the enormous Snowman, but definitely not as small as Zeb's.

Chris' admiration of his cock brings him back to

Keeley. Although he has washed in anticipation of a sexual event, he knows and enjoys the fact that this is highly unlikely with Keeley. Keeley isn't like the rest of the girls. She doesn't give in to the cider-smelling propositions behind Old Tommy's chip shop. In fact Chris doesn't know anyone who has actually kissed her. This doesn't surprise Chris greatly for as far as he knows she has had very few requests, considering her beauty. Although Keeley hangs around with the girls in the year, although she dresses like them, follows the codes that exist in being able to belong to them, they don't really belong to her. She hardly ever goes out. He can't remember seeing her more than twice behind the Old Folks'. Whether this is through choice or strict parenting he can't be sure but he does know that she is different. There is something about her that is entirely alien to the rest of the girls and Chris is in no doubt that even though perhaps only a sentence has passed between them in his lifetime, he could love this girl.

Still, he knows so little about her. She is such an enigma that whilst having these thoughts he actually finds it hard to recollect a clear image of her. Every time he pictures a part of her, the rest goes out of focus as if she is held in close up. He can see her eyes, dark brown irises – large with the milkiest muscle surrounding them. But this creaminess diffuses into her dark hair, bobbed straight and shiny, never worn up or plastered into a parting, just falling naturally. Her hair then morphs into her legs, short but beautifully sculpted – a scale model of perfection. Her legs dissolve into the colour of her skin, just the colour, a strange tinted whiteness filling the whole screen of his consciousness until he blinks it clear and gives up on trying to put this picture together. He hasn't got long to wait.

Graham sits in his front room, a large box of Ralph Lauren jackets between his widespread legs. He has just got out of the shower and smells great. His cropped hair is slightly fluffy like a used tennis ball and his stubble has disappeared.

Gold still hangs heavy and threatening. Feeling this threat are Kish and Zeb. They look around the front room with a mixture of awe and bewilderment. A shabby old sofa is all there is to sit on and so they crush themselves in either side of Graham as he pulls on a cigarette. He blows the smoke out of the side of his mouth as if attempting a comedy Popeye impression. This should tickle Zeb as he watches the smoke rise grey-blue into the air and spread across the browning ceiling, but it doesn't.

The whole room is in a state of terrible repair and this surprises both boys greatly. Large cracks extend from the over-painted cornice and down the under-painted walls. The carpet is almost threadbare, the manky blue skin allowing hessian smiles to creep through. Only a plug-in radiator warms the whole room. Graham picks up the box of coats and puts it on the coffee table. It is large, mahogany and looks like something from old films about the landed gentry. Pure antique luxury. But this doesn't impress the boys; instead their gaze is drawn to the plasma screen hanging on the wall. Both boys have only ever seen them in magazines and are excited about actually being in the same room as such a piece of equipment. In the fireplace are a cable TV decoder, DVD player, two videos and a police scanner. There is no sign of the wife and two children that left Graham last year.

He stubs out the cigarette in the heavy stainless steel ashtray on the table and turns to each of them.

'So, who paid for this lot then?' Kish nods and raises a reticent hand. Graham pulls out one of the jackets again and has a look. He turns to Kish, looking him squarely in the eyes. 'How much?'

Kish pauses like a young fan meeting a pop star at the stage door.

'Two fifty.'

Graham immediately flings his head back and bursts into a chest-rattling laugh, his gold teeth flashing and strings of saliva joining his lips as if they are the only thing stopping the top half of his head from falling off altogether.

'Two fifty? Serious?'

Kish nods an embarrassed affirmation and turns to Zeb, who is still surprised that he isn't even having to *try* to keep quiet. Graham puts the jacket back in the box and stands up. He makes his way over to the fireplace. He dips into the back of his jeans. These have been changed and are now a pair of black moleskin Versace's. He pulls out his cigarettes and offers them to the boys, who decline. He then goes into the top pocket of his shirt – a very fancy fitted Hugo Boss affair, again in black, and pulls out a Zippo lighter to light himself a cigarette. He takes a long drag and again blows it skyward.

'Was it a smackhead?'

Kish is taken back by this question. He has no idea. The person he purchased them from certainly didn't look like a smackhead; it was one of his Uncle Sukraj's friends from the Cash and Carry who had heard about his cheap sweets scam and earmarked him for a potential business partner. Or so he said. Kish shakes his head.

'Well, that was your first mistake, son. Always, I repeat always buy from smackheads. They're cheap and they're desperate. They also know the market better than anyone else because they have to. For them it really does feel like a matter of life and death so they keep in touch with exactly what people want. If half of them had gone legit, you're talking about another hundred thousand Dickie Branson's on this Island at least. A smackhead could have found this lot in the street and not touched it. It just don't sell no more. Five years ago, yes, but now, no chance. They're far smarter than us fences, work a lot harder too, but the desperation bit fucks them up. We've only got our cool exterior keeping us in business. Remember that. Your second mistake is bringing them to me. Right now, I have less respect for you than I do for a smackhead. Yes, you're desperate *and* you are fucking clueless. I'm sorry if that hurts but you're better off learning it now from me than going to jail a couple of times before you do. However. Hang on.'

Graham leaves the front room for a minute and Kish and Zeb look at each other with complete disbelief. They both feel like they are going to cry but manage to stop themselves before Graham returns, complete with DKNY leather jacket that he throws on with ease. Kish thinks he looks like something from *Donnie Brasco*.

'However, your second mistake is also the best decision

you could have possibly made. Confusing, I know but that's how it works sometimes. Every cloud and all that bollocks. This is because I am currently developing new business and I'll need someone to train up and take over the fencing side of my operations. Now, this does not mean that I will definitely take you on. I've watched your little sweeties' scam in school but we will not be dealing with sweeties. We will be dealing with TVs, videos, cameras – quality merchandise – and I have to know that: one, you've got the balls and: two, you'll be loyal. How am I going to know if this is the case? Well, instinctively I reckon you're the sort. Remind me of me when I was your age. Only much fatter. Anyway, even though I trust my instincts more than anything, there is going to be a test.'

Graham reaches into his inside pocket and pulls out a huge dummy of twenty-pound notes. He curls off ten and throws them on the table. Zeb and Kish look on. They have never experienced anything like this. Graham takes another drag of his cigarette. A fingertip of ash has burned down during his speech and he flicks it to the floor.

'There's two hundred there. That means you've lost fifty. No point in pretending you haven't had your fingers burnt, after all you learn from your mistakes and that. Problem is, in this game you cannot afford those mistakes, so this one is a Brucey Bonus. Enjoy it. But. Ha! Got you there eh? There is always a but, boys. Here comes the test. This two-ton isn't for the jackets. I'm taxing them and I'll probably give them to Oxfam. The money is for a job I need doing. And I want to know if you are up for it. If not, walk away now, no hard feelings. So what do you say?'

Kish looks at Zeb. Zeb shrugs his shoulders. Kish doesn't know what is more frightening. The performance Graham is giving or Zeb's silence. He clears his throat and speaks.

'Well, cheers and everything, Graham, but –. Well, it depends what it is, don't it?'

'Good! Someone's learning already. Fuck reputations. What's in it for me? Good, you do have to lose that shit-scared look though. Right, well this is the job. I've had a bloke paying me protection the last few months. Nothing big, just enough to keep the kids from bugging him and that, only today he asked if he could opt out. Obviously, I've told him that's fine. It was nice while it lasted and all that, *but* he has to be persuaded that although I will let him opt out, opting out means that protection disappears. That's where you two come in. What I want you to do is simple. Tonight, later on, I'll pick you up and give you disguises. All you have to do is to pay my mate a visit – not from me – but from the chaos that will take over his life without me. You go in, make as much noise as possible, scare the shit out of anyone in there and smash a few things up. Easy.'

Zeb sits up and smiles. He actually likes the sound of this. Kish notices Zeb's excitement and manages a smile himself. Maybe this isn't going to be too bad after all. They've terrorised businesses throughout the town for years, this is just a little bigger, a little more mature. Yes, Kish is now very much thinking this is a good idea. Not only does he get two hundred pounds (well one fifty, he'll give Zeb some for helping him out) but he also gets into

Graham's business. And he remembers what Graham said. 'Take over operations.' Kish nods with the thought of him being an integral part of Graham's Empire, the connections he'll make, the tricks he'll learn. Zeb looks at the plasma screen and thinks 'I want one of those!'

'Alright. No problem. Who is it we're hitting?'

Kish enjoys the sound of that sentence as it leaves his mouth and floats towards the ceiling like Graham's smoke. Graham smiles an expensive grin.

Chris finishes drying, wraps the tangerine towel around his waist, and tucks in the top to keep it secure. Steam rises from his hot clean body and forms droplets on the clean surfaces around him as if his very essence is taking over his environment. He then picks up the cassette player and slipper and heads to his room.

On his way down the landing he bends to unplug the cassette player and catches through an opening in her bedroom door a glimpse of his sister lying on her bed, her T-shirt/nightie riding up over her buttocks as she continues to play with her mobile phone. Chris quickly turns away from the sight of the naked flesh. It seems to him more and more these days that he can't walk around the house without being flashed by a thick thigh or a bulging tit falling over a towel. His sister has just grown up all of a sudden.

He heads into his room, removes the tape and puts the old cassette player and slipper under David's bed. Whilst under there, he takes out a bottle of L'Eau D'Issey aftershave and splashes on a liberal, painless amount as he has no need to shave yet. As he places the aftershave back, he sees a brown shoebox and knows this is where David keeps his spare cash. He pulls the box out and, sitting on David's bed, opens it. He takes out a ten-pound note and finds a bag of weed beneath it. He puts the tenner on top of the stereo and takes the blue Rizlas from in between *A Northern Soul* by The Verve and *The Velvet Underground and Nico* in the CD rack. This is where the skins are always kept. He then decides he needs to hear the rest of the tape that he was listening to in the bathroom and puts it into the space-age tape deck.

The stereo recognises the broken tabs on the top of the tape and begins to play it immediately. The sound of *Heart Of The City* by Jay-Z rocks the room. Chris wraps up a joint while rapping word for word with the song, his head nodding, lips twisted and one eye squinting as he belts out the chorus.

Billy is stood at the jukebox in the Trouble and Strife. David has sent him over with two pounds to choose some music while he grudgingly eats the pub meal that has replaced his mother's delicious curry. His instructions are clear – 'none of that rap shit or boom boom boom music'. Billy feels the pressure as he knows David takes his music very seriously.

The track lists rotate inside the machine as Billy tries to decide what David would like to hear. It is difficult, with most of the CDs being chart compilations and Best In The World Evers. Besides, Billy doesn't really know what David likes nowadays. He switches off whenever he is in work and doesn't hear anything that comes out of the stereo system David rescued from his room.

David takes another bite of his minted lamb burger and scowls. He's going to kill his mum when he gets in. Why should he be here eating this piece of shit when he could be at home enjoying a curry? As he chews the spurious meat he decides he'd get more pleasure eating a beer mat. He is also annoyed that he hasn't had time to change after his sunbed and can still feel ball bearings of sweat drop from his armpits and hit the top of his arms. Just as he thought things couldn't get any worse, he is shaken to the core by the music that sighs its way out of the jukebox. He throws his burger down in disbelief and shouts Billy over to their table.

'Oi! Dickhead!'

'What?'

'Get your arse back here.'

They are sat in the corner of the pub next to the pool table. The prime spot. The pub itself is attempting the old spit and sawdust ideals but looks like a Landlady Barbie Doll's House. The furniture – tall stools, tables and benches – are all orange cushions with cheap lightweight wood painted a dark brown to add an air of authenticity. Pictures of local businesses from sixty years ago adorn the walls, along with confusing pieces of maritime memorabilia. The bar itself stretches from the far end of the pub by the jukebox up to about three feet from where David sits at the other end. Sitting against the browns and oranges of the décor are bright red and blue bottles of Aftershock, lurid rainbows of alcopops and ridiculous cardboard adverts for the latest fads and football matches to be shown on the big screen. Billy walks past all these and stands in front of David.

'What?'

'Sit down.'

'What, I've got another eight goes left.'

'Sit down, I'll do it when I've finished this piece of shit.'

'Fucking hell, mate, is it the time of the month?'

'Do not wind me up, Billy.'

'What? What's up?'

David pauses and takes a sip of his pint. He looks at Billy and then looks away before turning back and fixing him with a glare from beneath his heavy eyebrows.

'*Hotel California.*'

'What? It's a classic, this: "Welcome to the Hotel California!"'

'Fucking hell, don't sing it, you're making it worse!'

'I thought you like all this stuff. Real music. None of that boom boom boom shit, you said.'

'It's a singing drummer.'

David says this as if knowledge of this fact should deter anyone from going near the tune still offending him – in stereo – from every corner of the room. Billy looks puzzled, which only exacerbates David further.

'Singing drummers! Fucking hell, Billy, do you know nothing? Any band with a singing drummer, any tune with a singing drummer, is shit. Shit. All the songs Ringo sings with the Beatles. Shit. Nirvana – Dave Grohl on drums: great. Foo Fighters – Dave Grohl singing: shit. Genesis – singing drummer – shit. And who is that singing drummer? Phil

Collins. Cherry-on-the-fucking-cake. What I'm trying to say, Billy, is that if a band allows its drummer to sing, it's like charity. It's like buying one of those poppies for Remembrance Day. It's nice, but the actual product is shoddy.'

'What, even them big poppies with the massive leaf that they wear on the telly?'

'No. That's different. I'm talking about the poppies we get, the paper ones with the black button and shitty stem and – what the fuck! I wasn't talking about poppies, Billy, I was talking about *Hotel California*. Listen! Just listen to that solo!'

Billy sits back and takes in the inordinately long guitar solo.

'Sounds alright.'

'Sounds alright! Sounds all fucking right! Jesus, Billy. A guitar solo is meant to take the song somewhere. It is not meant to be one long wank....'

Billy shrugs a little at this suggestion.

'Think Mick Ronson's guitar solo on *Life On Mars* by Bowie. Think Johnny Marr just pushing those Smiths songs along, despite knowing he could play like Clapton. Think John Squire.'

'Oh, hang on a minute, David. Now I know you're the music expert and all that, but John Squire has done some fucking long guitar solos. Even I know that.'

'That wasn't Squire. That was the cocaine. And don't say anything bad about John Squire again, you hear?'

'Yeah.'

David picks up his burger again which is now cold, and

puts it back down. He feels desperate for an understanding face, an intellectual equal, anything to save him from the imbecile that sits opposite him ignoring his phone as it receives constant messages. David doesn't know why Billy doesn't just turn it off or as least put it on silent. Everything about him is beginning to annoy David and he feels guilty that his fingers are twitching and wanting to strike out and put him in hospital just so he doesn't have to spend the night with him. Just when he feels that all is lost, a cry goes up from the door of the pub.

'Evening, ladies!'

It is Graham and David's face lights up almost as brightly as Graham's smile.

'Graham, mate, take a fucking seat, what're you drinking? Looking pleased with yourself.'

'It's been a good day, boys. I'm feeling good.'

Beth is feeling worried as she spins the Mondeo into the grey crescent where Billy's parents live. Her whole drive through the Estate filled her with more and more dread, old memories floating up to the surface of her consciousness like long disposed-of corpses.

This Estate was her home once. Not where she was from, her parents lived opposite the school in one of the larger detached houses, but the Estate was where she grew up. In its glass smattered parks, its shop fronts, the back of its Old Folks' Home, back when Beth thought bettering yourself meant an inch of make-up and shagging a friend of David Carty's.

She never meant to fall in love, never mind pregnant, but she's glad she had Joey, for he seems to have put everything into perspective. Seeing herself from above, puffing and panting, make-up-less as he screamed his way into the world empowered her beyond all reckoning. She had the power, the power to bring life into the world and she'd done it all without Billy being there. She didn't need endorsement from the hanger on of a local celebrity; nature itself was on her side.

She catches herself in the rear view mirror, gritty sweat collected in her brow, as she pulls up to his parents' house.

'Where the fuck? Fuck.'

Joey is not outside as she had instructed. All the warmth she felt for Billy before dinner has been sweated well and truly out of her system at the gym and this turn of events has her distaste for him burn around her joints. She hops out of the car and down the stepped path to the front door. She raps on the door three times, praying that Billy's brother will answer and not one of the Hillbillies he calls Mum and Dad. She turns her back to the door just in case, before she hears it open. It is Snowman, Joey standing behind him with a Play Station control.

'You were meant to leave him at the gate!'

'What?'

'Joey. You were meant to –. Never mind. Come here, darling.'

'He's been playing Play St–'

'Right. Thanks. Erm. Here. Thanks.'

Beth goes into her DKNY grey velour tracksuit bottoms and gives Snowman twenty pounds to shut him up before heading back up to the car with Joey. Snowman looks at the twenty pound note in his hand and pulls out the one Billy gave him earlier. Forty quid for that. Easy money. The world belongs to Snowman!

The night belongs to Chris. He places the joint on the stereo and puts the weed, Rizlas and shoebox away before standing up and casting a pleased eye over his clothes laid out neatly on his bed. Black socks with a white Nike Swoosh riding their length; back Calvins; black Armani Jeans; the charcoal Stone Island jumper David has bought him for his upcoming birthday. In a departure from tradition Chris has given the same artist two tracks on his tape and Jay-Z is now extolling the virtue of *Girls Girls Girls*. He dresses with pure joy, swaying his shoulders, bouncing on his toes and slowly fanning his face to the beat. First the Calvins, snapped on and flourished with a Jay-Z inspired grab of his crotch. Then his socks, pulled high to stretch the swoosh as he rocks his head to whiplash inducing levels. Next the jumper, which catches the stubble of his cropped head like Velcro. This reminds him that he must get a haircut soon. Next the jeans, which trigger the memory of their acquisition: Chris and the Boys were around at a local dealer's flat scoring a little weed when a smackhead called Martin turned up, trying to trade some stolen jeans for a bag of brown. The dealer refused, saying he only dealt in cash and the smackhead should go and see if Golden Graham could take them off his hands. The smackhead was new to the area, didn't seem to know where Graham lived and so Chris and the Boys offered to show him the way. The smackhead thanked them and Chris and the Boys took their weed and followed the smackhead out of the flat and down the stairwell. Without warning, Zeb tripped the smackhead and he fell down a whole flight. Hurt and dazed at the bottom of the stairs, the Boys chased down after him, kicking his prostrate body before stealing his wares and fleeing out into the street laughing with excitement. Chris' reward were these Armani jeans.

It didn't worry Chris. All he'd heard about smack-heads from his brother was that they were the scum of the earth and so it somehow felt right to teach this Martin a lesson. It *felt* right, but now....

Chris sits down for the next episode of his dressing. He takes two safety pins from the windowsill, bunches the hem of his jeans above his ankles and pins them in place. This way he can show off his new Nicky Deakins properly. Now these are his pride and joy. They sit in the box on his bed, paper and silica gel still present, as they are his birthday gift from his mother and shouldn't be worn before unless it is a special occasion. Barbara has bought them early from the catalogue so that Chris could try them on and change them in time for the big day if they didn't fit. They are black ankle boots with soft leather and a crepe soul. The only clue to their brand is a stitched gold rose on the tongue with the name of the manufacturer underneath. Chris knows already that he'll never go back to Rockports again.

He disembowels the shoes' paper guts and transplants them with his size eight feet, tightening the laces before tucking them into the side of the shoe. They fit like a glove. Tonight is definitely a special occasion.

19.15

The autumnal evening has begun to envelop the town, darkness replacing the dusky shade of crimson; the street-lights hum on their stands, flickering to orange from cerise. The smell of a fresh, clean Chris cracks the crisp air.

He walks out into the back yard, ignoring Squire and deftly skipping around the little presents the dog has left all over the block paving beneath the leaves. Can't get those new shoes dirty now. His head is full of images he cannot control. Her face, her hair, her bright white Reebok Classics cupping the ball of her ankle. As he walks past the cars parked along the street he checks his reflection in their windows. Their angle makes him look tall and imperious and this makes him feel tall and imperious. As he crosses the road he doesn't even half quicken his step as a car skims past his heels. Untouchable.

Usually he would take a short cut at this point. He'd cut right across the Sheltered Housing, down in front of David's Garage and descend the short hill to the back of McDonald's. But tonight he is going to stroll the whole catwalk of the town. He will walk past Danny's Discount Shoes. He will strut past the HSBC, its cash machines spewing out weekend money. He'll cut through the Central Gardens, avoiding the Old Buck pub with its ancient clientele and contagious lethargy. But first comes the taxi rank.

It is an old shop front (could have been anything in a past life: a butcher, a baker, a bookies?) with a crudely painted Arrow Cabs sign. The door to the building is steel and bolted with three heavy locks and the windows are boarded up. You can't get into the office anymore. On the wall next to the door is an intercom, and from here you may order a cab if there are none waiting outside. And there are never any waiting outside.

Waiting outside tonight are a group of girls about fifteen to twenty-five years old in wraps of shiny material like a box of Quality Street. From their number and degree of excitement, it is fair to guess that they are awaiting a minibus into the city centre some eight miles away. Chris looks over, and one in a green dress – a Praline Triangle – whispers to a friend and they smile. Chris allows the corner of his mouth to turn up and he brushes his hand over his head and to the back of his neck. He looks skyward and then into the large window of Danny's Discount Shoes.

Danny's Discount Shoes is a huge yet flimsy looking building with a doorway indented from its glass margin.

These roof to pavement windows are littered with the spiderwebs of cracks. One panel is boarded up after a heavy night, while the others look jealously on – their only protection, curling Back To School posters and pictures of insanely unfashionable trainers with almost-right brand names to lure in less clued up-parents. Chris can smell old piss and spots the telltale finger of dried relief pointing at him from the corner of the doorway. The smell conjures a memory.

When he was in Year Nine, Chris had stood in the doorway of Danny's Discount Shoes with a girl he had met that night. Her name was Vicky. She was two years older than him and lived a couple of doors down the street. They'd been in the Central Gardens, drinking what ever they could get their hands on and he'd asked her if she wanted to go for a walk. She was wearing a white vest top, short white skirt and a pair of white sandals. Somebody had probably told her it would make her look more tanned, but it just accentuated the translucent whiteness of her skin and the freckles sprayed up her back and across her shoulders as if she had been on the back of a bike on a wet day. This didn't matter to Chris though. Just a week before, she'd allowed Zeb to finger her and Chris was determined not to be left behind. Besides, she was pretty in her own way; quite pixie-like with tiny green eyes, auburn hair, and teeth so straight and white that this memory has Chris wondering if he is idealising at least one part of her for posterity. She accepted his offer of a walk and they left the gardens – which were then nothing more than a few benches, a small croft and some hedges protecting those

147

inside from prying eyes – and headed around the back of McDonald's to avoid the leers of the old men at the Old Buck. The back street was a bad sentence punctuated with debris from the shops that hung from it – pallets, old crisp boxes, dead flowers. Once they arrived at this doorway, Chris looked into those tiny eyes. She smiled and pushed her hair behind her ear before kissing him. He held her waist and they backed into the doorway, the washing-machine movements of her mouth making him doubt if he was ever going to get to the bottom of this kissing malarkey. He allowed his hands to wander up to her shoulders before bringing his left down on her small breast. She didn't flinch and so he squeezed and grabbed what he could, counting out exactly thirty seconds in his head. During this time he'd sent his right hand on a recon mission, gently rubbing her thigh, his sweaty palms causing his skin to catch on hers. On exactly thirty seconds he made his move. Up to her hip. Still no flinch. Into the elastic of her pants. Still no flinch. Then he moved his hand around to the front. She pulled away from his kiss and he looked at her in panic. He knew he looked stupid; desperate, his bottom lip hanging low in the wetness around it. But she smiled and kissed him again. He found himself smiling as they kissed and he stroked her wiry pubic hair. He was surprised at how similar it felt to the hair that he was so proud of, sprouting in his own pants. As if to signal, she opened her legs a little wider, standing at ease and so he moved his hand down, cupped it beneath her and *CRASH*! The pair of them jumped and moved away from each other, looking around. Across the road, outside the taxi rank, a group of girls laughed as the glass from the bottle they had thrown into the road danced across the tarmac in tiny cubes.

'Told you it was Dave's little brother! Watch him, darling, he'll be a right little heartbreaker!'

Vicky made her excuses and invited him to come to her house next week while her parents were away. Chris never went. Vicky now has a two-year-old boy called Adam.

Chris looks over his shoulder at the Quality Street Girls outside the taxi rank.

'They're talking about you, mate.'

Zeb sits on the wall behind the Old Folks' Home, sipping a can of Breakers and smoking a joint. The eaves of the Home shoot over his head at an acrobatic angle, giving Zeb – sat on top of the wall – the unusual inconvenience of having to duck to fit the space he occupies.

He has changed from his uniform and now wears a black Nike sweater and dark blue Evisu jeans – their huge turn-ups sitting above a pair of black and red Air Shox. His head is bare for a change, no cap, no skully, not even the shapes and borders usually shaved into it by Curtis the local hairdresser. No, it is just freshly cropped hair that his mother has done for him on special request.

His observation is relayed to Kish, who is standing below him, against the wall. He looks almost the same, only his school trousers have been replaced by some black and silver Adidas tracksuit bottoms.

'Yeah?'

'Yeah, mate. She's not stopped looking over yet.'

They are talking about Chantelle, who after leaving Tantasia has managed to change into a grey Mackenzie hoodie and navy blue Adidas tracksuit bottoms, rolled up above the ankle over white, blue and orange Air Max 90s. With her are Tash and Martine, two of her closest friends. Tash is very pretty, half-Chinese with a delicate little face, hardened by luminous green eye shadow and dark brown lipstick. She is dressed similarly to Chantelle but her tracksuit bottoms are Nike, her hoodie navy blue and her shoes Rockport.

'What's that little twat looking at?'

The toughness of Tash's makeup is matched by her speech, and her assessment of Zeb is not without bitterness. He finished with her last week after getting what he wanted. Martine, a slim black girl in baby pink velour tracksuit, all-white K-Swiss and large gold-hooped earrings is tired of hearing about it.

'He's looking at you, Chan.'

'I wonder if Keeley's ready yet!'

Chantelle quickly changes the subject. She is much happier on the circumference of a discussion. The idea of any kind of attention, particularly sexual, embarrasses her. The afternoon's events with Graham and her sister have left an acid taste at the back of her throat.

There is a three-metre gap between the boys and the girls and this five seem a disparate band on the patio of the Old Folks'. Usually this space is crowded with kids, all looking exactly the same, all swearing exactly the same, all smoking and drinking exactly the same. Only recently, people have begun to disappear. Some have continued to hang around the summer haunt of the multistorey car park as the mild weather has allowed them to take advantage of the broken CCTV on the rooftop. They were the first cameras in town some three years ago and so were the first to be destroyed. Some people have started to hang around outside the shops with the younger kids so that they can force themselves to the top of at least one hierarchy. Some have started sitting in the flats that older friends have managed to acquire from the local council. They have also started smoking brown. No, although there are few here tonight, all present see themselves as the crème de la crème. Besides, Snowman hasn't arrived yet.

Neither has the minibus, and the Quality Street Girls behind Chris are starting to get agitated. He watches one of them – a Toffee Finger – bang on the boarded windows of the taxi rank, as he turns right outside the HSBC, and towards the Central Gardens.

The Central Gardens were another great idea from the local council, approved by the Residents' Association for the enjoyment of the community. It is mainly a khaki-coloured concrete ring, with shallow steps leading from one side, to form half of the circle. The top of the steps are ringed with steel railings. Opposite the steps, four benches (lovingly donated by local businesses to illustrate how much they care for the people with whom they share the town) form the circumference of the circle. The benches are sponsored by: the local detergent factory, a foam and plastics developer, the vinegar works and McDonald's. The only horticultural aspect of the gardens is a few hanging baskets on poles tall enough not to be interfered with by the natives. These poles also house CCTV cameras.

As these cameras follow Chris on his way, he stops and puts his hand in his pocket, struggling to pull out his phone between his index finger and thumb. He tosses the phone into his left hand, stuffs the inside of his pocket back into his jeans and then puts the phone back into his right hand to press some buttons, grin, press another button, frown, shake his head and put his phone away before his mouth makes the shape of a word.

'Fuck!'

Marie ladders another set of tights. They are the third pair this evening and she is well aware that she needs to calm down or she'll never finish getting ready. She pulls the tights off and climbs onto the bed to open the window to the right of her headboard. As she sticks her head out into the night, she takes a cigarette from the packet she has stashed in the music box on the windowsill. It plays half a bar of the Nutcracker Suite before she slams it shut and lights the Lambert & Butler. As its end glows, the streetlights burst into orange and the noise startles her. She feels strange, jumpy. She has done all day. Things have been slightly out of sync.

She looks out of the window and to her left can see a group of girls waiting outside the taxi rank. She too is meant to be going out tonight but the bastard is yet to call. All day she has waited. She even broke her 'never text twice without reply' rule for him but he hasn't been in touch. Still. He's a man. A real *man*. The Lambert & Butler fills her bloodstream with possibilities.

Just as she begins to enjoy the cigarette and calm down, she hears the unmistakable steps of her mother mumbling up the stairs. Marie tosses the half smoked cigarette out of the window and bounces down onto her bed. She picks up her mascara as her mother knocks on the door.

'What?'

'I've got your clean clothes.'

'Can you leave them outside, Mum? I've not got anything on.'

''Course, love. I'll just leave them outside your door.'

Marie sighs a sigh of slight resentment that her mother has made her waste a cigarette. If she'd have known she would capitulate so easily, she wouldn't have even bothered getting down from the window. As she hears her mother's steps descend the stairs, she gets up and opens her bedroom door. There before her, folded into a beautiful neat pile, are her clean clothes. She picks them up and takes them into her room to begin putting them away. As she puts them into the appropriate drawers and shelves of her white fitted wardrobes, she notices her black dress. The one that she bought from Oasis when she was out shopping with Tina.

She loves going shopping with Tina. She loves Tina. She couldn't see what Tina saw in David but she knew exactly what he saw in her. Marie thinks Tina is beautiful. She loves her long blonde hair, how straight it is, how you never see her roots. She loves the shape of her long body, her big tits, tiny waist and pert arse. Marie loves the makeup that Tina wears, the music she listens to, how she has such tiny meals and drinks glasses of wine. She also loves the way she dresses, so when Tina said that this black dress looked great on Marie, Marie just had to buy it.

This despite what Marie thought of it when she tried it on. When she tried it on, it accentuated everything that Marie was and Tina wasn't. Its blackness seemed to emphasise her dark roots as if it were made from the same material as a black hole and its gravitational pull was yanking at her hair and drawing it out of her head. True, it showed off her tits, but although they are large they didn't seem large enough when compared to her hips and her behind. Compared to her thighs, they were puny. It showed how short she was, not just of leg but of body as well. It was too tight: when she bent over, rolls of fat could quite clearly be seen around her midriff. The hem was too high, if she walked more than four steps it rode up and you could see the cheeks of her arse. Marie hated it, but Tina said it would look lovely with some knee-high black boots and so they went straight from Oasis to Dolcis.

Marie sits down again on the edge of her bed and picks up the mobile phone from the top of the chest of drawers. She wills it. She's never let a bloke fuck her about like this before.

'He better not fuck her about, you know.'

Tash, a picture of concern. All for Keeley. The weird girl she can't bring herself to bitch about. Chantelle reassures her, a knowing glance at Martine telling the real story.

'Nah. He's alright, Chris. I reckon he really likes her.'

Martine takes the baton.

'Don't worry, Tash; they're not all like Zeb. He'll get what's coming soon.'

If this is the case, Zeb shows little concern, his enthusiasm bolstered by the lager and weed.

'See! They're all looking, all three of them! You could be in here, mate. Big time.'

Zeb's enthusiasm isn't shared by Kish. Like Chantelle, the afternoon's events with Graham have left him out of sorts. It happened. The moment he seemed to have been waiting for since he can remember finally arrived. But not without cost. How could he do over Frank's Food and Booze? His Uncle Sukraj had taught him everything he knew, had told him in no uncertain terms that he, Kishan Singh, was the son he'd never had and would take over the shop when Sukraj felt the time had come to move on. Who knows, they might have even expanded the empire to garages! Can he do this to his Uncle Sukraj? Yes, he has to, but this doesn't make it seem any better. Kish doesn't know who the first man to climb Everest was but he reckons he knows just how he felt. A dream lies in front of him, a dream that has been at the core of his existence, but what happens if he realises that dream? What does that make of his life before the dream? It makes everything before the dream insignificant. That hurts. It is still your life, a life you have put time and effort into living. If that whole time is insignificant enough to hang on one decision, is it really worth anything at all? If that time is worthless, what does that make you, being its dependant for so long? Kish has a conundrum and as much as he wants to take his chance, he can't help but curse the hand that destiny has dealt him.

155

He isn't in the mood for Zeb's matchmaking.

'Nah. They're looking at you, mate. It's Tash. She still wants you.'

Kish drops down to sit on the floor and Zeb drops off the wall to join him.

Chris sits on the bench sponsored by McDonald's and looks out towards its sponsor. His phone is still in his hand, face down to the bench as his other hand clutches the bench. He looks to the sky before turning his phone to face him once more. The message is still there:

gonna b l8. meet @ tindle park 8.30. xxxK

He can't believe she is going to be late. Why? She knew the time they were supposed to meet, she knew the place, she knew how much time she had. Why? Chris can't understand why anyone is ever late. This is because he is never late. He erases the message and stands up to put his phone back in his pocket before changing his mind. It had been such a struggle to get it out that he decides he'll carry it for the rest of the night. He wonders to himself how he can kill another hour and his stomach replies with a low grumble. Because of his earlier sulk, he is yet to eat and so the sponsor of his seat seems like a good option.

Chris strolls over to McDonald's and opens the door with his shoulder. Sat around are some younger faces from his and other schools. McDonald's is where a lot of the younger kids meet up before going out to wander the streets and stand outside shop-fronts. They used to hang around the Gardens before the CCTV. As Chris walks down the runway to the counter he raises his eyes to the menu while his consciousness settles on the looks he is receiving from the youngsters. A couple of Year Nine girls in the corner, made up far too heavily and in identical outfits of jeans, white vest tops and denim jackets look on and whisper. They know who he is and who he is meeting tonight. With them is a boy in a blue cap and blue and silver jacket. He takes a cigarette out of his jacket pocket and tucks it between his temple and his cap – the filter beneath the peak. He whispers something to the girls. It is the Third Boy.

'Whose Auntie Barbara's favourite little boy then, eh? Eh?'

Paul is confused by this question. Surely it is David – he is the eldest of her sons. Or maybe she prefers Chris. Then it hits him. They aren't little any more. But compared to them, he still is. He smiles reluctantly, a little insulted at the term, but after the delicious meal he has just had, he feels he owes her at least that.

To be truthful, Paul wants to go now but he can see that his mother is well and truly camped out here for a while yet. She has even resorted to smoking her own cigarettes that she found with feigned surprise underneath the lining of Jenny's buggy. With Jenny herself fast asleep, it might mean a couple of hours, so Paul gets up and goes to walk out of the kitchen door on another slime-busting mission. As he walks towards the door that leads into the hallway he hears a scratch and a sniffle. He stops. Had the aliens survived his bomb and come down the stairs to attack? He positions himself against the wall, a finger gun cocked beside his head. The noise continues. He is going to have to confront this monster – whatever it is – and knows from his TV viewing that a door opened quickly is better than a door opened slowly. He pulls the door and almost gets to let off a round of ammo before he is knocked flying across the kitchen by Squire. The poor dog had been tantalised, wound up like a spring for hours now and just couldn't help itself when presented with its Holy Grail – leftovers! Squire heads straight for Barbara but Barbara's face has contorted into a shocked, rewound scream.

'Paul!'

Paul lies on the kitchen floor, dazed. He cracked his head on the radiator and now all is fuzzy after a brief burst of colour. A smell of sulphur.

A melée of colours, shapes, smells and flavours attack Chris from the ceiling-mounted menu of McDonald's. He continues to look at the menu well beyond the half-hearted greeting from the baseball-capped burger boy.

'Erm....'

Just as his brother had done earlier in the day, Chris pretends not to know what he wants. When in fact, he knows exactly what he wants.

'Erm. Large McChicken Sandwich meal. Coke. And a couple of ketchups.'

'Anything else?'

'No thanks, mate.'

Zeb has skinned up another joint and Kish has once again

refused it. But Snowman won't: 'I'll have a bit!'

Snowman saunters around the corner looking... different. He is wearing light grey Nike tracksuit bottoms and a dark blue sweatshirt with no discernable logo but he looks different.

'Alright, Snowman. Get your lungs around that.'

Snowman takes the joint and has a long drag. His eyes narrow as he pulls on the roach and he takes another sharp breath of the night air as he takes the joint from his lips. At this, he notices the girls in the corner and nods his hello to them, blowing out a cloud of smoke that rises into the air, illuminated by the security lighting. Snowman passes the joint back to Zeb and cracks open one of the four cans of Stella he has brought with him. Stella! Even the girls are shocked.

'Anyone want a can?'

Snowman holds out the remaining three by the empty plastic ring that held the fourth.

'I've got four more in the bag, so –.'

Nobody can quite believe what is happening, that Snowman has turned up looking different, with eight cans. Of Stella Artois. Finally Zeb takes a can.

'Cheers, mate.'

'No problem, Zeb. No problem. Anybody heard from Chris?'

Chris throws his McChicken Sandwich in the bin, half eaten. He walks out of the restaurant, wiping his mouth with a serviette before throwing it on the floor. It is almost half seven. Still an hour to go. He looks over to the Archer

Centre opposite. He could see if anyone was on the multistory car park but –. No, he didn't want to be hanging around with any of the idiots from his Year tonight. They'd just lead him astray. Instead he turns right and sees the Trouble and Strife. He checks himself in the window of McDonald's. Yeah, he looks the part tonight and he has heard from other lads in the Year that it is possible to get served in the Strife as long as there isn't a big gang of you. Well, Chris is alone. Perfect. He rubs his head down to the back of his neck and rolls over to the doors of the Strife.

Chris feels like anyone does walking into a pub for the first time. Everyone has done it, everyone in the pub has done it, so nobody in there really gives a fuck about the kid who doesn't need to shave stood in the doorway. They are all just looking at the bird by the bar, the oddly-coloured pint, the situation on the pool table, the shit on the juke-box, the nudges on the fruit machine or some cunt that's looking at them and better stop it or they'll be looking at a hospital ceiling.

He cruises up to the bar and leans an elbow on the top, stroking his nose and trying to make eye contact with the barmaid. He imagines it is done this way. When the barmaid approaches, he tries to think of what to buy. The only thing he recognises from the off license is Smirnoff Ice so he asks for one of those. He hands over the fiver he'd taken from David's box and then takes his change and his drink to a corner of the pub where he can hide. As he walks over, bottle slung low by his side, head down and eyes up, he feels a tap on his shoulder. He stops and mouths the word 'shit'. Exactly what has happened forms quickly in his head: they'd taken his money and now they were going to throw him out.

'Excuse me, are you old enough to be in here?'

Chris turns around slowly and sees. David.

'Does Mum know you're in here?'

'Does Tina know you are?'

David smiles. His kid brother is sharp: that was a good response.

'Come on, sit down with the boys.'

David leads Chris over to the corner near the pool table where he was sat with Graham and Billy. As he sits down and nods his hellos, David immediately takes up the role of older brother.

'What the fuck are you drinking there?'

'What?'

'That there, what the fuck is it?'

'Oh, erm, Smirnoff Ice.'

'Smirnoff fucking Ice! Fucking hell. Have I not taught you anything?'

'What?'

'Tell him, Billy.'

Billy leans back in his chair and fixes Chris with a shake of his head.

'Fucking woman's drink, that, Chris.'

David ups the ante.

'Fucking poof's drink.'

And Graham delivers the final blow.

'Tart fuel.'

Chris looks at his drink and then looks at the three

faces in front of him. They look genuinely perturbed, disappointed to say the least. Then Chris notices a slight chink in Billy's lips.

'Fuck off!'

All burst into laughter and Chris pretends to have been got, but that is the price you pay for being the youngest one there. Still, Chris knows the score: the piss taking is like a handshake really, and the fact you are sat with these people, in a pub, having a drink (even if it was 'tart fuel') well outweighs the piss taking when it comes to telling your mates who you were with, where you were and what you were doing. It was good to have the piss taken out of you at this table.

20.15

Stella Artois sprays the air, a hand slaps the table, a head shakes with a wry smile and Graham sits back in his chair, his head dropped backwards at a right angle, blowing a tunnel of ganja smoke into the air. He snaps his head back into its usual position and fixes the grinning Chris with a stare.

'Can you believe it, Chris? Fucking hell, eh?'

'Yeah.'

Graham has just been regaling the assembled boys with an anecdote. They have all heard it a thousand times but every time bless the teller with the same hysterical reaction. Chris doesn't understand why, the joke is wearing off for him now. Billy wipes his mouth after his Stella splurge and finishes a text message he has been trying to write for the last fifteen minutes.

'I swear, Chris. His arse was red raw for about a fortnight. Couldn't sit down, the poor fucker.'

Chris nods again and takes the joint that has made its way around the circle and back to him. He places what is little more than the roach and some browned paper to his lips and tokes but he only manages to burn his lips. He spits as if ejecting sour pips from his mouth and throws the dead spliff to the floor. David, his hand still gripping the edge of the table, looks at Chris. The look says it all: 'Serves you right for nicking my weed'.

Checking the clock on the wall, Chris allows the end of his beer to sit on his lips for a second before downing the dregs. It is his second pint of Stella on top of the earlier Smirnoff Ice; the boys insisting that he have a man's drink if he was to sit with them. He feels a little woozy, has to find something to focus on and so picks a photo over his brother's left shoulder. It is a photo of the Central Gardens from sixty years ago. He finishes his pint and stares.

Barbara has finished the ironing. It sits in a neat pile on the now clear kitchen table: towels, shirts, socks, jeans, underpants – Barbara's children will not be creased. She had finished it with such speed to fend off the feeling of guilt that is consuming her since Paul's injury. She knows it wasn't her fault but can't helping thinking, well, that it was. She should have at least gone to the A&E with Jean but Jean had assured her that giving her twenty pounds for the taxi fair was compensation enough. There was no need for two of them to spend the whole night in a four hour wait. Maybe longer. It was Friday night, after all.

Resting on a pair of Simpsons' jockey shorts is a packet of Lambert & Butler cigarettes. Two cups of finished tea sit on the draining board and Barbara wants to make herself another but she can't because her daughter is upstairs running a bath and this has obliterated the water pressure downstairs. Instead, Barbara slides another cigarette from the packet on the ironing and – where is the lighter? She lifts up the ironing to look underneath and then fingers her way through the pile item by item. No. She gets up, checks the surfaces, the top of the fridge. No. She goes into the front room and hunts on the windowsills, the mantelpiece, down the sides of the sofa, in the TV cabinet. No sign.

Frustration is now beginning to form a hard ball in Barbara's throat. It is impossible. There must be half a dozen lighters in the house and she can't find one of them. Where have they gone? David wasn't in long enough to take one with him; Jean, well Jean will have stolen at least one but that goes without saying, so what about the others?

Barbara sits down and tries to think, the cigarette between her fingers but not yet born. She thinks of using the gas hob but then remembers that the spark has gone and she'd need a lighter to light the gas anyway. It is as if the whole house is conspiring against her, the living room, the kitchen, the bathroom, that bloody radiator. Upstairs, of course – upstairs. She jumps up from the table and bounds up the stairs, the thunder of water masking her assent. She goes into her bedroom and checks the tallboys. Nothing. She checks the variety of boxes and drawers that pepper her dresser. Nothing. She checks the windowsill and all that is there is a picture of Jack. He is standing with Barbara, his arm around her as they are framed by the entrance to a restaurant in Majorca. It was a Tex-Mex restaurant called El Rancho and that night Jack finished the biggest steak either of them had ever seen. The boys had burger and chips followed by Neapolitan ice cream. Barbara had a mixed salad because she wasn't feeling too well. Marie was on the way.

After putting the photograph back on the windowsill Barbara walks solemnly out onto the landing. The bath is still running and she can hear Marie singing along to the tape player that leaves its trail of wire from underneath the bathroom door to the landing socket. As Barbara's eyes follow the trail she notices a laser pink thong on the floor outside Marie's bedroom door. She smiles and bends down to pick it up. Marie must have dropped it when she took her washing in. She opens Marie's bedroom door and puts the thong in Marie's knicker drawer. The window is open and the autumn breeze has Barbara reach for her arms and hold herself. She steps over to the window and pulls it too and there, on top of the music box that was one of Marie's Christening presents is a lighter. Barbara looks down to her right hand and notices the cigarette is still there. She walks out of Marie's room and over to the bathroom door. As she approaches, the taps fall silent and only the tape and the screech of the water pipes can be heard. Barbara has the lighter in her left hand. Its function has changed. It is no longer there to give life to her cigarette; it is now an inkling of doubt hanging over her only daughter. Barbara knocks on the bathroom door and calls Marie to quash this misgiving.

'Chris. Chris!'

David's shouts break Chris' trance and he meets his brother's eyes with a stoned expression.

'You're going to be late, sunshine.'

Chris checks the clock again. Eight minutes have passed since he first focused on the photograph of the Gardens. Eight minutes he'd been staring at the wall.

'Fuck! Shit. Cheers. Right, boys. Cheers.'

'Oi!'

David commands his brother to calm down and Chris straightens himself as he prepares to leave.

'Before you go. Take this.'

David dips into his back pocket and pulls out his wallet. He flips open the heavy leather and puts two fingers inside. Chris watches him with a tingle of excitement as David pulls out a condom. He tosses it across the table and sings.

'Tonight is your night, bro!'

The others join in.

'Tonight is your night! Tonight is your night, bro! Tonight is your nighthahhahhhhaaa!'

Chris shakes his head, picks the condom up from the table and smiles as he gives them the finger and leaves the pub.

He walks out of the Trouble and Strife and turns left past McDonald's. Having snapped out of his fuzzy trance, Chris now finds that the booze and weed have filled him with courage. He walks the same route of a few hours earlier, a route that had lead to the bowling green, and continues up past the Trouble and Strife. Whereas before he had looked into the large McDonald's window for a sense of himself, this time he looks into the Strife's smaller, dirtier window, giving a wave to David and the boys. Each of them he is sure are aware of the glory that has just shone in their presence. Chris is a little caned.

He takes another left, walks past the Argos depot, the multistorey car park coming up on the left, the bowling green up there somewhere on the right. Chris is on his way to Tindle Park, near the Old Town Hall, the Old Town Hall which was now nothing more than an empty shell because nobody had an idea who made the decisions that affected their lives. Tindle Park, where the Sunday League matches were played, where everyone who'd almost made it picked up injuries that kept them off work, the kind of work that didn't pay sick leave, the kind of work they wouldn't have to do if they had made it. Tindle Park near the Lodges, where the police would always stop the kids fishing, drinking, fucking, smoking but they'd still come back for more. Tindle Park, to meet Keeley, Keeley who had never been touched, quiet Keeley, the endangered species, the girl who you couldn't say a thing about because you had no idea.

By now, Chris was only a minute away from the Park and so he sits on the benches outside the Longbow pub. On the side of the Longbow, there is a huge sculpture of a longbow man, drawing his bow towards the detergent factory on the other side of the roundabout, in front of the woods. He looks ready to let fly.

Graham's ready to take flight. He swills the end of his pint and checks his gold watch. It is almost time.

'Well boys. I'm going to have to love you and leave you.'

'Where you off?'

'Billy. Ask no questions.'

Graham taps his nose and stands upright. David reaches up and shakes his hand.

'You going to be about later?'

'Yeah. Maybe. Give us a bell.'

'Right. See you after, then.'

'Ta da boys. Don't do anything I wouldn't do.'

With that, Graham heads out of the pub and into the now dark evening. Billy sits back in his chair.

'He is one rum bastard, he is.'

David smiles.

'Yeah. But if you're ever in trouble, you know he won't let you down.'

Billy nods and drains the end of his beer. He thinks about what David has just said and hopes that he is spoken of in such affectionate terms when his back is turned. He can't decide one way or another.

'You having another?'

David looks at his watch. It is getting on a little and he does need to get home but he is still irked about Jean being over at the house again.

'Yeah, go on then.'

At long last, Kish has relaxed enough to accept a pull on a joint. He takes it from Snowman and inhales deeply before looking skyward and blowing the smoke into the heavens. It feels good. Already the heady mix is streaking through his veins and his whole body slumps. He takes another puff and smiles. Snowman smiles back.

'What're you up to tonight, then?'

'Ah, this and that. Got a bit of an errand to run and then – probably be back on here. What about you?'

'Ah, just chilling. Try and get me some bitches.'

Zeb immediately bursts into howls of laughter.

'What? What?!'

Kish smiles at Zeb who in turn tones his laughter down to a grin.

'Nothing, mate. Nothing. Don't you think Chantelle is looking good tonight?'

Snowman, not fully sure whether to let this one lie, notices something odd in Zeb's eyes. He is darting them between Chantelle in the corner and Kish sat next to him. It is as if he has become an Action Man figure and Kish is flicking the neck switch that controls his eyes. It is then that Snowman manages to make sense of the situation. Of course – Kish and Chan!

'Oh. Yeah. Yes. She is, mate.'

Zeb manages a relieved sigh and prompts his slow friend further.

'And she has been checking out my man here all night, mate.'

This time Snowman swells with pride at his sharpness.

'Yes. Definitely. Can't keep her eyes off you, Kish. Reckon you should go over, you know. Here. Offer her a can of Stella.'

Kish looks at both of his friends and forces himself to his feet. The weed has taken the edge off some of his cynicism and he feels a boost of confidence in what they say. Besides, he thinks if Snowman is saying so, it must be true. He is too stupid to wind Kish up. Stupid enough to suggest offering a girl a Stella Artois.

'No thanks, mate. I can handle this.'

He passes the joint back to Zeb and walks over to the girls. There is a mild flurry of activity between the trio before Kish speaks.

'Evening, ladies.'

Martine answers, followed by the pouting Tash.

'Alright, Kish.'

'You took your time.'

Chan glows with embarrassment. Martine chuckles.

'Take no notice of her, Kish. She's just jealous.'

Kish stands there. He has already run out of things to say. He wasn't expecting this response. In his head it had all played out differently and now with the reality of the situation in front of him, things are going pear-shaped. He smiles.

'Does anyone want a beer?'

'You trying to get us drunk, Kishan Singh?'

Tash begins to chortle at her own remark and Martine joins in, slapping her arm.

'Ah come on Tash, let's go and –. Let's go.'

Martine leads Tash, still laughing, to the other side of the patio, her laughter stopping the instant she crosses Zeb's path. Kish looks at Chantelle.

'Chris will have met Keeley by now.'

Chantelle continues to look at the ground.

'She texted me. She's going to be late.'

'Oh.'

Kish can't believe this. He can't think of anything to say – he, Kishan Singh, the businessman, the matchmaker, the hustler supreme can't sell the one thing he knows best – himself. He puts his hands behind his back and looks at the sky. The clouds have become steadily darker and their darkness makes them look thicker than they are. Why is he here? What is he doing? Why did he come over? He is having to take each of these thought processes one at a time – his instincts shot to pieces. Instincts. That is it. He is thinking about this too much; he needs to go with it, say what comes.

'I like your hair.'

'What?'

'What are you doing later?'

'Don't know.'

He is making a right horse's arse of this and he knows it. He feels trapped. He wants to say goodnight and leave Chan to her own thoughts, cut loose now before he does too much damage, but Zeb and Snowman are stood behind him and expecting some kind of result. Added to this, the weed has now turned from calming sedative to paranoiac stimulant and he can feel beads of sweat hitting the rolls of fat on his stomach. He gropes for something to say, anything, something that might sound a little like something a normal person would say and then Chan says, 'Why?'

Kish is taken aback.

'Why what?'

'Why did you ask what I was doing later?'

'Just wondered if you want to hook up sometime. You know. Meet me.'

'Not tonight, but tomorrow, yeah.'

Get in! There it came, out of nowhere, the answer to all of his doubts, why he is here, what he is doing, what he came over for – he has asked Chantelle out and she has said yes. Now is the time to remain focussed, though.

'I'll text you tomorrow, yeah, to sort it out.'

'Fine. Text me tomorrow.'

'Alright. Best get...'

'Yeah.'

Kish walks back beaming and Snowman and Zeb return the look. Now all they need is for Chris to get the job done.

Chris sits on the bench, waiting until it would be cool enough to turn up. A commotion comes from behind him. The door of the Longbow flies open and a group of lads tumble out laughing. At first, Chris is confused as it looks like David and the boys back at the Strife, that somehow they'd beaten him here. But then he sees Spoonhead's brother Cod-Eye: huge, bald, with a squint, in grey Stone Island and Paul Smith jeans. Panicking, Chris turns his head the other way, but in his stoned confusion, he turns back and repeats the exercise slowly, so as not to attract attention. He watches them in the reflection of a windscreen in the car park opposite. Its angle makes them look tall and imperious. They are crossing the road, down towards the bingo hall, heading back into the town centre. Chris watches them. They're about to disappear. Phew. He is in the clear. Then his mobile goes off.

All of them turn around, and Chris can't help but turn around to face them. Spoonhead has been patched up but he gives Chris exactly the same look he'd given him as he lay in the ditch on the bowling green. Then he makes a noise.

'Oi! Oi! There's one of the lads that battered me today!'

Chris doesn't even bother running: he just stands up and puts his phone in his pocket. They were all walking over, and now he recognises them all. Housing List Celebrities. Knowing he couldn't outscrap them and it was too late to try and outrun them, he opts for honesty.

'Spoonhead. Come on. I didn't even touch you. I pulled Zeb off you, for fucksake.'

Spoonhead doesn't answer. Cod-Eye swings his shoulders towards Chris, moving to the front of the flock, pushing his chest out until he is about an inch from Chris' face.

'That right? You help my brother out? You pulled this Zeb off him?'

'Yeah, honest; I never even touched him.'

'But you know this Zeb yeah, know where he lives?'

'Yeah, well, yeah.'

'Right, well you can give him this message then can't you.'

Cod-Eye steps back and cracks Chris with a right hook to the temple. Chris stumbles as he follows through with another punch to the back of his head. This puts Chris down on the concrete. The next thing he feels are some expensive so-called walking boots kicking holes into his back and ribs, switching between whichever part of his body is exposed. He smells his aftershave, David's aftershave wafting down across him among a flurry of oaths and promises. Just the smell of it stings his face. The commotion stops and Chris allows himself one look up. Spoonhead is stood above him, a smile creeping across his teardrop face. Then he raises a Rockport.

'YOUFUCKINGCUNTIFYOUEVERFUCKWITHME
AGAINIWILLFUCKINGKILLYOU!'

Paul sits in the corner of Jean's kitchen, a huge bandage around his head. Jean is pinning it with a safety pin, a cigarette dangling from her lips. They haven't been to the hospital. A taxi home from Barbara's costs £2.50 and so she has made a clear £17.50 profit from the £20 she was given.

'There you go, love. Good as new. Mummy's big brave boy.'

Paul likes the sound of that. That's more like it, even if his head hurts and he still feels a little dizzy.

Chris comes around. He lies on the ground for a while looking at the sky. All he can think about are Mr Buckley's pigeons. He is imagining them, circling around the sky, swooping, banking, Mr Buckley reeling them in with a shovel of corn and an expert call. An expert call. A call. That's when he remembers the phone. He props himself up against the bench he'd been sat on and presses to view his inbox.

b there in ten minutes. xxx K

Chris looks at the message and shakes his head. He even has a little laugh to himself. He stands up and starts back for home, using his radar, typing in a message to Keeley.

sumthings cum up. cant make it. sorry. xxxC

He presses send. Fucksake.

20.50

Chris looks at the white UPVC door in front of him. His vision has now almost returned to normal but with ordinary vision comes extraordinary pain – the numbness is wearing off. As soon as he walks into the house he knows all hell is going to break loose. He reaches out to the faux-brass handle, pushes down and opens the door.

The warm lights of the living room reach out to him. He can see the door to the kitchen opposite, shut to, its edges painted with clinical iciness by the strip lighting spilling out through the sides. But the living room lights are warm; the marshmallow settee is beckoning him with promises to take the weight. Chris steps through the welcoming doorway with these welcoming thoughts in his head, eyes closed, trying to force them out through his nerve endings, out into his limbs, lips and face. From behind his eyelids all is dark and peaceful and he begins to believe that everything might be alright, that in the darkness he can hide from the world – that by not being able to see it, it couldn't possibly find him. But the darkness is disturbed. A wash of red permeates his eyelids and he cannot ignore the warning sign. The strip lighting from the kitchen has filled the room, changing the whole of the landscape. Chris turns to the mantelpiece for solace but only finds a cheap market stall selling a family's last possessions – early birthday cards, statuettes of nobody in particular, photos of times long gone, of a family complete. Next to it the TV looks like a stealth fighter that has crash-landed in the corner of the room – shot down by a small boy outside McDonald's with a straw and a wet piece of paper.

The kitchen door is now wide open. Barbara stands small in the doorframe and Chris sees what his mother looks like for the first time in a long time. Her clothes are not old but not young. The tracksuit bottoms are shiny new and she wears them rolled up to mid calf as her daughter would. But her jumper looks too real to be new. An ancient chain knitted sweater, the sleeves rolled up to the elbow not as a fashion statement, rather a statement of intent. She wears a little make up, rushed and applied for an errand rather than a meeting, and her hair is cut into a straight bob, the rusty orange covering the grey. But it is her eyes that are the real giveaway, sloping like an aged boxer, a boxer of a lighter weight who fought with greater frequency than the heavier pugilists. She has a fighter's eyes. That always makes eyes sound fiery; ready to take people on at any cost. The eyes of a real fighter. Hers, though, are tired, paranoid and turn down at the sides like a resigned smile. Still, they are the only smile on Barbara's face now. Her mouth is blurred in the rapid movement of her cracked lips. She is talking incessantly, trying to fit as many words into the silence as she can and wrap Chris up in her noise.

The roar of a car engine and the glare of headlights bounce off the back wall of the Old Folks' Home, causing all assembled to turn in synchrony. Drugs are quickly stashed behind the wall with beer cans and youngsters begin to walk quickly towards the left hand exit.

'It's alright! It's Graham.'

Zeb being the swiftest of the mass had crept the opposite way to make sure escape was necessary and his report stops all in their tracks. Relief and excitement replace panic and animation. Snowman retrieves his Stella and struts out towards the car. The electric window buzzes down and Snowman leans in.

'Alright, Graham?'

'Yeah. Zeb and Kish about?'

Snowman is surprised at this response, hurt by his quick dismissal.

'Yeah. They're just –'

'I see them.'

By now, most of the Old Folks' crew has stolen around after Snowman to get a look at Graham. Whispers and rumour abound as they try to catch a glance without looking, try to watch without staring. Zeb and Kish slowly approach the car and the whispers flurry like bees sensing a threat to the hive.

'Could you give us a minute?'

Snowman takes his head from the car window and steps back. He doesn't want to rejoin the group but is aware of how foolish he looks stood between them and the object of their desires. Kish's head replaces Snowman's in the window.

'You're not caned, are you?'

'No. No.'

'Pissed?'

'No, Graham.'

'Good. Get in.'

Kish stands away from the window as it hovers back to closing and opens the back door. Zeb gets in first and shifts along the back seat to allow Kish access. Graham says nothing. He puts the car into reverse and pulls away. The crowd burst into action: incredulous gasps of maybes and guesswork. Chantelle is stood at the back, her friends looking at her with new respect as her boyfriend to be drives off with the famous Graham. She isn't impressed. In fact she wonders what the fuck Kish is doing with that wanker. Snowman just wonders what the hell has happened.

'Baby! Oh, my baby son! What's happened? Quick quick, here, sit down, lie on the couch, let me take your shoes.'

Barbara puts one hand on Chris' elbow and one on his left shoulder as she helps him towards the settee. She shoos Squire away, leaving the cushions clear, all the time speaking. Chris sits down slowly, Barbara easing him back so that he is lying across the three seats, feet hanging over the arm.

'Come here love, oh son. Let me take off your shoes. Oh your nice new shoes; look at them. Don't worry, I can send them back, we'll lift off the sole, send them back, get you another pair.'

Chris notices the state of his new Nicholas Deakins as Barbara tries to undo the laces. They are scuffed and scratched but nothing registers with Chris – he is still struck dumb by the realisation of his mother. She fumbles with his laces. He reaches up from the settee and puts his hand on hers as she continues to fail.

'*BASTARDS, THE BA*-ah-sterrrds,' her shoulders shake, starting with rage, ending in desperation, 'I'm sick of it, Chris. I can't take this much longer. It's killing me.'

'Mum, Mum, I'm fine. It looks worse than it is.'

'It's not just *looking* like that Chris. It's not just coming home being on the wrong end of it. Everyday I hear about someone else's son. Every time you go out of the door I'm thinking, worrying, I can never think of anything else. Sometimes, when your David used to come home, you could smell it on him. I can smell it on you.'

Chris sits up, pats the cushion next to him and takes Barbara's elbow as she sits down. He's never seen her like this. Not even with his dad and everything. She's completely broken and seems to be getting smaller and smaller in the seat. He puts his hand over her shoulder and looks the other way. He doesn't have the noise in him to wrap around her.

'*LET IT ROLL BABY ROLL!*'

David and Billy are making more noise than the rest of

the Strife's clientele put together, David taking charge of the jukebox and *Roadhouse Blues* by The Doors causing the commotion.

'*LET IT ROOOOOL. ALL NIGHT LONG!*'

Both David and Billy finish the song with a flash of pool cue guitar before returning to their game. Sat at their table are two young girls who joined them just after Graham had left. Neither David nor Billy can remember their names, nor have they attempted to impress the girls in any way, but still they sit and watch the two men wish they were the bastard sons of Jim Morrison and Alex Higgins. Billy settles down to the table. It is his shot and there is the black ball and one stripe left on the table. Billy is on stripes.

'And Willie Thorn bows at the green baize. It's a big shot. One of the biggest of his career at the Crucible and the pressure is telling in his face...' Billy hates it when David commentates on the game. Especially as David always refers to himself as Higgins, White or O'Sullivan, and Billy as Thorburn, Griffiths or Thorne. '...Ask any of the professionals on the circuit and they'll tell you that Thorne is the best break builder around on the practice table. A true master of the cue action. But on the big occasion, he is equally famous for going to pieces...' Billy lines up his shot and smashes the ball into the bottom left hand pocket, finishing perfect on a black ball to the middle. '...But tonight Thorne becomes a rose. Surely the game is his now.'

David slurps the end of his pint. Already he has tried to break Billy's roll of six straight pots by insisting on the earlier sing-along and constantly coughing, whistling and of course commentating. Now comes the final trick – the last resort. He walks around the table as Billy lines up the black and puts his cue in the rack on the wall.

'Game, mate.'

Billy knows exactly what David is up to as he sits down with the two girls and pretends to start talking to one of them whilst watching Billy through the corner of his eye. He is trying to make Billy believe he doesn't care. That he is resigned to defeat. That the only way he can win is if Billy makes a real fool of himself now. And Billy really doesn't feel like making a fool of himself now. He strokes the cue ball gently. It cuts the black at the perfect angle, rolling it towards the pocket, rolling, rolling, creeping and –

'Maybe not!'

The black ball hangs over the edge of the pocket, falling just short. Billy's face sinks into the cloth and he stands upright, exasperated. David approaches the table.

'A valiant effort by Thorne but it seems the Hurricane may have another gust left in him yet!'

David leans over the table, cueing with intense concentration. Just as he is about to strike the ball, he lifts his head and looks Billy straight in the eye. David pots the ball without looking and drops to his knees to cry mock tears of joy. He motions to an imaginary wife to join him, to pass an imaginary baby into his arms. Billy puts his cue back and goes to the bar. The two girls stand up from their seats and clap and cheer.

'Where's my baby? Where's my baby?'

'Where's my boots?'

Chris and Barbara are still sat in silence. Squire has stayed in the corner. It feels like they are going to stay like that forever, that in years to come, people will excavate the town and find these two figures, preserved like the people of Pompeii. But the real eruption hasn't happened yet. The next round is coming down the stairs.

'*Mum! Where's my boots?*'

Marie hasn't reached the front room door yet but her noise has made Barbara jolt upright. She recovers instantly, clasping her hands, regaining control of her lips and her words. But you can still tell it was pre-recorded. It isn't live. She answers Marie and then speaks to Chris, 'They're in the cubby-hole love. They're in here. I'll get you a cup of tea. Nice sweet tea, that'll make you feel loads better.'

Marie strides in with two towels, one wrapped around her head like an African headdress, one around her body – squeezing out her tits, skirting her arse. She walks straight past Chris on the couch and turns left into the cubbyhole. The lights go on and destroy the mountain of shoes that has formed in there. Chris looks down at his Nicky Deakins. He can't really bend down to undo them so he puts toe to heel and fires them one at a time across the front room to crash by the TV. As the second shoe skids across the skirting board, Marie emerges from the cubbyhole, one hand pinching two black, knee-high boots by their tops. She strides past Chris and heads towards the door. As she opens it, she looks back.

'Who was it?'

'Spoonhead. Cod-Eye. That lot.'

'Yeah?'

'Yeah.'

'Dickhead.'

Chris' sister strides out with little elegance, the sure-footed strut of a girl who doesn't want to give a fuck. She is mature beyond her years, in the physical sense, taking after her father. Her frame is large: broad shoulders, large breasts and hips, wide midriff and solid legs. This is not to say that she is fat, or chunky, or any of those quantifiable adjectives. She is a russian doll; the one you open first. Large enough to house many other dolls but proportionately the same. Her mother is the final doll, the small one that is hard, but not impossible to break if you try hard enough.

'There you go, son. You took your shoes off! Good lad. Sit back now, I'll get the little table so you can put your tea on it and watch a bit of football.'

'Cheers.'

'Cheers, Graham.'

Graham closes the boot of his car after passing Kish and Zeb a balaclava and a baseball bat each. They have parked on a patch of wasteland where a new motorway is being planned and an old petrol station has been levelled in readiness. With nothing of worth around but the land, this is a CCTV free zone.

'Now, you know the drill. Keep the bats up your sleeves as you're walking and keep those hoods up. There's that many cameras around here at the moment you can't swear without being pulled, so make sure your faces can't be seen.'

'Why don't we just stick the balaclavas on?'

Graham shoots Zeb a flash of gold.

'Because Zeb my boy, you've got a good half mile to walk and balaclavas attract more attention than any face. They don't, I repeat, they do not go on until you reach the shop. Understood?'

Both boys nod.

'Right. I am going back home. I should be back in five minutes. Don't set off for at least ten. I want to be safely speaking to my mother on the phone while this happens. Keep your dicks up, boys – tonight you become men.'

Kish and Zeb both nod, despite Zeb wanting to laugh at the ridiculousness of Graham's final words. Despite Kish feeling a cold crush gripping his heart.

Chris doesn't feel like watching football, and doesn't feel better for finishing the hot sweet tea. He just wants his Mum to feel better. Chris knows deep down that this is impossible because of what has to be done.

'I'm sorry.'

'Don't be daft, son. Eh? There's nothing you can do about it now is there, eh?'

'Nah. Nah, there isn't.'

'We'll send your shoes back. Just lift off the sole, pretend they've fallen apart. But I don't know about your jumper. I can have a go at fixing it but –.'

Chris hadn't noticed the rest of his clothes. His jeans are full of dust from the concrete – nothing that a good wash couldn't sort out – but his Stone Island jumper is ripped from the neck right down to the embroidered logo.

'No, Mum, you can't fix this. I'll have to speak to our David.'

Billy hasn't said a word to David since the pool game. He disgusts him. All the shit David feeds him about keeping on the straight and narrow, loving his fiancée and the importance of marriage. All the 'my mum and dad were together for twenty years and would still be today if it wasn't for the accident. Only death could part those two.' And here he was, slavering over a couple of his groupies. At least Billy had the decency to admit he was a letch.

'Tell you what, girls. I haven't had anything to eat yet. How do you fancy going to Don Juan's for an Italian? Billy?'

Billy nearly chokes on his pint.

'Nah, erm – thing is, Dave. I've heard it's really gone to shit, that place.'

'Well I'm fucking starving, mate and this Stella is no good on an empty stomach. Besides –'

'We could have a curry.'

David shoots Billy a glance.

'We can't take a couple of classy ladies like these out for a curry! These kind of women need to be wined and dined.'

'We'll need to check if they're booked up.'

'Booked up!'

'It's a Friday night, David. Like you say. A classy place like that. I'll see if I can swing us a table.'

Billy winks at David and David thinks he understands.

'Oh, 'course. 'Course. Tell them David Carty wants a table if they're full. That should swing it.'

'Will do, boss.'

Billy stands up and walks to the door of the pub. He plays with his phone but instead of ringing, sends a text. He puts the phone to his ear and shakes his head. He begins to get animated before pretending to get annoyed. He signals for David to come over. Hesitantly, David approaches.

'You're not going to believe this, mate. They're booked up.'

'What?'

'Fully booked. No tables at all.'

'But I was meant to be taking Tina –. Hang on.'

'Honest, David. Tell you what. It's a good job you didn't.'

'Yeah. Fuck. Right.'

David and Billy both walk back to the table.

'Change of plan, ladies. Just spoke to a friend of ours and he has told us that Don Juan's has really gone to the dogs. But I do know the head waiter at a very nice Indian restaurant.'

David clasps his hands and looks at the girls. They can't believe the great David Carty has failed to get them a table. They look at each other thinking the same thing. This guy is old news. He's not the man he used to be. He is trying to fob us off with a Balti.

'Sorry, David. We've got to meet some friends. We're going to town, Club Eternity. Is that the time? Cheers, lads but we best be off.'

'See you later, Mum.'

'Hang on lo–'

The slam of the front door shakes the floor of Chris' bedroom as he reaches for the brown tape recorder under the bed. Marie has gone out, none of them know where. Reaching down under the bed reminds Chris of how the night had started so well: nice aftershave, a fiver and a bit of weed. He was looking forward to meeting Keeley so much. Of course it wouldn't have happened anyway but Chris had the weird feeling that if Zeb hadn't beat up Spoonhead, Keeley would have still turned up. But then again, if Spoonhead hadn't beat up Zeb and – Chris could go on forever to find the cause for the action but truth be told, the trigger to these events is like our time in the womb. It must have happened but we can never recall it. And now. Well, Chris can't see Keeley tomorrow – he has business to take care of. He'd worn David's aftershave, spent his money and smoked his weed and knows that when he comes in, when David finds out about what has happened, Chris will have to follow his lead. Gladly, of course.

He drags out the tape recorder and dips into the tape box for his old Tupac tape. Chris is feeling scared and Tupac always puts things straight for him. He puts the tape next to the recorder and begins to strip off: jumper first (still with care despite its ruin), then jeans. He has a large bruise on his left hip from where he'd hit the deck. He scans the rest of his body. There are red marks in full bloom and the buds of bruises all over his chest. Grazes on his hands and shoulder blades. Chris is a mess. His eye is yellowing like a dandelion. A real mess. He kicks off his socks, picks up the tape and the recorder and heads for the landing, stopping on his way to pick up the slipper.

The bathroom shines. It really shines and gleams and sparkles and blinds. It is neat and folded, tended and cared for and those who enter feel tended and cared for. It is clean but not clinical, spotless and soothing. It gives everyone a fresh start. Chris begins to run the bath and then goes through the usual rigmarole of setting up the tape. The first song to come on is *Thug Passion*. Tupac makes a mistake during the intro and starts laughing. Chris smiles.

Snowman frowns as he leans against the wall of the Old Folks' Home. The buzz of Graham's arrival, of Kish and Zeb's departure has just about died down but not enough for him to join back in with the conversation. A wave of mobile phone messages has brought all of those who had decamped to the shops back to the Old Folks' in anticipation of the possibility of another visitation by Graham. All the old faces are back, along with some younger new ones. Snowman, at fifteen, feels old and useless. Already he can see the upstarts – the people who will one day replace him in a role he is yet to take up himself. Why does that feeling of invincibility he so fleetingly gets always wear off so quickly? Because someone always ruins it for him. Snowman needs someone who'll make him feel invincible – he can't just rely on himself anymore. He's been alone in his struggle for too long. He sips his Stella and slides down the wall to sit on the floor.

Chris sits on the toilet and looks over at the bath. He has run it as deep as he can but there isn't enough water after Marie got ready, so the bath is only a quarter full. Sat on the toilet seat, Chris has a good look around the bathroom. He thinks to himself about how little notice of things he takes – how much is habitual and robotic in his life. The bathroom hasn't been decorated for ages but it is still sparkling clean. The whole house is clean, clean all the time. Chris' Mum never stopped scrubbing, polishing, dusting, mopping, washing, spraying, buffing. But Chris can't remember seeing her do any of it.

He climbs into the bath and it stings like sunburn. He grits his teeth and splashes the water up all over himself, trying to get as much of his body wet as soon as he can. He's learnt this trick swimming in the canal every summer. Nobody was bothered about the old bikes and the stories of weeds dragging kids under, killer pikes that bite your cock off. It was the shock and sting of the cold that filled you with fear. So the trick was to jump off the lock, straight in, right under so that everywhere felt the shock at the same time. You felt all the pain all over and it was all done with quicker. Chris uses what little water there is in the bath to try and cover his hurt before sinking down to relax.

Less than a quarter of the pain stops. The water only comes up to the bruise on his hip. It doesn't even wet his pubes.

Then it happens: Chris begins to cry. Chris never cries – but right there, in six inches of water, stinging like sunburn, listening to Tupac, he cries about everything ever. He cries about the time his sister blew out the candles on his cake on his eighth birthday and his dad put some more on a Bakewell tart so he could blow them out on his own later that night. He cries about the time Squire's Mum Joplin had a litter of puppies and they had to sell them all except for Squire. He missed the puppies but his father was so happy that he took all the family to the Beefeater with the profit. Chris didn't even finish his scampi. He cries about the time his dad came back from the vet's saying Joplin had been put to sleep. He cries about the time his dad got home after losing on the horses and argued with his Mum, kicking her in the leg so hard that she dropped the chip pan. He remembers wanting to cry that night in the nearly silent house – the echoes of the fight still bouncing from wall to wall. Because they never fought, his mum and dad. He was afraid they'd divorce, that he'd lose his dad just like most of his other friends. He didn't cry at the time, but he is crying now. Sobbing, snot swinging from his nose, his lungs whooping, trying to keep up with all that he is breathing out. He pulls the plug.

21.40

Marie has been sat in Don Juan's restaurant for the last forty-five minutes. He should have been here an hour ago and she thought fifteen minutes was long enough to keep him waiting. She hasn't even been able to get a drink as she hasn't got any ID. Just last night she was in Club Eternity drinking Bacardi Breezers and doing coke and now here she is in Don Juan's, munching at a bread stick and sipping Pepsi.

She is sat in the small bar area at a table on her own. A small family party is taking place in the main room behind her and she can hear the whoops and laughter ricocheting off the white plaster, collecting in the Mediterranean trinkets cluttering the walls and loosening the wax melted by candles in old wine bottles. A map of Italy on a tea towel isn't keeping her interest and a waitress in black and white uniform slumps behind the bar, giving

Marie dirty looks. Does she not know who Marie is? Does she not know her brother? For the last three quarters of an hour Marie has been hoping nobody in Don Juan's did, just in case, but now she wants to ram the information down this slag's throat and insist on a Watermelon Breezer.

Instead, Marie gets up and goes to the toilet. She sashays through the main room – couples holding hands, old folks eating steaks, the family party – and batters her way through the toilet door. She doesn't actually go to the toilet. Instead she puts her hands on either side of the old sink as if she is going to vomit and looks into the mirror. The mirror is smeared and speckled with the fresh paint job the bathroom must have had recently. On the wall is a condom machine offering extra safety and Marie can't believe that it is left up to women to sort that out as well. She looks again in the mirror. The wreckage of this morning has been covered with fresh foundation, silver eyeshadow and lipstick. The spot on her forehead has been covered with concealer and her eyelashes are longer than usual. She looks great but feels –

'Fuck it. Fuck. It. I'm off.'

Marie stomps out of the toilet and past the laughing party. A waitress almost calls something but stops when she sees Marie's fearsome strut. No questions to ask about that walk. The drinks are on the house for that walk.

Kish and Zeb are walking quickly, trying – as hard as they can – not to run.

'It'll be alright. We've done it, 'course he'll let us in. Chill out.'

194

Zeb's words do little for Kish. It is not the worry of getting caught or Graham letting them hide out at his house for a while that is propelling Kish – he is being thrown clear by the shockwaves of the destruction that has just hit Frank's Food and Booze. Somewhere it all went wrong. Kish trawls his memory to pinpoint the exact moment, to find the cause of all this, the trigger, the Big Bang. They'd waited the appropriate length of time, they'd donned their balaclavas in utter synchrony, ahh, yes, but when they'd got inside the shop Kish just froze. He couldn't do it. He just stood with the baseball bat at his side and watched as Zeb set about his Uncle's beloved shop. First went the refrigerated drinks crashing under the weight of Zeb's fervent swing. Then went the tins and dry goods, obliterated by his sweeping strike. Then –.

'Slow down! Slow down. Fucking hell Kish, we've got to stay cool. Stay fucking cool. Think.'

Billy is trying to. He knows he should go home to his wife, maybe even catch Joey before his extra late weekend bedtime but the pull of the City is too strong. He is on the bus. Being reasonably early, this doesn't seem strange but still he feels that all eyes are on him. All on the bus are in their best going-out clothes, a fog of Issey Miyake clouding the long deck and even though Billy too looks ready for a night out in town, he just doesn't look as clean. He doesn't smell as fresh.

As the bus begins to approach the city centre, the signs of urban renewal are still a mile or so away. This is the untouched north of the city – a far cry from the press

195

fanfares and cutting edge architecture sweeping its south, west and east. The north has been left untouched and so there is a strange chastity to its sleaze and decay.

Sleaze and decay suit Billy. Or so he thinks. His thoughts have become muddied by the regard in which he now holds himself and all he can do is play out the role that he has created. He is sick, he is scum and so this is the kind of thing the likes of him should be doing. It's the reason he is here at all. It's home.

David strides towards home with purpose. He reaches the white plastic door and pushes down the handle dragging the white plastic bag of takeaway curry behind him. The door opens and David's frame, much bigger than Chris', fills the doorway. The front room bursts at the seams with David.

'Alright, Mum! Only me. Is our lover boy home yet?'

He shuts the door behind him with heavy digits, a large gold band – his father's wedding ring – on his middle finger, and then runs his hand through his greased and ready hair. His fingernails have the never-clean crust of the mechanic, his hands shiny with Swarfega, his knuckles uneven. He has the hands to match his mother's eyes but his own eyes dance above a strong and steady nose: straight, parallel, leading to full lips framed with sandpaper stubble. It is the face of a living classic: Michelangelo's David, stepping outside the gallery and having to fend for itself in the real world. David's face is a portrait of this world and his mastery of it.

Or maybe not. He saunters towards the kitchen, the

steaming Balti Hut bag swaying jauntily beside him.

'Mum? Mum?'

The stairs shudder with Barbara's panicked arrival.

'Sorry, love. I was just resting my eyes. You're home early.'

'Well I'm starving, aren't I? Fucking Red Cross this place. Fucking CAFOD.' Barbara says nothing. Usually she'd try to defend herself, make an excuse – maybe even fight back – but Barbara's ominous silence has David speak again. 'Yeah. Well. Is there any clean plates for this lot?'

David knows the answer to this question and winces at having asked it. He really didn't know what else to say and so he sits at the wooden kitchen table and takes the grease-blotted brown paper bag from inside the plastic. As he *psshts* a can of Dr Pepper open, Barbara puts a clean plate and a fork in front of him. He lifts the silver trays out of the bag and pulls back the edges of each to reveal chicken balti and pilau rice. By now, he should have at least a spoonful in his mouth but he can't bring himself to tip the mess onto his plate.

'Mum. Where's Chris?'

'Upstairs, love.'

She doesn't have to say another word. David is out of his seat and heading for the stairs.

Marie is heading for the Old Folks' Home. She can't believe she's been stood up and so she goes to the Old Folks' for some comfort. When she arrives a huge mass of JD Sports-sponsored kids has gathered and she looks out of place in her black dress and boots. Her confident walk slows up at this realisation and she scours the place for a fellow outsider. By the back wall with a can of Stella is Snowman. She makes her way over to him.

'Give us a beer, Snowman.'

Snowman stands up quickly, shocked from his sitting position by the sight of Marie's thong. This is a strange reaction, given that such a sight is something he has dreamed of for a long time. Snowman has had eyes for Chris' sister for about a year now, ever since she'd grown up all of a sudden, and the sight of her here on the Old Folks' Home is an odd but pleasing one.

''Course, 'course. Here you are.'

Snowman hands Marie a Stella. She *psshts* the can and takes a long deep gulp. Snowman watches the shape of her neck as it devours the contents before her lips curl away from the can's.

'Ahhh. You've not got any spliff have, you?'

Snowman can't believe it. For once in his life he doesn't have any weed on him and this one time is the one time he really should have.

'No. Sorry. Erm.'

Then he remembers his back pocket. It was meant to be a party trick to impress Kish and Zeb but seeing as they had just ditched him for Graham, he decides to use it on Marie. After all, she's worth it.

'But –. I've got this.'

Marie catches the Lottery ticket wrap that has been tossed her way. She looks at Snowman, his sorry eyes looking for some kind of recognition.

'Is this –?'

'Yeah.'

'Snowman. Come on, let's leave these fucking dicks behind.'

With that, Marie trots off towards the bowling green and Snowman trots dutifully after her.

Duty is something Zeb knows all about. As far as Zeb is concerned, all they have just done is their duty but for Kish it was obviously a little more complicated. As the two of them continue their speed walk to Graham's, the sound of police sirens creep in from behind them. They slow to almost snail's pace as the walls around them light up in reds and blues before a white flash of police cars whiz past them. They let out a collective sigh as the distorted wail of the siren makes its distance known. And then they start to run.

Within seconds Zeb is streaking away in front of Kish.

'Zeb! Zeb, slow down, mate. Give me a fucking chance!'

Zeb slows to a jog while Kish keeps up at full pelt over his right shoulder. Kish looks at Zeb's back and the memory returns. As Zeb cleared the tins, his Uncle Sukraj walked up behind the frenzied Zeb. Kish stayed frozen by the door. Kish didn't move, just watched as Sukraj approached but then he saw what his Uncle was carrying. He had a crowbar in his right hand, the same crowbar they used to break up the damaged pallets that the Cash and Carry would ask them to dispose of in return for some cheaper goods. Sukraj lifted it above his head to strike Zeb but Kish suddenly found the power to move again and brought his baseball bat crashing down across his Uncle's shoulders, cracking one of the ceiling lights on its way down. Sukraj fell to the floor and Zeb span around. The two looked at each other, then at Sukraj's prostrate body before letting their bats go limp.

And they ran.

And still they run until they reach Graham's door and stop.

'You knock.'

'No, you.'

Billy stands at a heavy black door at the side of an international phone café filled with Nigerians, Somalis, Bengalis, and Turks. Above the shop is a brothel. The same brothel he visited on his stag night. He looks at the building. That night he was drunk as Lord, celebrating his last night of freedom, cheered on by his friends. How has he arrived here, drunk as a skunk, mourning the last of his dignity, bombarded by unknown tongues speaking to people on the other side of the world? The building itself has changed. It was always dirty but now it seems even dirtier than before. The windows once hidden behind light blue blinds are blacked out and open half an inch to allow the sweat of commerce to creep out. But the heavy black door is the same, opening silently to allow Billy to creep in.

He climbs the stairs in twos, his head down, the smell of skunk heavy in the air. The black girl is no longer behind the desk – it is now a swarthy, moustachioed man with too much Kouros on. The girls have also changed, no more middle-aged fun-time girls just a series of depressed and tired looking young Eastern Europeans. No welcome, no phone line, just a list of services and prices on a chalk board on the back wall. Billy is about to walk out. He cannot have fallen so far as to stoop to this but something stops him, something familiar from a happier time. Through some saloon doors he hears a voice singing but it is not the sweetness of the voice that draws him in, it is the coughing that punctuates it. He turns to the moustachioed man.

'Is Kaya in tonight?'

'Kaya?'

'Kaya.'

'Kaya?'

Billy shakes his head. This man only speaks sex English – he obviously knows no other words. Luckily for Billy, one of the girls does.

'She is Kaya not more. Now she is Chanel. She is just cleaning her. She will be out soon.'

Chanel. Billy likes the sound of that. He smiles at the girl and walks over to the large mirror on the wall before taking a seat.

David is sat opposite Chris now, diagonally. He looks at him for about ten seconds and then runs fingers down his rack of CDs. He's wearing what Chris had seen him wearing in the pub and once again Chris thinks his brother looks fucking cool. A charcoal grey Stone Island jumper. Not one with the big buttoned-on label on the arm, one with a smaller embroidered logo. His jeans are black Armani and his trainers Adidas Stan Smith. Again black. Chris thought they looked like PE pumps in the shop but on him they looked class. None of it was stolen. David insists on paying full price for his clothes, even though Graham could get it for a third of the price, with the labels still on. Graham says he could even get the right carrier bag to put it in if he wants, but it does no good. David always pays good money for his clothes.

He finds the CD he is looking for and puts it on the stereo. It is The Stone Roses. He looks at Chris.

'Fancy a bit of skunk?'

'Yeah. Yeah, cheers.'

David ducks down under his bed between Chris' legs for his moneybox, the one with the weed in. He pulls it out and looks at the bag. He looks at Chris and then back at the bag. He puts the lid back on the box and empties some weed onto the top. Slowly, he breaks the compressed weed into small pieces. David is going to take his time rolling this. Chris feels like he is waiting outside the headteacher's office. You know that something is going to happen, something big, but it had to wait. And you had to wait. You weren't in control.

'You got any baccy?'

'Just some cigs.'

'You smoking now?'

'No.'

'Good. Filthy habit. What are they?'

'Lamberts.'

'Fuck. Has Mum got any?'

'Yeah, they're Lamberts as well.'

'Fucksake. Going to the dogs, this family, I'm telling you. Give us a cig then, beggars and all that.'

Chris leans over to his jeans and pulls the cigarettes out of his pocket. He passes the silver box to David and he flicks the bottom of the box to take one out. He licks along the seam and splits the cigarette open with his dirty fingernail, emptying the tobacco onto the shoebox in a small pile next to the weed. Without sitting up, he pulls some king-size blue Rizlas out of his back pocket and tugs two of the thin papers out of the packet. He puts the packet at the back edge of the shoebox, flush with the lid. Carefully he takes one of the papers and bends it down at the narrow edge, making it look like a Stanley knife with its blade drawn. He licks this edge and tears it off quickly. He then licks the gummed edge of the torn paper and sticks it to the narrow edge on the piece of paper that is still intact, forming a small ice pick that he folds not quite in half. Placing the skins on the box, he begins to mix the tobacco and weed together, thoroughly, all the time silent. He then takes the mixture and begins to sprinkle it along the folded papers, loading the end of the pick closer to the head a little more than the handled end. Almost there now. He picks up the papers and begins to roll, crushing the mixture into the cone. Then he puts it down and reaches for the Rizla packet, tearing off a small stamp-sized piece and rolling it into a tight spring. He takes the roach and places it at the thin end of the cone, wrapping the papers around it until he has a perfectly formed spliff. But there is one last thing. Even though Chris and David are going to smoke it there and then, David twists the top, making sure none of its contents can spill out. Then he shakes the spliff, giving it one final mix.

David taught Chris how to skin up like this almost exactly two years ago.

Marie is knelt by a bench on the bowling green, chopping out a line of cocaine just as she was taught to when he first took her out. But she isn't with him now. She is with Snowman. Snowman has just had one. He sits back and allows the rush to stream through his body, small drops of powder falling from the top of his nasal cavity and down the back of his throat. He's beginning to understand why Graham said this stuff was like gold dust. Still, he is in some state of shock at how adept Marie is at chopping the stuff out. She'd prepared his line for him and now she is priming her own much fatter line. Snowman watches her knelt there and his cock begins to throb. He feels it growing in his tracksuit bottoms and bulging at the pocket. All kinds of thoughts filter through his mind – aggressive, unthinkable thoughts of rape and abuse. The sound of Marie's snorting does little to remove these feelings and in fact as she looks up and rubs her nose like a character from Peanuts, these feelings grow as strong and hard as his penis. Still kneeling, Marie looks at him.

'You feeling horny, Snowman?'

Snowman nods and Marie reaches into his pants. For revenge.

Jean reaches into her handbag for a lighter. It is Barbara's lighter – the one she stole earlier along with her money. Well, the money wasn't stolen. It wasn't ring-fenced for Paul or anything. She takes out the lighter and sparks up a

Lambert, inhaling deeply and blowing the smoke towards the ceiling. Above the ceiling Paul and Jenny share a room. Jenny has been asleep for some time but Paul's mind is racing. His head is still clumsily bandaged and he is wearing his Incredible Hulk pyjamas. He is thinking about his dad. He is thinking about Jenny's dad. He is thinking about his cousins' dad. Where have all the dads gone? But he can't even imagine them – he can't invent their faces, where they live, the kind of jobs they do. He cannot imagine it. For once in his life, Paul just cannot imagine it.

Graham doesn't even want to imagine it.

'What the fuck have you two done?'

'What you said. Just what you –'

'Shut up, Zeb. Kish. What happened?'

'Nothing, Graham. Like he said. Just –'

'Well how come half of the local fucking constabulary are on the fucking scene?'

Graham points to a police scanner in the corner buzzing with police chatter. Neither of the boys had noticed it when they came in.

'You don't get that much action for a shop being done over. Now. What is going on?'

'Right. And that's all you did. Watch?'

David is looking Chris straight in the eye, spliff smoke pouring out of the side of his mouth.

'Only if you're lying, Chris –. Well, there's going to have to be serious payback on this one and I need to know I'm in the right.'

'I swear, David. I just watched. I pulled Zeb off him!'

'Fucking Zeb. I told you he was fucking trouble, Chris. Christ.'

David passes the spliff to Chris. Despite his show of worry and indignation, a feeling of shame and betrayal is what is really stinging David's synapses. The afternoon's events are swirling through his weed-embroidered mind, some lived, some imaginary, but he can't help but feel it has been a day of shame. From his business having to close for the half day; to letting down Tina; to throwing yet another dinner-time tantrum; to leaving Tantasia, fully knowing what Graham was going to do when he'd gone; to almost going out for dinner with those two skanks Billy had brought to the table, to this. David feels ashamed and knows he must rebuild his reputation. For nothing says more about a man than this, and David's reputation goes before him.

'Right. We'll get this sorted. Don't worry, I'll sort this out.'

Saturday 8th November 2003

Saturday 8th November 2003

10.07

David is looking for Graham. He doesn't know why he has to find him or why Graham has to be involved in this at all. Planning to kick someone close to death is for most a stark enough warning but David is a little low on confidence and needs the added threat of someone like Graham behind him. Besides, he has heard Graham bitching about Cod-Eye's crew for a while now – about how they haven't got enough respect to pull off what they're up to and how they are due a fall. This means Graham *must* be up for it. If he needed any extra motivation, that is. Any more motivation than loyalty.

David is meant to be getting a bottle of wine. It is Tina's cousin's son's christening today and he is meant to get a bottle for the do afterwards. He isn't looking forward to it – all screaming kids and flakes of mini sausage roll pastry finding the creases in your best shirt. He doesn't like Tina's family – the McIntees. They are typical Estate bums. Dad Terry is on the sick – never seen in public without his rubber-toed walking stick. Mum Denise has never worked a stroke in her life, apart from an afternoon in a sandwich shop but the latex gloves gave her a terrible rash so she couldn't go back. Older sister has had two kids by different blokes: one eleven, one eight and both hanging diseased and sour on the Estate's grapevine already. If the *Daily Mail* wanted a cover for a piece on The State We Are In, the McIntees' family portrait that hangs in soft focus above their fireplace would be perfect.

The thought of them sends a shiver down his spine. She's so lucky to have him, so lucky that someone can save her from all that.

The air is still, cold and dry, the sky white and the sun like a torch behind tracing paper. David rolls the Beemer slowly down Graham's cul-de-sac – not because of speed bumps or the glare of the fresh tarmac but because Graham's house is approaching and he doesn't want to miss it. This is another of David's recent neuroses. Falling behind. He is continually aware that more and more things are passing him by – his younger brother's steps into manhood, his younger sister's steps onto manhood – all very frightening. Maybe he should go to the doctor. Maybe he's depressed. He's driven right past it.

'Ah bollocks!'

Kishan collects another box of dented Heinz Ravioli tins, only for the bottom to fall through the box he is collecting them in. The tins roll around the floor like bound and blindfolded prisoners trying to escape.

He takes the box and stands it by the entrance to the shop. The Open sign is facing inwards toward him – the first time this has happened at this time of the morning since his Uncle took over the shop. But the damage done yesterday is more serious than anything that has happened before. Worse than when some skinheads from another town sprayed racist graffiti and pushed dog shit through the letterbox. Worse than when the BNP were flyering outside and singing the National Anthem all day. Worse than when it was held up by some local armed robbers, because in that there was at least some sense of justice: they were promptly caught after getting photos of themselves developed posing with sawn off shotguns and the booty from various ram raids and robberies around the city. This was the first time Sukraj knew there could be no justice. He hasn't even told Kishan to save the damaged tins for the bargain bin. He just sits behind the counter watching the window.

Jean is at the counter in Tantasia trying to wangle a freebie by way of a spurious connection to Graham. Tammi is filing her nails. Chantelle is playing with her phone. Toni is having none of it.

'I'm not being funny, but do you have any idea how many people round here reckon they know Graham?'

'Ring him. Go on, ring him'

'I've never seen you with him.'

'Why do you think I'm here? There's fucking loads of

sunbeds on this Estate, I've even got my own at home. I'm here because Graham invited me. I've known him since he was this high. Since he was her age there.'

'Right, I'll ring him up then but he's a very busy man.'

Jenny looks up at her mother and opens and closes her hands. Jean bends down and wipes her mouth. She has been eating chocolate buttons and most of them are smeared across her face and hands. Paul too is about to get a wiping. A Snickers bar is slowly melting in his right hand, as he stands quietly bored. He is uninterested in the barber's station, the products on display, the strange glow coming from the back of the room. Not even him noticing the two older girls have the same face manages to spark his imagination. He hasn't even touched his breakfast.

'He's not there so I'm afraid you'll have to leave Mrs –'

'Wait till he hears about this you pair of... I'll have you sacked, you –'

'Have a nice day.'

David parks the Beemer outside Tantasia and sees Jean strut out with the kids. She doesn't notice him parked there and he is relieved. He'd have felt shit about himself when he backed down from telling her exactly what he thinks. Instead he hangs back in the car a while, slides out a tablet of blue Extra and checks his hair in the rear-view mirror. As she disappears past the Red Lion, he climbs out and locks the door. With no Graham, he can't be sure round here. This part of the Estate is Smackhead Central and one is loitering around now outside. David gives him a look of warning and rolls the sleeve of his Hugo Boss sweater down over his Rolex. He pushes the door, eyes still fixed on the young addict, hearing Toni before he saw her.

'Hiya, David'

'Alright, Toni, Tammi. Alright, Chantelle.'

Chantelle smiles, blushes and gets back to her phone. She has been busy texting Keeley. Apparently Chris didn't show last night and Keeley is really worried if he is okay. Chantelle has told her to stop being wet and asks whether she wants her to go over and bollock him for standing her up. Keeley says no, she doesn't want that. Something was strange about it all. She doesn't think he meant to stand her up. Chantelle tells her all men are the same. Keeley says Chris is different. Chantelle wants to say so is Kish but she hasn't told any of her friends she is meeting him yet. Not because she's embarrassed of him. It's just; it isn't a Chan thing to do, meeting boys. Matchmaker, yes; but to find a match for herself? Instead she just says if you say so and tells Keeley she'll have to text back later because someone is in the shop. She carries on pretending to text while secretly listening to what her sister Toni has to say to David.

'So, back for more are you?'

'Erm, no. Not now, like. Just wondering if you'd seen Graham about?'

'Bloody hell, he's a popular boy today isn't he?'

'Eh?'

'Some old trout trying to get a freebie just left, says she knows him.'

'Yeah. That was my Auntie Jean.'

Toni looks to the floor with embarrassment and Tammi laughs inside. Just as the laugh begins to force a smile onto her face, David tries to put Toni at ease.

'Shit, not like I'm bothered, Toni. She *is* an old trout. She doesn't know Graham from Adam, the scrounging cow. Don't you give her a fucking thing. In fact charge her more, the fucking cheating slag. Do you know what she... so, has Graham been in or what?'

The ferocity of David's rant leaves even Toni quite reticent in answering him and so Tammi finally gets a word in.

'Sorry David. He hasn't been in yet. He'll probably be in later.'

'Right. Shit. Can you tell him I called in?'

'No problem, David. You alright?'

'Yeah, fine.'

'Want a massage or anything?'

'No, no thanks. Love to like, but –. Just let him know I called, yeah? See you later. Tammi, Toni. See you later, Chantelle. Right. Bye.'

David leaves Tantasia in a panic. What is happening to him? What the fuck is going on?

'What the fuck is going on here?'

Sukraj tries to stand up behind the counter but Graham motions for him to stay where he is. Most of the glass has been cleared up now but the rest of the shop is still a mess. Shelves have been broken, magazines litter the floor and a few tins of ravioli still try to scale the perimeter.

'Was it those Nazis again? Fucking bastards. They can fuck right off. Good people on this Estate, they'll get no fucking votes round here.'

'It was not them, Graham.'

'No?'

'No, it was kids. Just kids.'

'Any ideas?'

'No. They wore masks. The pull-down ones.'

'What about the cameras?'

'Nothing. The police say they came out of a blind spot.'

'Fucking hell, eh? All that money they spent on those things and – someone'll know them, Frank. I'll keep my ear to the ground for you. What about you, oi, you. You heard anything?'

Graham looks straight at Kish who can't believe the balls this man has. Graham's face paints a picture of apoplexy – absolute contempt for the bastards that have done this to his local shop. Kish shakes his head.

'This is my nephew, Graham. A good boy.'

'Pleased to meet you, son.'

He holds out his hand, a large gold G catching the strip lighting above and temporarily blinding Kishan before he reaches out to shake it.

'Kishan.'

As he grips Graham's hand, the light above creaks and falls, causing the two to jump back hastily and separate.

'Jesus! Fucking hell. When it don't rain, eh?'

Graham dips into his pocket for his mobile. He takes it out and looks at the multi-coloured screen. There are missed calls, one from Tantasia and many from David.

'Shit. Right, better be off. Bit of business. You need anything, Frank, just give us a bell.'

'Okay, Graham. Thanks.'

'Don't mention it. Nice to meet you, Kishan. Stay out of trouble now, eh?'

Graham winks and flashes that smile.

One of Billy's eyes is stuck closed and his mouth dry. He tries to take in the data of his surroundings, compute and collate some idea of where he is. He hears the bang and wave of the Garage door. He sits up.

Billy is in the back of a Honda Civic – an MOT that was done yesterday morning but had to be kept in for essential repairs that didn't exist. He holds his head and tries to remember why he is here.

He finished business at the whorehouse just after midnight and then went to a Shebeen to drink away some of the shame. Kaya – no – Chanel told him about the place. She said it was open as late as you like and if he mentioned her name there'd be no trouble. After a history lesson from the cab-driver on the way there – about how this part of the city was one of the most sought after addresses around until the blacks moved in; how a postcode here used to mean you were part of the aristocracy and now it meant your job application went straight in the bin and too right, he wouldn't have one of this lot working for him either – Billy remembers getting out of the cab and hearing the throb of some indefinable music thicken the air. This was a part of the city he'd usually avoid at all costs but he wanted to go somewhere illicit, somewhere where the terrible sin he'd just committed would be just another stain on the collective souls in the room. He felt he'd come to the right place.

The Shebeen was in an old terraced house, one of those left alone by the slum clearance scheme for use as immigrant housing. Inside there were Yardies with underage white girls on their arms, a couple of skinny crackheads hitting the pipe on the kitchen floor. Or so Billy imagined as he looked in through the sliding hole in the steel door. A blue light filtered through the green smoke that hung in the air like piss in a swimming pool. Then came the scowling face of an Asian-looking man.

'Sorry, no.'

'But –'

'Good evening, have a nice night. You ain't coming in here.'

'I know –'

'I don't give a fuck *who* you know, I don't know *you* so fuck off.'

Billy turned around and went back into the street. He started to feel scared. The district he was in was notorious. The odds of getting a cab around here were longer than getting stabbed or a bullet. He decided he would chance his luck and walk back into the city centre for a cab, but he had no idea which direction he should go in. He walked out of the avenue and decided to turn left. 'If in doubt, turn left,' he thought and then thought, 'What the fuck am I talking about?' He walked for what seemed like hours before arriving at a Balti House that looked to be closing up. He went up to the glass door and mouthed the words 'are you open?' to a waiter. The waiter looked at his watch before calling to someone who looked like the manager. The manager slid back the bolt and opened the door.

'Can we help you, Sir?'

'I was wondering if it was possible; can I order a taxi from here?'

The manager shook his head.

'We phone only for patrons, Sir.'

Billy thought about it for a minute and decided that the only way out of this was to order some food and then get a taxi. He'd get an onion bahji. A chicken bhuna at the most.

'Can I get some food then?'

'I'm sorry Sir, we are closing –'

'I'll make it worth your while, mate. I'll order the most expensive thing you've got.'

The manager shouted something back to the waiter who sighed and shouted something back to the kitchen.

'Certainly, sir.'

'Right. Do you take credit cards?'

So that's what the smell is in the car. He hears the bang again and steps out, squeezing his way past the driver's seat and out into the Garage. Light is creeping in through the sides of the corrugated door. He walks towards the door, looking down at his Armani shirt and jeans, his brain suddenly springing into life – he will not get away with saying he's working in this get up. David would kill him for sneaking in. He doesn't even know he has a key.

As quickly as he can, he grabs a pair of overalls from the peg by the door and lifts himself into them, almost losing balance as he forces his feet down their legs. There is another bang on the door and he shouts an unintelligible acknowledgement before sliding the door up and open. The instant flood of light blinds him and it takes a few seconds for him to even register the hazy silhouette before him.

'Yeah? Yeah?'

The silhouette shrinks and becomes lucid, vivid, horrific. It is Beth.

David pulls into the Kwik Save car park. The wine will have to be from Liquor Save because he's fucked if he is going to pay Frank's prices across the road. He takes a look to register this thought and sees Kishan carrying a bin bag out. Kishan waves a hello and David nods back sheepishly. He feels bad now – being rumbled going into Kwik Save while young Kishan's shop is only over the road. He decides he's going to need all the good karma he can get so he crosses and heads over to Frank's Food and Booze.

As he approaches he notices the closed sign on the door. He can't remember this shop being closed since he was a kid and the actual Frank had it. But he remembers the day Frank left with absolute clarity. David was in the pub with his dad. His dad often took him to the pub on a Saturday to watch the racing with his friends. They'd send him round to the bookies with their bets. They had a wedge of slips behind the bar so nobody had to leave the pub in order to have an extra flutter on something they might have missed in the morning paper. David became the Bookie Boy, taking the slips round with the old men's money – them giving him twenty pence to put in the pool table if there was any change. If he put a winner on for them, they'd give him a pound and he'd get a bag of scampi fries from the bar as well. The bookies didn't mind a ten year old kid putting the bets on – they all knew who he was and what he was doing. David was something of a child star.

One day, someone came bursting into the vault where his father sat with his friends and shouted that Frank had done a runner from the shop and left the door open. David had never seen a pub empty so quickly. He ran after the men, out of the pub, across the road and into Frank's Food and Booze. They stripped the place – beer, spirits, cigarettes, cigars, tins, bread, chocolate, crisps, milk, butter, cheese, pop – the only things that were left behind were the morning papers. When they got back to the pub, they all had a cigar and David was given as many free goodies as he wanted. He remembers those days. His dad was pissed every night for a month. His dad was a happy-pissed.

David shields his eyes and looks in through the window over the stickers for international phonecards. The place has been devastated. He knocks on the window and Kishan comes out.

'What's happened here, Kish?'

'Some kids. Smashed it up last night.'

'Did they take anything?'

'Nah. Just smashed it, like. Smashed it up.'

There is an uncomfortable pause before David spots the old man behind the counter. He is sat staring at the floor and his shoulders are shaking.

'Is your Uncle alright?'

'Yeah. One of them hit him with a bat but I think he's okay.'

'You sure, he –.'

Kishan turns around. He can't believe his Uncle is

crying. He feels like he should go in and comfort him but he hasn't got the face. He hasn't got the balls that Graham has.

'He's been like that all morning. Best to just leave him alone, you know.'

'Yeah. Any ideas who did it?'

'No. Not a clue.'

'You want to speak to Graham. He'll sort it out.'

'He's just been in.'

David's ears prick up.

'Yeah?'

'Yeah. Said he was going to sort out some business.'

'Right. Shit. Better go. Erm, tell your Uncle I hope he's okay.'

'Yeah. How did Chris get on last night?'

David nearly tells him but then thinks that the poor lad has enough on his plate without having to deal with all that as well.

'Great, yeah, fine. If you need anything, give us a shout, yeah?'

Kish wants to tell David he's meeting a girl tonight as well. That he can get a girl too. But he's embarrassed. It's Chantelle. He'd probably take the piss.

'Yeah. See you later, David.'

David bounds back across the road and into the car. He completely forgets about the wine.

11.46

Chris doesn't wake up covered in sweat. Neither does he wake up gasping or short of breath. Rather, he just wakes up – a shitty mouth, a brain picking its way through the day ahead while trying to make sense of the one just passed, never forgotten, always nagging somewhere at the back, a shadow shifting in the sun, only constant during complete stillness underneath artificial light – the usual morning feeling. Apart from the nagging that Chris needs to remember something.

The surroundings of the bedroom offer no respite as they are now almost tattooed to the environment. Sky blue wallpaper covered with *FHM* and *Maxim* posters of air-brushed beauties, a smiling football team, old tickets of gigs David went to as a youngster – The Charlatans, Oasis, Black Grape – a signed poster of the second Stone Roses album and finally Chris' patch of wall with Jay-Z, Nas, Tupac and a photo of his dad. There are no memories on these walls, just the past.

He gets out of bed and the physical reminders are quick to prick his nervous system. The marks of his beating are still too young to fade out or burn away: head sore as he stands, grazes stretched as he reaches for the ceiling. Outside the sun feels bright through his half-closed eye but a quick glance through the curtains shows him a blotted orb leaking into a pale sky. Nothing's changed apart from the street. It's a Saturday and so the road isn't full or empty, it is a mirage of movement wherever Chris looks. The pavements are finger-painted by the uniform young. They are all walking past Chris' house towards the Archer Centre to hang off balconies; stand around telling the same old stories with different names; coo over babies that so and so's sister has allowed so and so to take out for the day; try to impress boys, try to impress girls; tax some kids who live on the new estate, talk about what happened last night. Friday night. Saturday. Nothing's changed.

The other bed is made and neat but aftershave spices the air. He must have been up early and left without even stirring Chris. What must have been so important during his sleep that he'd miss his brother? David always woke him in the morning, it had been a tradition he'd pretended to hate since David left school and started getting up extra early for a paper and a proper breakfast before work. So Chris walks across the room in his jockey shorts and out onto the landing, the seed of a limp rubbing in his now

223

purple hip but yet to sprout in his gait. Behind him, Marie's door is shut.

She is awake. The ceiling has held her gaze for most of the night as Snowman's cocaine was cut heavily with whiz. Her lips are chapped and chewed, the inside of her cheeks like busted Tootie Frooties. She traces her tongue across the roof of her mouth and thinks of those pictures beamed from Mars that were always on Newsround. Both the drink her mother left her and the one she fetched herself before going to bed are long gone through boredom more than need, drained back in the first few hours of her sleepless night. She remained thirsty, not wanting to raise suspicions during the evening with constant trips to the kitchen and the toilet. Paranoia. So much so that she wouldn't even crush the long hours with cigarettes out of the window. Besides, there was no sign of her lighter anywhere. She must have left it on the –?

She wishes she could remember this and forget the rest but the rest is crystal clear. It seemed like such a good idea at the time. Ah fuck. She knows she should get up – keep active until sleep descends on her in its own time. She has been here before. She's never been a weed girl. Smelled it wafting from the back of the bus or from her brother's room too often for it to have any kind of allure. Marie has always been about chemicals, from the head-shrinking sniff of poppers at ten, to the spine-tingling taste of billy at eleven. From the sick burps of her first pill at twelve, to slow erosion of teenage doubt through charlie – her most recent enterprise. She is now used to the lips, the inside of her cheeks, the dryness, the boredom, the paranoia. What she has never got used to is the shame; a shame that seemed to grow with every step, every year, every morning after. A shame that fills all of the empty hours before real sleep finally comes. And being Saturday, a day of nothing to do, it doesn't matter which hour repose chooses – she has the whole of in-between to sit and think about what she has done. Shit. What if he did turn up at Don Juan's? What if there was a perfectly reasonable explanation? What if everyone was already talking? What if it was already written in a bus shelter? Why did she have to choose –

Snowman. Despite not sleeping a wink he walks confidently to the Archer Centre where he may stand knowing, but say nothing. Not even Zeb. Nope, Snowman's lips are frozen shut.

Last night was a dream come true. Marie was so fine, so out of Snowman's league. She was a strange girl in school, solitary and arrogant, standing out from the crowd by refusing to be part of it. Not gorgeous but there was –. It was well known she went for older lads, went to older clubs, did older drugs, so he couldn't quite believe it when she turned up on the Old Folks'. But she did and she saw something in him. For sure, he had no doubt about it at all. She looked at him sat away from everyone else and said to herself, 'Now there is a man among boys.' And Snowman knew exactly why.

Ever since he said yes to Graham, people have looked at him differently. They don't even know that he has said yes or what he has said yes to but it must be in the way he now carries himself. Must be something about *him*. At the moment he is just stashing the stuff, it'll be Snowman's door they come knocking on, but Graham has said he has big plans. People must be able to see that bright future in Snowman's eyes. It's happening too much. Not only has Marie Carty sucked him off, but Kish and Chris backed him up when he twatted Zeb with the pan – totally backed him, not a doubt in their minds who was in the right. Then Billy asked him to mind Joey, and he understood Zeb's subtlety when trying to leave Kish and Chan alone; all this was a different Snowman to the one he'd had to grow up as. No more clothes from the Discount Sports sale rack for him now, it'll be JD Sports all the way. No more getting knocked off Man United tops – he'd be decked out in the real McCoy with embroidered badges. In fact, he hadn't used his prescription shampoo last night, instead he'd used some Lynx stuff that he'd got from Billy and Beth for Christmas. Perhaps even the dandruff was going!

Snowman stops and tries to calm himself down a little. Like Graham said, it's better he starts small. At the moment he still has a lot to learn. But it is hard to stay clam because he is desperate to learn. He is willing to watch and study and put his all into this because ever since he said yes to Graham –. Yeah, Marie saw it. It wasn't just the drugs.

That's what makes it worse. I mean, what did he think it was – love, respect, lust? Eugh. The very idea of her lusting after Snowman brings a wave of nausea to Marie's ribs.

The boy has nothing going for him. He was just the right one in the right place to give her what she thought she needed. The fact that he was there alone while his friends were all off somewhere else, sat there with cans of Stella like that made him a rich man or something. Fucking Stella. No, she's being unfair now. He's not that bad. A little stupid, gawky, but his dandruff seemed to be getting better. And he had a big dick. In fact it was massive but Marie isn't part of a gang – she has no gossip to spit. So who the fuck is she talking to?

She gets out of bed and heads to the bathroom but the door is locked and she can hear someone brushing their teeth: 'You going to be long?'

'Hmmsn.'

'Fucksake.'

She recognised the mumble as Chris' so she'll be in for a wait. She thinks about going downstairs to watch CD:UK but that would mean facing –

Barbara can hear movement upstairs. They have lived another night and another night she has stayed awake, worrying about her babies.

Chris' face when he walked in brought back so many memories. No, memories aren't right. Deja-vu? Not quite. Premonitions maybe. Everyone she spoke to talked of the violence of youth. Of how the world is a much more dangerous place now than when they were young. But Barbara isn't sure. It feels like she has always been scared. She grew up in a violent household, her mother's face often painted by her father's frustration. Brutality had always been there and that's why Jack made such a difference to her life. He was a gentle man mostly – a breath of peace aired itself about him when he spoke.

They met at a local club, at a time when this town had them, and he asked her to dance to a Motown record. She wishes she could remember the exact one but she can't. She always asked him what it was and now he has gone she has no one to remind her of it. The children remind her of him. Chris and Marie look like him, they walk like him and in their early years she felt the same peace and beauty in them. But as they have grown older, as the world has tightened its grip on them and pulled them away from her, that peace seems to have drifted away like cigarette smoke and left behind an urgency that scares her. The urgency to grow up, to right wrongs, to prove themselves. She has seen this urgency hurtle them forward in her daydreams and nightmares, propel them to disaster and her to loneliness. Just as it did with Jack. And just as the assurance Jack gave her has disappeared, so too has the memory of a peaceful time. The world feels like it has always been this way, even though she knows in her heart that there was a time of peace sandwiched in between her brutal youth and middle age. But with no reminder left, peace has become just like that forgotten Motown record.

She is in the kitchen wondering what to do for breakfast. The cupboards are full, stocked heavily with favourites but she doesn't want to second-guess her children's desires, as that has led to so much conflict in the house recently. She wants a quiet house today. After everything that happened yesterday she needs a quiet house and so decides to wait until they have come downstairs to start on breakfast. Instead she takes her Lambert & Butlers from the top of the fridge and lights a cigarette. Squire is sat quietly in the corner. Even the opening of cupboards hasn't spurred him into action so Barbara calls to him, knowing something is wrong.

'Squire. Come here, boy, let's get you some breakfast, eh.'

At least she knows what –.

He wants to tell the world but knows he mustn't. If too many people find out the trouble would be much worse than a bollocking from a teacher. But Zeb is impatient, excited. Last night he did something special, something out of the ordinary and he loved the buzz, the adrenalin rushing through his veins as he smashed up the shop – tins rolling, shelves snapping, lights crashing. He felt part of something.

Right now he is alone. His mother didn't get home from work until the early hours. He can hear her cough every now and again upstairs so he has the TV on with the sound turned low, waiting for Football Focus. He'd played this morning for school but couldn't concentrate on the game and was substituted just after half time. After the cold space of the football pitch the house seems hot and small, the green settee taking his weight on its edge as he leans forward checking his phone every couple of minutes. Any minute now Snowman will be here. Any minute now Snowman is always here. Good old Snowman. Good old reliable Snowman. Only that he isn't anymore. Snowman is starting to change. What happened yesterday with the pan and his Grandmother's clothes would have been another classic Zeb moment any other time, but something is going on. Zeb feels like he is losing his grip on everything. Has done for a while now. A few things have helped him along, the game of Hairy Arse Furry Balls, beating up Spoonhead with Chris and last night. It was just another occasion where Zeb could say someone was with him, really with him. Another occasion where he could honestly say he was not alone. Unlike now. Yeah, he knows his mum is just upstairs but he is on his own. Has been most of his life. That's why he listens to her cough. I mean, he loves his mother, he has fought too many times to defend her honour for anyone to question that but being up early without her is a part of everyday life. She has never dressed him, never made his breakfast. She does much cooler things like cuts his hair, cuts his friends' hair, listens to really good music, still goes out clubbing, smokes the odd spliff around the house but her work has meant she has never wiped the sleep from his eyes before he went to school. This was what made him so popular at first. He was the only kid in Year One that made their own way to school, wasn't dropped off by their mother in a dodgy tracksuit, or smoking a fag or giving out embarrassing kisses. But that was what he wanted. More than anything else.

'Zeb! Zeb, the door, love.'

He hadn't even heard the knocking.

'Sorry, Mum.'

''Salright baby. You off out then?'

'Yeah. Be back later.'

'Okay son. Love you.'

'You too, Mum.'

He opens the door and Snowman is stood in front of him.

'Fucking hell, mate, took your time.'

'Sorry, Snowman. I was washing my hair. You want to try it sometime.'

Ah. Good old –

Zeb. Could he blame Zeb? He didn't have to follow him did he? He didn't have to stand and watch him kick Spoonhead in the face. But I suppose he did, really. You can't just leave your mates like that, that's what being a mate is all about. Being there for each other. That's why Chris knows tonight is going to be special, because now his brother is involved, his brother who taught him all the rules.

He spits out the toothpaste into the bowl and washes it down the plughole, watching his own blood sluice away. He smiles because he knows that blood doesn't do that. Blood doesn't just drain away and get washed out to sea. It congeals, sticks, hardens, knits us together. Like David. David is sticking to him now, sticking up for him, righting his wrongs because of blood. David is his blood. Blood and David. This is when it comes back. The thing he has been trying to recall since he opened his eyes almost fifteen minutes ago. The nagging hole in his consciousness.

The reason he'd found it so hard to pin down is that it didn't happen yesterday, or the day before, or last night. It happened in a timeless place where past and present and future unites like toothpaste, blood and water. In his sleep. The thing that Chris had been searching to remember was a dream. It was a bad dream. Not one of his usual nightmares – the sloping cliffs and falling, the running and getting nowhere – this was a weird one. He was stood on top of the multistorey car park looking out over the bowling green across the road. The bowling green was full of Old People, nothing unusual there, but it was the way that they peopled the green. The Old People were laid on their backs in black suits, head to toe, shoulder to ankle. Their arms were fixed to their sides like the diagrams of the slaves packed onto ships that Chris had seen in history lessons. And they were completely still. Not a movement or a breath. Next to Chris on the top of the multistory car park were Spoonhead to his left and David to his right. They were stood as he himself was – straight, feet together between two narrow white lines. The whole car park was filled with everyone that Chris knew, all stood in their own white lines. But unlike the bowling green, those in the car park were stood hand in hand. Or rather, hand to hand. They were all playing mercy; the childhood game he played grappling hand to hand with his opponent, trying to bend back their fingers and wrists until they cry mercy. Everyone, right across the car park was doing it, everyone Chris knew. Apart from his mother and Keeley. Barbara wasn't there. Keeley was nowhere to be seen.

Chris' left hand was pinned to Spoonhead's right and David's left to his own. Spoonhead was being managed comfortably, kept in his place easily but he was still only as close to capitulation as Chris. It was stalemate. Neither could win. But David was murdering Chris. Chris could hardly remain standing as his brother's fearsome frame bore down on him but Chris could not give in. He could not plead for compassion. Not from any sense of pride or sibling rivalry but because he couldn't. His vocal chords wouldn't physically form the words. He was desperate to give in, there was nothing he would have rather done, but he couldn't. And the pain was too much. He couldn't take it any longer. He had to do something.

So he did. Without even thinking about it he dragged his brother into his own space before ducking and lifting him fireman-style onto his shoulder. David was light, as if his body were made of balsa wood or that they were in a world without gravity. Spoonhead had let go of Chris to watch and this set off a chain reaction, every member of the car park players letting each other go. Except for David. David still wouldn't let go and now Chris' right hand was somewhere unseen behind his own back at an angle as impossible to comprehend in the real world as David's weightlessness. David carried on applying the pressure so Chris lurched towards the edge of the car park and slung his brother over the edge. The force was clear and David felt heavy again as he was launched from Chris' body. It was only then that David let go. It was only when the floor had disappeared from beneath him, when his weight had returned, when gravity had come home, that his brother let go.

And he fell, he fell straight and hard until he hit the tarmac below.

When Chris looked down to see what he had done, two figures were stood around David's body – the figures of his mother and Keeley. They both looked up at Chris who couldn't meet their eyes and instead tried to stare blankly past the bowling green. But something was happening over there. The Old People were moving. Not as Old People usually moved in Chris' head but serpentine. They slithered and snaked their way down the green and like slugs they stuck to the wall before plopping onto the road. At the front of the crowd, leading the way, was Jack. Chris' father. He wriggled with evil sibilance over to the body of David before carrying it away with the rest of the pack, back to the bowling green. There they lay once more with David at his father's side – not still as Chris had first thought, but dead.

As soon as the bowling green became still again –. As soon as the show was over –. Everyone on the car park placed their hands back together and got back to playing mercy. Even Chris.

Remembering all this makes Chris wonder why he didn't wake up with a gasp. Didn't wake up with a start. He feels guilty for not waking up covered in sweat.

13.14

Chris is being very helpful. So far, since he got up (looking very smart in the Nike sweater Barbara got him last Christmas, some Adidas tracksuit bottoms and those white ankle socks she got a very good deal for at the market), he has made her toast with Nutella (which was naughty, but she ate it to make him happy) two cups of tea, washed up the plate (and the knife but not the cups) and has now offered to go to Old Tommy's for some chips (his shout) for her and Marie. (She couldn't possibly accept, after all he's done.)

'No thank you, love.'

'You sure, Mum? It's no trouble.'

'Positive, love.'

'Marie?'

Marie picks her nose, wondering what Chris is up to.

But not for long, he's hardly worth the effort of figuring out, so she just shakes her head. The look of shock on the faces of her mother and brother has her almost plea a defensive 'Fucking hell, I'm not fucking hungry, alright?' but she manages to control herself. She has decided to stop eating so much.

She thought about it while waiting for Chris to finish brushing his teeth and decided it was the right thing to do. It isn't just the comedown from the whizzy fraction of the cocaine either; it is a conscious decision about her lifestyle. She is getting a bit chubby. Half a stone would probably be enough, a stone at most but she wants to get it sorted before it gets any worse and too difficult.

Not because of pictures of pop stars or models or anything like that – Beyoncé's got massive thighs anyway and J-Lo's arse is huge! – no, she's doing it just for *herself*. Not for anyone else. She wants to be healthy.

A crispy piece of snot is stored underneath one of her longer nails. She pretends to bite her nail in order to transfer the crispy snot into her mouth surreptitiously. The snot tastes of paracetemol. She spits over the side of the sofa.

Billy sits on a reddish-brown display sofa dozing off in a hung-over funk. He is in Ikea. He'd been promising to go there with Beth for weeks and had forgotten that this was the weekend she'd pinned him down to. She could have reminded him last night but then again –.

After Beth whisked him from the Garage and dropped off Joey at her mother's she made him go home to change. Beth insisted that he look right and had already picked out his Levis and a Next sweater that he hated. He had to protest to make it seem less suspicious – 'It's only a furniture shop, it's not like there's a dress code' – but secretly he was glad he'd be able to dispense of the whiffs that hung about him like a cape of culpability. Still, he wasn't wearing that Next shit, and instead changed into a CP Company knit.

He got undressed in the bathroom to avoid Beth seeing last night's togs, stuffing them to the bottom of the washing basket next to some of the cum-stained socks and pants that collected there until he had a clandestine launderette run. He knew he had to rush, as Beth was very excited but everything seemed to move in bullet-time. He stood underneath the shower for five minutes while brushing his teeth, looking out towards the frosted glass of the bathroom window. He wondered what old Sue was up to. It was a Saturday. Her old man would be at the Club in the afternoon watching the races so he was sure she'd be putting on a little patio window show before the 2.35 from Chepstow. Ironing? Hoovering? Cleaning the laminate floor! Yes, that would be the one. Her in that nightie, no knickers on, hands and knees while she wiped the floor with a damp cloth, first bent down facing the window, her floppy tits swinging like two shopping bags after a ten items or less trip, a glance up to let him know she knew he was watching before turning around and putting her nose to the ground to really inspect her floor as the hem of the nightie collected over her hips uncorrected and –.

After watching the semen swirl down the plughole, he stepped out of the shower, dried off, burped up the vapours of last night's curry, sprayed on some L'Eau D'Issey and got changed.

At least she was driving. She wouldn't let him drive her car but he never told her he wouldn't be seen dead behind the wheel of a Mondeo anyway.

Graham sits behind the wheel of his car outside Tantasia. He has already beeped once and he is damned if he is going to do it again. The car is an old Sierra Cosworth 4x4. White. He never wanted the obvious criminal car – the Beemer, The Merc, the Jag. Christ, even those big Volvos had got in on the act recently – no, this car was perfect. It spoke to him of his youth and of goals achieved.

As a youngster he and his friends would play a game called 'No Shares' on their way to school, on their way to town, wherever they went, they would play. Looking back it was a silly game; they would watch the roads for special cars, cars that could be seen as dream cars and the first to see one would claim possession of it by screaming 'No shares on that'. It got so competitive that people would arrive at each other's houses swearing that they had claimed a Lamborghini Countach, or a Ferrari F40 on the way. Of course, they usually were lying but never pulled each other up on these lies as they were lies that *all* wanted to believe. Believing that people believed them wasn't the issue, just saying it was enough. But one day, Graham saw a white Sierra Cosworth 4x4, its oversized spoiler making it look like it had flown straight out of Battlestar Galactica, the engine's throaty vibrato sinking into the tarmac like a rich liquor. And he didn't even claim no shares, he knew

238

he'd have it one day. That he would sit behind the wheel, as he does now and a beautiful girl would climb in the passenger side, as Toni does now.

'Alright, darling?'

'Yeah. Where we going?'

'Surprise.'

Toni can't believe it. He's taking her out for lunch. She's been dying for him to take her out.

Ikea has recently opened and Beth has been dying to check it out. But she didn't want to come in the first few weeks; all those crowds, all those people jumping on the interiors' bandwagon – not real enthusiasts like her. Just driving into the car park sent a shiver down her spine. She'd had the catalogue delivered before the store had even opened and had completely devoured it, post-it noted and dog-eared pages before the free copy arrived in the post as part of the promotional campaign.

Everything she looks at she wants – the sofas, the storage units, the kitchenware. But the bedroom is what she really wants. She wants to change that little girl's bedroom. She has resigned herself to the fact that they are not going to be able to move for a while and she can't face another year with those tie-backs, the trim on the wardrobes, that fucking bedding. The whole scene reminds her of how far she has come since she first dreamt of that room. Growing up, she was very ordinary. She hung out with the girls with the perms and jewellery, the fake tan and boyfriends. One of these older boyfriends was Billy. He hung out with David Carty and Graham Bennett and all that crowd and shit...

everyone wanted them. But being just ordinary – not spectacular like Tina or beautiful like the twins Toni and Tammi, Beth settled for less with Billy. She set her sights lower, knowing full well that the likes of David and Graham were out of her league. She scraped five GCSEs and then sat a couple of GNVQs in Lower Sixth before leaving with her sights on a flat and a kid with Billy. But then something happened. She got a job at a call centre in the city. By accident really – dole wasn't paid out until she was eighteen and she wanted something temporary till then, so she went to a temp agency. When she was shown around on the first day of training it all clicked into place. The water tanks; the coffee machines; the name badges; the computers; the plastic plants; the slogans on the walls; the security passes; the glass lifts. She never thought she'd be in a place like that and as soon as she realised that she could hack it, that they respected her work, that people asked her important questions about their finances and at the click of a button she could read them the information they needed, that after six months she didn't need to even bring up the help files – she could tell them what they needed to know off the top of her head – due to her *product knowledge*, she jumped at the chance of a permanent contract. Now she knows her worth and she is worth much more than that fucking bedroom. It's all marked out in the catalogue, laser-printed on her brain – she can even remember the product numbers of everything she wants. But where is Billy?

'Billy!'

He wakes and tries to work out where he is. What's

this place? Who is that shouting his name? Is it heaven? It's bright and big enough and he feels very comfortable on this... ah, he sees the Ikea tag on the sofa. Bollocks.

Chris can't hide his disappointment. He needs to get out and this would be the perfect excuse, but Barbara picks up on this straight away.

'You stay here. I don't want you going anywhere today, now sit down and make yourself comfy. If you want chips, love, I'll go.'

She gets up from the sofa and looks at herself quickly in the mirror above the mantelpiece to see if that Nutella has somehow already inflicted its terrible damage. She walks through the kitchen, out of the door and turns left up the stairs.

The house has the clean Saturday smell that Barbara loves. Of course, she always keeps on top of it, but on Saturday she has a day off cleaning so she can really enjoy the satisfaction of living in a tidy house. She knows it's always tidy, she knows that she keeps a good house but it is like she becomes detached from what she's creating while she is involved in its creation. All she's thinking about is doing a good job and by the time she's finished, she doesn't even have the will to enjoy that which has taken up her efforts. That's how Barbara feels everyday, except Saturday, when she can just concentrate on *enjoying* it.

She kicks off her slippers and has to stop herself putting them away in the wardrobe. No tidying today. She opens the wardrobe and takes out her trainers. All of Barbara's clothes are stacked neatly on the shelves inside the wardrobe – her few pairs of shoes lined up neatly at the bottom rather than dumped in the cupboard below the stairs with everyone else's. She closes the wardrobe door and sits on the bed, pulling the trainers on and fastening the laces. She's tried to wear them like the kids do – tucking the laces under the soles of her feet – but she just couldn't get used to the discomfort. She'd got used to so many discomforts, perhaps it was her body telling her that the laces were just one too far. She stands up and looks out of the window to gauge whether she'll need a jacket. She decides she'll take something light, just in case, and goes back to the wardrobe – ignoring the slippers – to pull out a silver windcheater. She chuckles to herself – she'll be like those old people soon, wearing their big winter coats on the hottest day of the year *just in case* the weather changes. The caution of old age, she can feel it tapping her shoulder much more regularly than wrinkles or bad joints, she can feel its fingers round her neck most nights.

Graham's knuckles whiten on the steering wheel.

'Urrrrrghhhh....'

Toni swallows and sits up. She has no idea why he insisted on the car park but he knows exactly why – power and perks.

He lights a Benson & Hedges, offers one to her that she refuses, and buttons back up. It's been a good day so far. A very good day. Graham is in demand.

'I'm not due back till two.'

'Yeah? Fucking hell, what do I pay you for?'

They both laugh, hiding their true thoughts until Toni

lets hers spill absent minded from her lips.

'Do you fancy going to Wetherspoons for something to eat?'

Toni can't quite believe she's finally said it. Graham has been fucking her on and off for years but they haven't been out. You know, properly. As a couple. She knows he's busy and whatever but... a girl can't wait forever.

Ever since Tina bagged David back in school, Toni has had her eyes on Graham. He's been A-list since she can remember. Always the one to be seen out and about with for the public paparazzi to snap with gossip and dirty looks and she thinks she deserves a proper outing. Wetherspoons for lunch would be perfect. Everyone is in there Saturday daytime, killing the day before they live it up at night.

'Sorry, love. Fucking mad busy today. I'll bell you tomorrow, yeah?'

'Yeah. Alright.'

There is no fucking way he is taking her to Wetherspoons. Everyone would be there and it's bad for business to be attached. Like those boybands who pretend they're single when they're actually married with a kid. Or queer. Not that Graham is queer. No way. Graham has to look loose, free; as soon as he is seen to settle they'll think he's got soft, taken his eye off the ball. That's what happened with Elisha, his ex-wife.

He'd met her at a shebeen on the other side of the city. She was the younger sister of an infamous bank robber and hung around with a very tasty lot. Graham was there trying to network, he'd heard there might be some driving jobs for him but all he came away with was Elisha. It was weird taking her back home, nobody expected him to be with anyone from out of town, he had claims on all sorts of girls here but he remembers feeling proud as he walked into the Strife with her and introduced her to the boys. That was when he was seventeen. They got married the day after her brother was sent down. Took pictures of himself with his spoils, the daft twat. She had Graham's children. He loved her so much.

Of course, she divorced him because of his shagging around but even when he was sticking his dick into everything that moved, his heart wasn't in it. It was just for show. And everyone could see it, the love in his heart for his wife and his boys – it shone through. Everyone could see the tarts on the side were a sham; that Graham was in love. And that's a dangerous place to be in his game. You show you've got a heart and it becomes easier for your rivals to stop it. He's never going to make that mistake again.

Toni closes the car door behind her. She's not upset. She doesn't care. Even when she hears the engine fade into the bright tarmac behind her.

Chris hears his mother come bombing back down the stairs, ready to ask if he is having his usual, ready to check if Marie is still passing up on chips and batter bits. This makes a mockery of all of Chris' helpfulness. Earlier this morning after having his shower and going back to his room – which itself was a dangerous activity with Marie stomping past him calling him a poof, knocking his bad hip, him calling her a stupid slag – Chris looked at the clothes his mother had placed on his bed: the cheapo Nike sweater and Adidas tracksuit bottoms she'd got him last Christmas. Those dodgy market stall ankle socks. His reflexes had him grab for the sweater first, getting ready to hide it at the back of his drawer, hopefully never to be found again. But this brought an orangey yellow feeling in his kidneys – the same orangey yellow colour as his mother's homemade curry – a feeling he knew only too well as guilt. So he took the sweater and put it on first, then pants and socks and then tracky bottoms. Even if David took the piss out of him for looking like the rest of the 'pondlife' who hang around in the Archer Centre, it would make his mum happy.

'I asked you to do one thing. One fucking thing would have kept me happy.'

David is getting it in the neck for forgetting the wine.

'We can pick some up on the way.'

'That's not the point, David. You always do this.'

'Do what? It's a bottle of wine, Tina.'

'Yeah, but you always let me down.'

He feels the silverblue of rage streak down his neck and into his arm. He could hit her. He could just backhand her now, leave her sprawling across the carpet with half her make-up done. She wouldn't cry at first. She'd look up at him stood there, half naked and glaring at her, his hand still straight like a paddle. Then she'd hold her lip and a tear of blood would fall onto her knuckle. She'd look at it and then she'd look at him. And then she'd cry – her fresh mascara deltas down her face as he left the room to continue getting ready. She wouldn't even mention it at the Christening. She'd tell her family a hilarious story of how she acquired the purple swelling blossoming on her jaw and hold him close and everything would be as it should be. But he can't. As much as he wants to, he can't. All he can do is say he is sorry.

'Sorry, I just –.'

'Quick, over here.'

Billy is still coming around and hasn't caught up with Beth yet. All around him couples are milling about. He wonders if they're as happy and interested in each other as they seem to be. Do they long for a time when things were so much simpler? Do they feel ashamed every time they lie next to each other? Do they still want to do exactly what they've done to feel this shame, over and over and over again because they can see no way out, no way to exist without it? Do they rely on shame to fill them with a sense of duty? Is it only guilt that keeps them together? These old couples nicely dressed and trying to buy young, these first time buyers getting excited about their first house together and marvelling at how a lampshade can make them feel so close. These middle-aged types whose kids have finally left home so they can claim the place for themselves again, rediscover each other. These young student types with frayed jeans and Daddy's credit card, playing at being grown ups. People all around him sharing their lives in a flatpack warehouse. It's fucking awful – he sees his whole future flash before him and he nearly vomits.

Graham feels sick. A sickness he hasn't felt since 1994. He pulls up two doors from his house as his driveway and the adjacent kerbsides are blocked by police cars. What the fuck is going on? He flicks his Benson out of the window and shakily puts another in his mouth before getting out of the car and slamming the door shut. Now he must return to role.

He leans on the bonnet and lights the Benson, enticing one of the policemen over to him. There was no way he was giving them that satisfaction.

'Graham.'

'Alright, boys?'

'You mind if we take a look around?'

'Got a warrant?'

'Yes. But it's polite to ask.'

'You'll have to hang on a minute. I don't smoke in the house. It stinks.'

Graham takes long, slow drags and looks at each of the police officers in turn, trying to psyche them out. He is used to this. He is always coming up against these bastards but they are always shit-scared of him. They're not scared of him pulling a gun and blowing one of them away, of him sending word from his cell to acolytes who would take his revenge out for him on their friends and families. That wasn't Graham's style. They were scared of the humiliation he invariably served upon them. How many times have they pulled him in only to find nothing, to be told in no uncertain terms that he *is* cleverer than them? Every time he meets this lot he can see it in their eyes – the vermilion of fear. But not this time.

Why? He is so careful. He never has anything on the premises. Even with the new enterprise he is about to embark upon, this has always been his essential rule. It is what has made him the fence he is. The goods he has are gone before they become a risk or burden. He can't have made a mistake. What are they fucking grinning about?

He stamps out the Benson and walks towards his door. The policemen flock around him. They've waited a long time for this. He slips the key in the steel door and unlocks the many bolts and mortises. As he walks in, they follow him confidently. He's very worried now. Something is definitely wrong here. He stands aside and watches them in as they all take different rooms. One stands by him to make sure he doesn't run and he expects a long wait.

But it doesn't come. It is over in seconds. One of the policemen appears from the front room with a box, a box almost too big to carry and although he can't see his face, Graham knows the bastard is smiling. The box drops just short of Graham's toes. The policeman folds back the flaps to reveal the contents. Beige Ralph Lauren jackets.

Barbara zips up her silver windcheater. She looks like a runner who has just finished a marathon.

'Right then, usual for you then, Christopher and are you sure you don't want anything, love?'

Marie thinks for a millisecond.

'Yeah. Go on then Mum. Chips and batter bits.'

One last blow out before she starts her diet.

'Right, then. Won't be long. Oh, nearly forgot.'

Barbara races out of the front room and back upstairs

to her room. She picks up the slippers from the floor and puts them neatly next to the space for her trainers. It's the same every Saturday.

She just can't help herself. Jean stares at the flashing lights of the fruit machine, one final twenty pence in her hand: all of the money Barbara gave her to get a cab to the hospital has gone. She puts in the last twenty pence and her eyes light up. Three nudges are flashing. She squats down in order to look up, to see which fruit is ready for harvest. Jenny is in her buggy, crying.

'Shh Jenny, Mummy's working.'

One eye closed, one scans the rolls. Three gold bars, three gold bars, three gold bars! The jackpot, twenty quid is three nudges away. But then her concentration is broken. Jenny is actually speaking.

'Mummy! Mummy! Paul. Look, Paul.'

Jean turns to her left. Paul is on the ground, his eyes closed, the bandage wrapped around his deathly pale head.

'Paul! Paul, love. Paul!'

People in the Arcade are staring at her as she shakes her son. He won't wake up. She looks back at the fruit machine: three gold bars, three nudges. She stands up, her daughter crying, her son lying unconscious, and hits the first nudge.

14.15

Zeb is holding court. He stands, leaning back on the aluminium-tubed balcony rail of the second floor of the Archer Centre. The Centre is teaming with youngsters. All of them with tracksuits and hoodies, knocked-off Evisu and Burberry, trainers and Rockport boots, baseball caps and McDonald's milkshakes. Possible romance and probable violence crackle alongside the static of two-way radios – security staff whispering out of the sides of their mouths, jaws leaned on collarbones like fiddling Neros. They march around, attempting an air of intimidation and authority, but they can't disguise their knowledge that this is an enemy that will never be beaten. This battle has already been lost. Saturday in the Archer Centre belongs to the kids. And the kids on the balcony outside WH Smiths belong to Zeb.

His audience takes deep lungfulls of yet another truish story about Snowman doing something stupid. Zeb has been telling such stories since they got here, stories they have all heard before but pretend to be hearing for the first time, shying away from the truth so that life continues to be fresh, new and exciting. With Snowman and Zeb are Tash and Martine from the Old Folks' last night. Zeb's skill in storytelling has Tash giggling, slapping his arm, looking at him with a tilted head and playing with her large hooped earrings. Martine notices this and silently curses her. The two-faced bitch. All last night she was slagging Zeb off, telling anyone who'd listen that he kissed like a washing machine; that it took him ten minutes to find her fanny and then it felt like he was sanding a piece of wood; that his cock was the size of a disposable lighter when hard. And here she is flirting with him when she knows Martine really likes him. Fucking Tash. Two-faced bitch.

Stupid bitch. David is so angry he nearly says it out loud. Only the fact that he is in a church stops him. Stupid bitch. Having him running around for wine all morning. He expected a moan but shit, she hasn't said a word to him. Still! He's a busy man and at least he's here, isn't he?

David looks around the church but has to fix his eyes on the crucifix in order to quell his rage. It is a very sterile crucifixion scene. The cross is lightly-coloured hardwood, the INRI plaque beautifully curled like a painted scroll, the loincloth Daz white. Jesus himself looks slightly disappointed rather than in the final exhaustive throes of death. The nails *do* pass through his palms, the scar in his side *is* dry and a *trickle* of blood is present beneath the crown of thorns, but the turn of his hips, the crossing of the knees – David decides that Jesus isn't dying for our sins, he is dying for a piss. He knows the church well – St Peters – not because of religious obligation but because this is where everyone receives their quota of sacraments. It is the church where David and Tina will be married. But that doesn't give her the right to give him the grief he's had all morning. It's a Saturday, for Christ's sake. Works his fucking arse off all week and, shit, she works round the corner from Tesco. She could have popped in any time. And what does she want wine for? As if any of her family drink wine? Bet the rest of them have brought cans of Special Brew.

Old Tommy opens the fridge and pulls out two cans of coke. The radio is providing an in-depth post mortem of England's disastrous innings on the final day of the Test. They have to follow on. Usually this would cause Tommy hyperbolic and vocal despair. He has always loved cricket. Was a pace-man as a youngster himself – played for the town team. The town doesn't have a team now. It isn't the kind of place that should have a cricket club. Since that Estate was built.

The real shame of this in Tommy's mind is that it wasn't just about the sporting occasion or the beauty of the game. There was a community aspect to it. It seemed that half the town would turn up to watch them play on a weekend and then afterwards drinks at the bar. Fundraising dances. And without talking himself up, he was a ladies' man back then, something of a catch. Over six feet tall, handsome and well built, respected by the wider community, sole heir to a successful business. A fine cricketer. Hardly a week went by without Tommy's name peppering the back pages of the local paper for his bowling prowess. When he arrived at the bar for drinks after the game, he never paid a penny, as it was his performance that had earned the victory. He was a celebrity in those gentle times but now he doesn't read the local paper as it invariably angers or depresses him. Crime, drugs and old friends filling up the obituaries. He is still tall, still reasonably built, far from ugly, but now his skills, his attributes are not those that gain respect. He is yesterday's man.

'Was coke, wasn't it, Barbara?'

'Yes thanks, Tommy. One proper, one diet.'

It was at the local cricket club that he first met Barbara. She was beautiful: red hair, green eyes, full lips. He stood at the bar drinking a Chester's Mild and was mesmerised. She was younger than him; much younger, but Tommy couldn't approach. This wasn't the kind of woman you have a fling with, Barbara wasn't that kind of girl. She was the kind of girl you married but Tommy didn't have time for that at that moment. He put it off, and put it off and then a fellow who had been moved from the inner city slums to the new Estate in town came along. Jack. He liked Jack. Jack was a decent man and his death was a real tragedy. Back then Tommy felt he was too busy to waste time courting. Now though, time is slipping through his fingers like salt.

Snowman is just biding his time. Despite the bashing he is

getting he still feels unbeatable, and although he can't tell them why (although he wishes he could, he wishes he could just spew the truth all over the Centre floor that makes their trainers squeak) he does have something up his sleeve and is just waiting for Zeb to reach his crescendo so he can bring the little shit back down to earth.

'Eh, Snow, do you remember when you tried to rob your gran?'

Zeb's question is rhetorical. Of course Snowman does. Everybody there does. Even if Tash keeps up the pretence that she doesn't: 'You robbed your gran?'

Snowman just shrugs his shoulders. Fucking two-faced bitch. She wouldn't even look at Zeb last night.

'Telling you. He did. I saw it with my own eyes. Me, him and Chris, we're sat there, yeah, in Snowman's room. We'd been having a bit of a smoke, like and we had the munchies big time. We rang up a pizza to be delivered but no cunt would deliver 'cause... well... for some reason, Snowman is always getting takeaways that he knows nothing about sent to his house, aren't you, Snow?'

Snowman smiles, his tongue between his teeth.

'Anyway, this one place – was it Kebab King? Yeah, Kebab King; they say they'll deliver so we order a proper feast: hawaiian, pepperoni, chicken, onion rings. donner, chicken nuggets, chips, the lot. Even Kish wouldn't have got through it! So we're all sat there, excited, starving, another jay on the go and we realise we haven't got any money. We're like, shit, we'll just have to hide and that, but Snowman's going mad, like, "No way boys, this is the only place in town that still delivers to me, I'm not getting blacklisted by them as well," proper deep, like you do when you've had a smoke. Me and Chris are just puffing away trying not to giggle, so we pass Snowman the last few tokes and he smokes it right down to the roach. He throws the dimp out of his window and then turns round, like swoosh, "I've got it boys. I'll rob my gran." We were like, "Whoa! Snow, don't be at it. You're taking the piss yeah?" and he goes, "Nah. It's perfect, She got her pension today and you know she's fucking blind as a bat. All I've got to do is disguise myself." Anyone got a cig?'

'Yeah, hang on.'

Martine hands Zeb a cigarette and lights it for him, much to the annoyance of Tash. Fucking flirt. She knows Zeb's her man.

'Cheers. So we're there, mashing up his wardrobe, trying to find some old clothes and stuff that he can put on. I mean it, you should have seen the shit we were pulling out. Fucking hell! But he gets to this old bin bag full of his brother's stuff. Shit. None of us had seen anything like it. What did your Billy call it, Snow?'

'His acid house gear.'

'What's acid house?'

'Fuck knows. So Snowman starts putting it on – big baggy hooded top in all mad colours and a big map of Africa on the front, these jeans – massive jeans – black with big red squares on the back, daft fake Ray-Bans you couldn't see through and this floppy hat with, what did it have written on it?'

'Reni is God.'

'Who's Reni?'

'Shut up Tash, let him tell the story.'

'So he's there and he looks even more of a clown than he usually does. But he needs a weapon. So he goes under his bed and pulls out this machete. A real machete. A dirty big fuck-off machete. We were going, "You can't do this Snowman, it's only a fucking pizza," but he's like, "I've got it all planned boys, I'll climb out of my window, down the drainpipe and then smash through the front door." Why? "Because then she'll think it's a proper robber." Well, before we could stop him he's out the window, monkeying down the drainpipe with this machete, like, *chh*, *chh*, but as he slides down – check this out – his hood gets caught on the gas vent. You know them square metal things? He can't move. He tries to get himself free and he loses his grip on the pipe and just swings, screaming but dead quiet so he didn't disturb anyone in the house. The hooded top catches under his armpits – that's the only way he didn't fucking hang himself! Me and Chris were just pissing ourselves.'

At last he takes a drag on the cigarette. The girls are cracking up and Snowman is just about to form a response but Zeb's velocity in these situations is unparalleled.

'Hang on, it gets better. So he's there, swinging from the vent by this hooded top and who pulls up outside? The pizza. The only takeaway that'll still deliver to Snowman's house pulls up outside and there's some loon in sunglasses and mad clothes *with a machete* dangling from an air vent. Never seen anyone move as fast. Poor bastard was in his car and off like *reeeoooowwwww*! By this time, people on the street have noticed and curtains are going. Mums are calling their kids in off the streets! And, *and* someone's called the police.'

'No way.'

'On my mum's life. Me and Chris see the cop car pull up and we shut the window quick so they can't smell the weed. Next thing we hear is the police, megaphone, the lot: "Put the machete down. We understand. Nobody is going to hurt you!"'

'Come on now, Graham. We've got the kid on camera, we've got the box of jackets in your house. Do us a favour and let's get this wrapped up, eh?'

'When my brief gets here, we'll have this wrapped up in no time.'

Graham looks the police officer takes a sip of the water he requested. He has rung his solicitor and left instructions but this show of confidence is exactly that. A *show*.

This could not have happened at a worse time. He has three kids roaming the streets all capable of getting him in an awful lot more trouble than he already is, he just hopes he can get someone to them before the police do. He can't believe he has been so stupid. He's let all of his big plans blind him to the all-important details of his everyday operations and now it looks like the big plans might be over before they began. For some reason, all he can think about is Elisha and the kids. He knows they're well, word gets back to him on the grapevine every now and again.

She's living with a real nobody. Graham is happy about this. The nobody is a carpet fitter: works hard, looks after her and the kids – the kids call him dad. When

Graham heard this he thought it would bother him, but it didn't. Even when he was around, he wasn't around. Not for the kids. He didn't know them, never had them in his life and he still believes you can't miss what you have never had. You can want, you can lust after it but you can't miss or long for it. So why, what, is this orange glow in his chest? What is the feeling swelling up inside? Guilt? Yes. It's guilt. He can't believe he is feeling guilty. Has never felt guilty for anything that he has done but now the feeling glows in his chest and begins to rise into his shoulders, creep up his neck, making it flush red. It envelops his ears.

'No!'

'Sorry Graham?'

'Nothing. I'm fine.'

Graham takes a sip of the water on the table in front of him and tells himself to pull himself together. The colour recedes. His senses cool. He recovers just in time. The show must go on.

The gang on the balcony are only just recovering from Zeb's story. Tash pretends to wipe a tear from her eye while avoiding her mascara and Martine slaps Zeb on the back. Zeb just takes self-congratulatory pulls on a Lambert while blowing the smoke out of the side of his mouth like Popeye. Snowman decides this is the perfect time. Now, just as Zeb has them all in the palm of his hand, he'll tell them about yesterday. About Zeb dressing up in his Gran's clothes.

'Ah, she was a good girl. My Gran. God rest her soul.'

The girls both stop laughing immediately: 'Oh, Snowman.'

'You alright?'

'Yeah. Fine. She was well old, like.'

'Do you miss her?'

'Yeah. But, you've got to get on with it, haven't you. And I've got good mates to help me through. Like Zeb. Did he tell you what he did yesterday?'

Zeb stops smiling. He knows what's coming. He can't believe Snowman is going to do this. He promised he wouldn't say anything. This isn't the way it's supposed to be. It's Snowman who gets shown up, not Zeb. He looks around, desperate for something to distract them from the story. Come on, there has to be something, someone. Ah!

'Chantelle!'

He screams over the side of the balcony to the figure of Chantelle who has just entered the Centre. Snowman curses for a second but then realises that this is even better. He can prolong Zeb's agony and increase his audience. Besides, seeing the panic in Zeb's eyes, hearing the terror in his cry, 'Chantelle! Up here!' –.

Chantelle waddles, huge through the automatic doors and looks up to the balcony to see the midget figure of Zeb waving to her. She stops and thinks about what he could possibly want, before waving back.

Tina gives a little wave to the mother of this child. David has actually forgotten how this child is related to Tina now but he can guess what the future holds for the poor sod.

He looks around the church. Every hangeron imaginable is there: relatives that haven't seen each other for years despite living on the same Estate, turning up for a free buffet. Fair play, everyone has made an effort. Even Tina's dad is wearing a suit and tie, his rubber-toed crutch underneath his arm like that of a returning war veteran. Tina looks stunning. It has to be said. She's wearing a long snug red number that she got with David's credit card. He doesn't know where she got it from – she used the additional card he gave her after months of bugging him. But it looks nice. Very nice. Low cut with long splits up the sides revealing her freshly-sprayed legs. No Tantasia for David's girl. St Tropez all the way. His thoughts turn from slapping her, to fucking her. Or maybe both at the same time.

Concentration is broken by the guitar line to *Fools Gold* by The Stone Roses. The whole congregation turn towards him. Fuck, it's his phone. He digs into his jacket pocket and pulls it out. It is an unknown number but something tells him he must answer despite the glare he is getting from Tina.

'Hello?'

Graham's solicitor is on the other end. He tells David about the situation. Tells him that Graham has been arrested and that David has to get down to Tantasia before the police do. There's something in the safe – Toni and Tammi know the code. He's got to get it. He also has to find three boys: Kish, Zeb and, Snow... yes, Snowman and reassure them. He has to tell them that whatever the police say to them, they can't prove anything and they are to keep their mouths shut. But first, he has to get to Tantasia.

The congregation stands and the organ farts out the opening bars of *Colours of Day*. David runs out of the church as the priest makes his way to the altar.

Chantelle makes her way up the escalator and meets up with the gang. Zeb rushes to greet her.

'Hiya Chan. How's it going? When are you meeting Kish?'

Chantelle, a little startled by Zeb's sudden interest in her life tells him she doesn't know, he hasn't texted yet. Before Snowman can draw, Zeb fires off another question.

'Have you spoke to Keeley? How did her and Chris get on last night? Is she going to see him again?'

Again, Chantelle is taken aback with Zeb's concern and tells him that they didn't meet up. Something came up and Chris didn't show. Tash and Martine jump on this information immediately, pummelling Chan with questions, cursing Chris Carty and who he thinks he is just because of his brother and he should remember it was him who asked her and poor Keeley, she can do better than him anyway and while all this is going on, Zeb and Snowman look at each other, puzzled. What could have stopped Chris from meeting up with Keeley?

'Yeah. Should be. Someone battered our Chris last night but he should be going out. I'll text you when the house is empty. Love you.'

He was sorry and Marie has forgiven him. Things came up at work and he couldn't get away. A little bit of business he has on the side. It was out in the middle of nowhere. He had no signal.

She lies back on her bed and looks at the screen of her phone, checking the last caller and seeing his name flash up every time. He's going to come over later, pick her up when no one is about. It's not that he's ashamed of her, nothing like that, but he knows what people are like. They won't understand the age-difference thing. He understands because if he's honest with her even *he* wouldn't have realised how much love can overcome such matters until he met her. No. He never said it. He never told her. She has to make sure Chris goes out. She has to make sure her mum goes out. Shit! How is she going to get her mum out of the house?

'There we go. *Diet* Coke.'

'It's for Marie. Says she's dieting. I think she's got a boyfriend.'

'Ah, young love, eh?'

'If only we were still young and beautiful eh, Tommy?'

'Some of us are.'

'Oh, leave it out, Tommy. I'm old and tired.'

'You haven't changed a bit.'

Of course, she has. Her skin is sagging now, her red hair is a chemical orange and her eyes... but it doesn't matter. Tommy has to do something about the regret. The regret of all those years. Every day he has missed, longed for something he's never had.

Tommy turns round to the till and looks at the letter by the radio. It has yellowed and worn from the fat, smoke and vinegar of the shop. But he can remember its contents exactly. He closes the till and reaches up for the envelope. Barbara is placing the two cans of coke into the plastic bag with the kids' chips. She slides the bag into the crook of her elbow and opens up her purse to pay for the meal. Tommy turns around, envelope in hand and waves away her money. Before she can offer the traditional protest, Tommy shushes her with a finger on his lips. She can tell by his look he is serious. He places the envelope into the plastic bag. Something has changed.

Snowman feels that the atmosphere might have settled enough for him to strike. But just as he is about to open his mouth, Tash jumps in to hit Chantelle with one more question.

'I thought you said you were working today?'

Chantelle stops and looks at them. She has all the aces today, all the gossip. Every bit of useful information is held by her. This can only be a good omen for tonight. Chantelle is in demand and for the first time in her life, she likes it. She starts her explanation of why she isn't at work. She had been at work, helping Tammi and Toni and then Graham came round to take Toni out for some lunch. (Toni is seeing Golden Graham? Raised eyebrows, impressed tones from all – Snowman's ears prick up.) Well, when Toni got back from lunch she looked upset, went straight into the Nails Room and wouldn't speak to anybody. Chantelle had looked at Tammi and Tammi had shook her head and mouthed that they should leave Toni alone for a minute, and they thought that Graham had done something. About ten minutes later sirens go. Tammi grabs a few things, Toni comes out of the Nails Room and the police barge through the door. (Snowman is really listening now.) They've come with a warrant and ask them to leave the premises and give them the keys. They ask who works here and Tammi says me and Toni, my little sister has just called over with our lunch. The police say Chantelle can go but Toni and Tammi have to stay, they might want to ask them some questions. Tammi says 'Questions about what?' The police look all pleased with themselves and say Graham had been arrested.

Snowman's starts to sweat, his head starts to itch again and dandruff flakes fall onto his shoulders. Invincibility is a short-lived thing. Zeb asks if he is alright but he cannot hear a thing over the buzz of the girls talking. Snowman wipes his face and makes sure: 'Chan.'

She hasn't heard him.

'Chan!'

Still no reply

'*Chantelle*!'

All stop and look at Snowman. He would feel embarrassed if it wasn't for the panic cells multiplying in his body.

'Chantelle. Sorry. Chan. Are you sure. Are you sure they've taken Graham in?'

'Check out Tantasia. The police are stripping the place bare.'

Snowman doesn't tell his story. Snowman doesn't get revenge. Snowman doesn't even say goodbye as he makes a run for home.

David pulls up at Tantasia. The police are stripping the place bare. Sunbeds, chairs, even the partition for the Nails Room is being carried out in the search. Shit. He spots Toni sat in the doorway of the now-derelict butcher's next door and makes his way over.

'What the fuck are they looking for?'

'I don't know. Is it true? Have they got him?'

'Yeah. He's at the station now.'

Toni begins to sob. She can't believe her man is going to prison. She was so close to happiness and then –

'What the fuck are you whingeing for now?'

Tammi has appeared, Lambert in one hand, other hand on hip.

'I hope it's for our jobs and not for him, the no-good bastard. No offence like, David.'

David is taken aback by Tammi's tone. She is livid. It takes him a couple of seconds to ask the question, 'Is there any chance of getting in there do you think?'

'No chance. The place is crawling. Why, you left something?'

Tammi sees despondency sulk across David's face.

'No. No. It doesn't matter.'

What is going on at the moment? Can he do nothing right?

'Do you two need a lift home?'

'Nah. We've got to hang around. The police might want to ask us a few questions.'

'Fair enough. Well. See you later, yeah?'

'See you, David.'

Tammi watches David slope off, cursing under his breath. Poor sod thinks he's let his mate down, left him in the shit. Poor sod, Tammi thinks. She can't do it. She can't be that cruel. She walks over to David's car and he winds down the window. She leans in, kisses him full on the lips and he feels something land in his lap. It's from the safe – the oily rag and its contents. David thanks Tammi and then gives a nod to Jesus.

14.57

Marie is watching Chris. He is playing with his food, sweeping up salt with fat chips, flecks of orange batter bits floating as flotsam on the vinegar. Marie finished her meal within minutes of it landing on the table. Her empty mouth is struggling for words to fill it and instigate conversation.

'So, what are you doing today? Then.'

'Eh?'

Chris has no idea why Marie is taking a sudden interest in his life but knows she must be up to something. He'd usually try to figure out what; work out if there's a chance of some kind of extortion. Today he can't be arsed.

'Out with the boys tonight?'

'Nah.'

Marie thought this would be the easy bit. You usually can't keep Chris in at the weekend but he's acting weird.

Maybe it's because of the fight. Violence is so much a part of the Estate's culture that even when her brother is on the receiving end it rarely interests Marie. Definitely doesn't impress her as it does some of the girls. But it could be a way in.

'You going to find them?'

'What?'

'You know. Whoever did it. Yesterday.'

'Ah. Dunno. Might do.'

Chris eats a chip and then pushes the plate away. He can't eat. His jaw aches as he chews and salt is stinging a loosened tooth at the back of his mouth. But this isn't the reason for his lack of appetite. Keeley is. He should be thinking about tonight's revenge, he might be thinking about the dream he had and its meaning, but instead he is thinking of Keeley.

He takes his phone out of his pocket and remembers her messages. The kisses she left him. He smiles to himself and thinks of texting her. But he can't. He can't do that. He stood her up last night. It wasn't his fault, but he definitely stood her up. She has no idea what has happened to him. She might hate him. The girls will have been all over the news, advising her, filling her head with negativity and thoughts of retribution. He doesn't think Keeley will listen. But he can't be sure. He's still never even spoken to the girl. He thinks about asking Marie what she would do in this situation but she too is looking at her phone, smiling, and if there was one person in the world he doesn't want knowing about his feelings, it is Marie. Who can he ring? Chantelle? He hasn't got Chantelle's number. Why would he? He scrolls through his phone book and arrives at Snowman's number. He might have it. She is in his league. He presses call and rests the phone alongside his sore jaw.

Snowman ignores his phone. He doesn't even look at the screen to see who it is. He is in the house alone, his parents at the Catholic Club, drinking.

He has been sat in his room since he got home, knees tucked into his chest, arse squeaking the loose floorboard that stores his fear. The high of the morning has been replaced with the crushing low of afternoon – like a hang-over that hides until you're sure you've escaped it. His room is still a mess. Usually when nervous, when frightened, he tidies it up to take his mind off things but his fear is so complete it has pinned him to the carpet. He begins to rock so that the squeaking matches the rhythm of his ringtone. He is staying put. He is not moving for anybody.

Chris hangs up.
    'Shit.'
    'Who you ringing?'
    'Snowman.'
    'Oh.'
    Marie glows bright red. She looks at Chris' chips. They are still reasonably warm. No, she can't. She really can't. Instead she takes a sip of her diet coke. Then she puts the coke down. She is dying for a cigarette. Maybe she should work on her mum.

Barbara is sat on her bed. She has put the letter down. It

reeks of vinegar but it is the sweetest smell. She smiles. She can't believe it. She goes to pick up the letter and re-read it when Marie bursts in and flops on the bed.

'Are you okay, darling?'

'Yeah, Mum. Fine. What's that?'

'Bill. Gas Bill. What's the matter?'

'Nothing.'

Both stay silent on Barbara's bed, Barbara sat on the edge, Marie lying down the side. Marie turns onto her front, her black dress just riding up over the cheeks of her arse and revealing the string of her thong. Barbara isn't shocked. She washes them often enough. She looks at the dress again. He daughter is becoming a woman. She already has bigger tits than Barbara. And she always looks so –.

'That's a nice dress, love.'

'Yeah.'

'Where did you get it?'

'Oasis in town. Remember, when I went shopping with Tina.'

Yes, Tina. Lovely girl. He's really done well there, David.

Fuck Tina. Why is he worrying about Tina. He has far more important things to do. David swings the Beemer through the streets of the Estate. He is heading for Billy's house. Even though Billy moved in with Beth ages ago, even though it belonged to Billy's Gran, it's still Billy's house. It always confuses David when Chris tells him he's going over to Snowman's. When David was Chris' age none of the boys went over to Billy's. It was the Old Folks' or nothing. Billy wouldn't have them over, even when it was the done thing to go to your friend's house for tea.

Those were good days. Whenever anyone came over to David's, his mum would cook Alphabites, fried eggs and beans. She hadn't mastered the curry then but everyone would wolf it down and then they'd go over to Tindle Park for a game of football. Some kids would always have booked out the Astroturf there and even at that age David had reputation enough to insist on a game with them. He wasn't even that good but his team always won. Those were definitely the days. But they never went to Billy's for tea. When they knocked on for Billy he would always be ready by the door so he didn't have to invite them. He'd open the door and slide through the smallest gap he could, shouting goodbye to his Nanna and heading out. Like he was ashamed.

Billy is ashamed. Always bloody ashamed. A new bookshelf lies strewn in flatpack parts across a dust sheet in the front room so it doesn't mark the laminate flooring. Now Billy is good with his hands. He's a mechanic for Christ's sake, he can put anything back together, but Beth won't let him near flatpack. Ever since he smashed up a TV stand from MFI in a fit of screwless frustration.

Beth is hopeless. She has every part laid out in neat rows in front of her, the instructions dead centre like a treasure map. She reads instructions, picks up the odd piece of MDF, a washer here, a bolt there, mouths the name of the part she holds and then puts it down again. Billy can see the instructions from where he is stood draining his tea. He'd have this up in five minutes flat. No problem. And this isn't just macho posturing. Billy would. But he can't help. He's not allowed to. Beth will take all afternoon doing this – that is why Joey is still at her mother's. She is under no illusion as to how difficult she finds these tasks, but she will not be beaten and she's damned if she is going to owe Billy a damn thing. Billy slurps the sugary end of his drink.

Chris sips at his coke. Who else would have Chantelle's number? He thinks back to yesterday, to when he asked Keeley out. When the message came through from Kish that she'd said 'Yes' he felt like he did when his Dad came home with his first pair of Air Max.

He'd been lusting after them for so long that the lust had become a strange sort of love. They were Air Max 97, £110, silver. He'd leaf through the catalogue and gaze at them for hours, imagine what he'd look like as he strode into school with them on. One day, his dad came home from the pub with fish, chips and a box.

'Son. I've got you a present.'

If he's honest, Chris wasn't that excited at the time. His dad was always coming home from the pub with presents but usually they were fake football shirts or jeans that would have fitted a giant. But that day he placed a red, black and brown box on the kitchen table, opened it up and put the trainers next to the box. Chris nearly cried. A brand new pair of Nike Air Max 97. He walked over to them and almost felt that he couldn't touch them. He leapt on his dad and hugged him round the waist. Like all trainers, he soon tired of them. Before long he was even wearing them on cross-country.

Kish! Of course, Kish who texted him with the good news, he must have Chantelle's number. Good old Kish. He'll give him a bell. Chris punches in the numbers and puts the phone up to his ear.

'Can I ask you a favour?'

Marie sits up on her mother's bed.

''Course, Mum.'

Barbara feels silly asking, but remembering her wardrobe that morning reminds her it is a necessity.

'Can I borrow a dress off you for tonight?'

Marie is almost speechless. But utterly opportunistic.

'You got a date, Mum?'

Marie leaps forward and lets out a quiet scream, just like the ones she has seen the girls do in *Friends* whenever there is exciting news. She takes her mother's hands and shakes them and Barbara tries to join in but feels a little embarrassed.

'Who is it? Where are you going? When are you going?'

'It's not a date. Me and a friend are going to Don Juan's tonight.'

'Tonight!'

More shaking of hands, more quiet screaming but Marie is working out a strategy and all of this noise and movement is just a distraction to prevent her mother noticing. She's got it. She lets go of her mother's hands and looks down to her left.

'Sorry, Mum. I can't.'

'Oh.'

'You can't lend a dress.'

'Oh. Right.'

She looks back up at her mother and beams.

'You can get on a bus into town, get down to the shops and buy yourself a brand new outfit straight away! Dress, shoes, the lot.'

'Oh, I couldn't.'

''Course you can! What time are you meeting him?'

'Half seven.'

'Well there you go. You've got ages. Go on. You deserve it.'

Barbara finds herself having an epiphany at her daughter's statement.

'You know what, love. I do.'

They hold each other in an excited embrace. Marie looks over her mother's shoulder at the mirrored wardrobe and allows herself a smile.

Snowman fights the urge to look out of the window. Someone has been banging on the door for the last minute or so and shouting his name. He heard proper shoes clapping down the path and nobody he knows wears proper shoes. It could be anyone.

David looks up at Snowman's bedroom window.

'Bollocks.'

He makes his way back to the Beemer and loosens the tie he is still wearing. He stops and looks at himself in the passenger side window. Black trousers, black shoes, crimson shirt and matching tie. He must look like a right twat. He gets in the car and whips the tie from round his neck, tossing it onto the back seat. Who was next on the list? Kish. Yeah, he knows where he lives. Chris used to always go around there for tea.

What did Chris want with Chan's number? He didn't even say how last night went. Kish can't work it out, but he isn't worried. It does remind him though. He has to text Chantelle about tonight. He takes his phone out and taps in the message:

half 7. outside tommys chippy. kish

He presses send and wonders whether he should have put a kiss on the message. No. He did well. He can't fuck this up. He's got to play it cool. He imagines her face when she receives his words. She wants him. It's a weird feeling.

Kish opens his wardrobe and selects his outfit for the evening. White tee-shirt, blue and white Orlando Magic basketball vest, Evisu jeans, blue and white Air Force Ones, flat peaked blue and white Yankees baseball cap. He lays the clothes on his bed in a deflated effigy of himself and smiles, nodding. He's going to look the business. Chantelle won't be able to keep her hands off him.

He goes towards his chest of drawers to pull out some underwear when there is a shout from downstairs. It's his mother. The strange thing is, she isn't shouting in English.

'Alright, hang on, Mum.'

Kishan takes another look at his clothes before stepping onto the landing. Before he reaches the stairs his phone beeps. He takes it out and checks the message:

c u there. x chan.

HA! HA! He knew he was right. Kishan Singh's time has come. He waddles down the stairs and to the door. His mother stands holding it open.

'Kishan Singh?'

'Yeah.'

'We'd like you to come down to the station. We have a few questions to ask you.'

David parks up just short of Kish's house. He sees Kish walk out with two policemen and duck into the back of the car waiting outside.

'*FUCK*!'

He smashes his fists into the dashboard. He's had enough of this chasing around. Who is next? Zeb. The little one with the big gob. Fuck knows where he'll be. Then it dawns on him – how stupid he has been all along. He should have just gone home to Chris. He should have got their numbers and phoned them, told them to meet him. He's David Carty for fuck's sake. He shouldn't be chasing around after these little scroats. Back home to Chris.

Chris opens the back door. There's no point in wasting his leftovers when Squire will have them. He has texted Chan with the details and asked her to pass them on. He couldn't bring himself to speak to Chan directly. He feels better now. Almost optimistic.

Squire bounds over and tucks straight into the chips, the grease from the paper coating his whiskers and the salt causing him to sneeze. Even the thunder of the stairs and Barbara peering into the mirror at the bottom doesn't distract him from the chips.

'I'm just off out, love. Should be back in a couple of hours. Those chips will do you till your tea won't they?'

'Yeah.'

Chris looks at Squire hungrily finishing them.

'If not, there's some of them Chicken Kievs you like in the fridge. Just stick them in the oven.'

'Right.'

Barbara plants a kiss on Chris' cheek.

'Now don't you be going out anywhere. Okay? See you later, love. Ta ra Marie!'

'See you, Mum. Good luck!'

'Thanks.'

Barbara turns back on herself and heads out through the kitchen and towards the front door. As it slams behind her, Marie arrives silently at the back door with Chris.

'She gone?'

Chris jumps.

'Yeah. Where's she going?'

'Town. You got any cigs?'

'Town? What for?'

'I don't fucking know, do I? Come on Chris, I'm gasping.'

'Top of the kitchen cupboards.'

Marie goes into the kitchen and grabs a chair. She had

to ask or Chris would figure out it's her that has been stealing them.

'That'll be thirty pee mind!'

Marie re-appears at the back door next to Chris and blows smoke out over his shoulder.

'Get fucked.'

They both laugh. It's been a long time since they laughed together. Chris feels a strange sense of warmth and love, yes love, for his sister. He puts his arm around her shoulder and she leans on his, smoking. Just as Chris is about to open his mouth, Marie hears a car door slam.

'Shit! It's David'

Marie passes the cigarette to Chris and runs inside and upstairs to her room. The back gate swings open and David spots Chris, cigarette in hand.

'Thought you said you didn't smoke?'

'I –'

'Never mind. You got Zeb's number?'

'Yeah. Phone's on the kitchen table.'

David marches in and picks up Chris' phone. He scrolls backwards one entry and finds Zeb's number.

Zeb is still in the Archer Centre. Or rather, he is on top of the Archer Centre in the now defunct ticket kiosk on the multistory car park. Tash is wanking him off while Martine keeps look out.

'Will you give us a blowjob?'

'No, Zeb. I'm not that kind of girl.'

'Come on. I could do that myself.'

'Want me to stop?'

'No. No. Carry on.'

Zeb winces as Tash continues furiously. He closes his eyes and imagines himself with Tina. She has just finished work and is walking up to the multistory car park when she spots Zeb.

'Hiya Zeb.'

'Hello Tina.'

'You off home?'

'Yeah, you?'

'Yeah. Do you want a lift?'

Now they are in Tina's Ka. She starts the engine and then turns it off. Without saying a word she puts her hand inside Zeb's tracky bottoms and starts to work his dick hard. His cock is a good ten inches long and very thick. She smiles and undoes her WH Smiths shirt to reveal her enormous –

'Urrrgh.'

'Zeb!'

Zeb comes all over Tash's new jeans. He looks away embarrassed and puts his cock away.

'Fucking hell, Zeb. You could have warned me. Shit.'

Martine shouts over to them.

'You finished?'

'Yeah. You got any tissues?'

'You're joking.'

'Little Zeb's had an accident.'

Zeb doesn't know what to say. He is embarrassed. Martine approaches and looks at Zeb in mock disgust.

'Zeb, you dirty bastard.'

His phone rings, saving him from the awkward silence he is too fuzzy to fill. It is an unknown number. Martine passes Tash a tissue and looks at him: 'Zeb.'

'Yeah?'

'You going to answer that?'

Zeb steps out into the car park. There is muttering and laughter behind him. Fucking slags. He answers his phone.

'Zeb. It's David. David Carty.'

Shit. In his post-orgasmic shame, Zeb believes for a second that David has somehow tapped into his imagination and realised what he has just done to his fiancée. Just for a second though. Dickhead.

'Er, David. Hiya.'

'Where are you?'

'Car park.'

'Right. Wait outside Argos and don't move. I'm coming for you.'

'Okay. See you.'

Tash and Martine approach and look at Zeb. Martine does all the talking as Tash dabs at stray spots of jizz.

'Well?'

'What?'

'Who was that?'

'David Carty.'

Tash stops and throws the tissue to the ground.

'Chris Carty's brother?'

'Yeah. So I've got to go. Sorry.'

Tash's tone of voice changes. Suddenly Zeb is the man again.

'It's alright. Give me a bell later, yeah? I'm babysitting for my auntie.'

Martine rolls her eyes. Tash'd just been laughing about

his tiny cock again a second ago. Two-faced bitch.

'Alright.'

Zeb walks off with a strut and stops to straighten out his cock. Yep, I'll see *you* later Tash.

'See you later Marie! Get something on your feet, Chris. We've got an errand to run.'

Chris looks at David. It is not the time to ask questions. He slips on his Reebok Classics and follows his brother to the car. Upstairs, Marie hears two car doors slam. She takes out her phone and types in a message.

all alone. xxx m

She presses send and lies back on her bed.

16.00

Marie is getting fucked from behind. It's his favourite. She doesn't know why. She wants to look at him while they make love and so he has repositioned the mirror as a gesture of good will.

He arrived about half an hour after she texted him so she had time to spruce up a bit – quick shower, bit of make up, perfume. She spent ages putting on a new outfit and he asked her to put on her school uniform. He was still burping up last night, had to call into the twenty-four hour garage for some blue Extras because someone had smashed up Frank's Food and Booze. He kissed her as soon as he walked in and they hardly said a word to each other. It was almost just like in the films. She tore at his clothes, and he told her to watch it – it was CP Company. He carried her upstairs but put her down halfway so she didn't hit her head on the overhanging airing cupboard.

Marie is sure he is a very good fuck. Knows what he is doing. Knows where things live and how to use them. At least she thinks so. It isn't common knowledge but she was a virgin until last Thursday – underneath the security lamp behind Club Eternity. It wasn't how she'd imagined it to happen but it was perfect in a way. She was a little bit high, the loose crush of cocaine falling down the back of her throat, the left side of her face quite numb. It was also the first time she'd done coke. Everyone in school thought she'd been fucking old, drinking expensive, drugging posh for years but truth be told she just hated all the fuckers at school and this was a way to make sure they left her alone. Now though, she was walking the walk.

'Get on top.'

He collapses onto the bed, red in the face and his centre parting flat with sweat. He can't come. He's been banging away indiscriminately for ages and nothing's doing. She is shit. Last Thursday he thought it was just the beer, just the charlie, was sure that in the right frame of mind, blood clean, he'd be able to do it, but he has fucked himself into ear-buzzing exhaustion and gets her to climb on top to give him time to recover.

She looks at his cock, the slippery condom stretched down its length. It reminds her of a newborn lamb, for some reason. Earlier he'd asked her to put it on for him and she swelled with pride when she managed it with ease. She is a little nervous now, though. She's never been on top but has seen how it is done on the DVDs David sometimes leaves lying around. She grabs his cock at the base and eases him in, groaning because he seems to like it when she does that. She slowly starts to rock, his cock throbbing intermittently as she does. His hands are on her tits, cupping them, his thumbs pressing her nipples. She groans again and looks at his face but he is looking into the mirror.

David speaks into the rear-view mirror. Zeb and Chris are sat in the back, Zeb playing with the armrest nervously as David delivers him the word of Graham. All Zeb can think about is his wank fantasy over Tina and whether David really can see into his mind.

'Are you fucking listening?'

'Shit. Yeah, yeah. Sorry.'

'Good, because it would really get on my tits if a little shit with ears as big as yours was ignoring me. I'd be tempted to bite them off.'

'No, David. I heard. Sit tight, say nothing.'

'Good. Now fuck off.'

Zeb gets out of the car and heads back towards the Archer Centre. He feels like shit. What should he do? Yes, go and see Snowman. That always cheers him up. David and Chris watch as he breaks into a jog towards his destination.

'He's a fucking liability that kid, Chris. You want to stay away from him.'

'Yeah.'

Chris has no idea what David has just said to him as he stares out of the window. He can see the tops of the trees in the town's small wooded area being gripped by the concrete fingers of the encircling roads like a new bride eager to toss a bouquet over her head. David swings the

Beemer into reverse and out of the car park.

In front of the woods is the large detergent factory that employs many unlucky locals. Chris remembers one summer a few years ago. He must have been eight or nine. It was one of the first hot days of the holidays and so kids were stripped to the waist for water fights. Washing up liquid had been poured away down the drains so that the empty vessels could be made into homemade water pistols. It was the same every year. But the year diffusing through Chris' memory had an added treat. It was the year of the Summer Snow.

As the kids ran around the streets, soaking each other, water bombing passing cars and older girls, a truly magical thing happened. Snow started to fall. Great white clusters collected on the hot bonnets of cars, drifted up against walls and suddenly the attention of the kids switched to the only thing more exciting than a water fight: a snowball fight. It was a surreal scene, half-naked children frolicking in the snow whilst the sun striped their shoulders and peeled their noses.

It was a powder that had escaped from the detergent factory. Parents were soon out, calling their kids in, sitting them down and watching for signs of symptoms, fingers ready on the speed-dial buttons for compensation claim lines. But the next day an article in the paper revealed the powder was harmless and the plant was simply to be fined for the mess that had been caused. A collective sigh of disappointment blew the powder from the streets of the Estate.

Snowman sits on the stash of cocaine. He too is reminded of the Summer Snow. His disappointment double that of the others, for it was a few days later that his chronic dermatitis started. His parents were too drunk to make a connection, his Gran too honest.

For the first time since he fled the Archer Centre, Snowman allows himself a smile. The irony of his nickname and his incipient if seemingly stillborn career has only just dawned on him. No doubt they'd have got him one day anyway just because of that. Because getting caught is part of Snowman's make up. He should have known this would happen from the start.

Resignation lifts him from the carpet. What can he really do about this? Nothing. He is beginning to settle comfortably into despondency. It's a part of the culture on the Estate. He pulls back the carpet and lifts the floorboard that houses the stash. He takes out the cocaine and smiles. It looks exactly like the Summer Snow. He shakes his head at how this stuff could possibly be worth the price it is. Sure, it was a good buzz but addiction is something Snowman has never got his head around. And it isn't just through watching the way his parents behave – nothing as predictable as that. Snowman just can't imagine relying on something. So he decides to give it another go to see if he'll get what all the fuss is about.

He pops a bag and takes a pinch of the powder before sprinkling it on the top of his portable TV. He takes out his wallet. The only card in there is his National Insurance Number that arrived over the summer. It'll be the first time he's used it. He presses the card flat onto the pile of powder and crushes out the bigger crumbs. He picks up the card, taps it on the TV top then licks off the residue stuck to its underside, wincing at the taste, a small grin appearing as his mouth begins to drain of feeling. It reminds him of last night. He chops the powder with the edge of the card, trying not to be too hasty, savouring each tiny movement as the signals to his hand echo through his brain and trigger off more bursts of memory, more synaptic souvenir snapshots. He parts the now dust-sized particles into two piles and begins to stretch them out into a wispy number eleven. When he is happy that they resemble the girth and length of last night's happiness he licks the edge of the card – eyes closed, tongue soft and slow, a tingle in his groin. He then looks around his room for some paper and finds a school exercise book on the floor. History. He rips out a page from the back covered in the names of his friends and doodles, then carefully tears the page into the size of a banknote and rolls it into a tube. He breathes in deep, sniffs up to clear his nostrils of mucus and then bows before the powder, pressing the paper tube to his right nostril and snorting the line on the left. He leans his head back, sniffing twice and swallowing before repeating the trick with the solitary comet tail. Again he leans back, opens his eyes and then closes them to allow the feeling to rise from his shoulders upwards. He waits for the still snatches of memory to flick into life, the frame rate to increase until he is watching a movie but instead he has a void, a black hole. He feels empty, alone and realises that he is missing something. Someone. It's his grandmother. He can't recall her face, can't remember the sensation of having her hold him as a young child, play horsy on her knee – and they've taken the canal turn, the chair coming up and ohhhh he's over and he's building up speed for the next fence, nearly went that time and next comes Beecher's Brook and he's all over the place how will he stay on?

He stands up, stretches his shoulders and shadow boxes. He can't shake off the need for remembering. Nanna's chips, always made fresh, little black bits peppering them. He needs to feel her again. The thick blue veins snaking her ankles like the expensive cheese she bought at Christmas. He stomps out of his room and heads for hers, stopping at the door to feel a rush of cocaine sprint the nape of his neck. The smell: the stale old smell of love. He opens the door.

Chris slams the door of the Beemer behind him.

'Fucking careful, dickhead. Collector's item, this.'

'Sorry, David.'

'Right. I'm off to find Billy. I'll pick you up at about half seven and we'll go and find Cod-Eye. Drinks in the Longbow, don't he?'

'Yeah.'

'Well that's where we'll go. Show the cunt not to mess with a Carty, right?'

'Right.'

David rolls off and Chris approaches the back gate. He stops for a second. He doesn't want to go home just yet. He wants to see Mr Buckley. Walking around to the front of the houses he sees that his sister's light is on but the curtains are drawn. The lazy bitch. He strides past his own door and up to his neighbour's old wooden door. He presses the bell but isn't sure if it made any noise and so flicks the brass letterbox three times.

'Shhh.'
   'What?'
   'Shhh! Right. It's okay. Sorry.'
   'Fuck. Tell you what, move the mirror behind you.'
   Marie reaches for the mirror and rests it beside her bedroom door. She was sure she heard David's car door slam, certain she recognised Chris' footsteps outside but she puts it down to her nervousness in the situation. He was just thinking he might be getting there when she stopped and shushed him and now has to start all over again. He's tried it with his eyes closed and now thinks a little more visual stimulation might help.
   'That alright?'
   'Hang on.'
   He twists to the left so he can see past what now feels like her quite considerably-sized body. She's going to have to be careful or she'll turn into a right fat bitch. He checks the angle of the mirror, his dick buried deep, balls hanging red and low. He tries a couple of slow test thrusts and she groans.
   'Yeah. That's fine.'

Chris sits down in Mr Buckley's front room after reassuring him that sweetener will be okay in his cup of tea. Mr Buckley shouts in from the kitchen: 'Diabetes see. And I don't get too many visitors so I don't bother with sugar no more. Still like it milky then, Christopher?'

'Yes. Please, Mr Buckley.'

No one ever calls him Christopher anymore. Not even the teachers at school. His mum does when he's pissed her off but Mr Buckley always calls him Christopher. The last person to do that was his Dad.

He looks around the front room. It is the same size as his own house but looks much smaller. The walls are covered with wallpaper, yellowed by liquorice roll-ups, and a large mahogany fireplace lies bare in the chimneybreast. The large, charcoal stand houses a tiny portable TV, an ancient one with two dials on the front, one for volume and one for the channel. The test match flickers on the screen in black and white with the sound down: England have had to follow on.

'Getting beat again are they, Mr Buckley?'

''Fraid so, Christopher. Some things never change, eh?'

This front room hasn't changed at all. Same scratchy yellow and brown settee, same pictures on the wall – New York workmen sleeping on the skeleton of a skyscraper, a woman with a blue face. One thing is missing, though. The old mahogany coffee table that held the antique scales Chris used to like playing with. In its place is an old pasting table with collapsible legs.

Mr Buckley totters back into the living room, trying not to spill any tea from the mugs held shakily in each hand. He places them on the pasting table and catches his knees before settling into his armchair with a cough. He takes a tin from the pocket of his grey cardigan, opens it and lifts a pinch of dark tobacco and a black cigarette paper.

'Yes. Got to be careful with the old food now, but at least I've still got one thing to keep me going. You want one?'

Chris shakes his head and feels a slight sense of awe as Mr Buckley's vibrating hands smooth a perfect cigarette from its raw materials in one clean press. He leans over to pick up his mug of tea and rests it on his lap.

'Good. Filthy habit.'

'Things been good then?'

'Aye, not bad. Went to Lourdes a couple of weeks ago. You know, with the church.'

Chris wasn't aware that Mr Buckley was religious. Maybe it was with him getting older, more frightened. His Nanna Dee Dee was the same. Got all pious in her old age when the light at the end of the tunnel burned too bright to see the entrance.

'Went there to see if it could do anything for my arthritis. And did it? Did it balls. Load of bollocks.'

Mr Buckley grins and Chris breaks into laughter. Mr Buckley has always had a filthy mouth. He stops as the laughter pains his ribs.

'You alright, son?'

'Yeah. Fell over.'

'Right. Not been beaten up then, by the shits that live around here?'

Chris looks ashamed that Mr Buckley has seen through his excuse so easily. He takes a slurp of his tea.

'Bastards, they are. While I was in Lourdes, my young

nephew Martin, you know our Martin? Martin Davies? No. Well lovely kid he is, he looked after the place for us. When I got back, he's sat in the kitchen, sobbing his heart out and yabbering on, saying sorry. Once I'd calmed him down, it turned out some lads had come around. There were a few of them like, and they'd been drinking and wouldn't leave. Battered him, they did. Kicked him in and nicked my table. Took my telly. They even took them old scales I got from my dad. Probably the same lot kicked him down the stairs in the flats that time. Poor kid. He couldn't say who'd done it in case they came after him, he said if I reported it to the police I couldn't say he'd been watching the house 'cause they'd come over asking him questions. So I didn't. I told them I'd just been burgled, plain and simple.'

Mr Buckley takes a puff of his roll-up and blows blue smoke skyward. The silver of his glasses glints in the sunlight dripping through the partially-closed blinds. Chris is bent with shame. He knows Martin Davies. He's a local smackhead, one of Graham's best. But he can't crush Mr Buckley with the news that he had just been burgled. Plain and simple. By his nephew.

'Shame. Nice table, that.'

'Yes. But all things must pass, Christopher. You know that more than most.'

Chris looks into his tea. There is an oily film on the surface. The spare mug has obviously not been used for a long time.

'You have to remember the good, see? That old table served me for years. I kept it polished up, not a scratch on it. It held my things, some good memories in that table.

291

That's what you have to remember. It's like the Dandelion Field. Do you remember the Dandelion Field?'

For the past four years, Chris hadn't, but now the memory rose from the warm tea in his belly and back into his mind. The Dandelion Field was exactly that: a field full of dandelions at the far edge of the tiny woodland behind the detergent factory. Not long after Chris began helping Mr Buckley with his pigeons, the old man took him out there to see the field. At first, Chris did it to humour him. The thought of a field full of dandelions did little to fire his imagination but when they arrived he was completely speechless. He'd expected a field of yellows and orange but what he found was the grey mist of a sea of dying dandelions, their white heads perching on their stems and forming a cloud stretching across the field for what seemed like a mile. Chris' immediate instinct was to run into them, feel their softness around him, watch the fluff float into the air as they did when he was a small boy and blew them in his Nanna Dee Dee's back garden to tell him the time. But sensing the boy's desire, Mr Buckley simply placed a hand on his shoulder – a silent signal to stay put just as the shake of a shovel brought his pigeons home.

'Yeah. The Field.'

'Well just think. That field only looked like that for the shortest of times. The dandelions were only that beautiful when it seemed like they were about to die. But in passing like that, they allowed the likes of you and me to enjoy that amazing sight. Someone is enjoying that table now, and while they can enjoy its beauty, I can still enjoy the time I spent with it in here.'

Mr Buckley taps his temple and some ash falls onto the sleeve of his cardigan.

'Time can't touch that. Time stands still in there for as long as you want it.'

David checks his watch. He has got so much to sort out but he needs to rest a while. He hasn't been in the house since he woke up. He needs to get home and relax before tonight.

He turns the Beemer around before he reaches Billy's estate. Billy can wait. He can count on Billy despite everything. He checks his phone. No word from Graham – must still be being questioned – but no worries, Graham knows what he is doing. He'll be out for tonight. Tina hasn't called either. He feels a bit sorry about Tina. Today was important to her but she's got to understand that shit happens. David is a loyal man but his loyalties don't just lie with her, he has family to take care of. He is the man of the house. He thinks of giving her a call but he needs to relax and he knows she'll just wind him up. He's just got to get back to the house.

Back at the house, Marie is on her knees. He is sat on the edge of the bed as her blonde head bobs in the mirror. The sex wasn't working, he just couldn't come. She just wasn't good enough so he told her to suck his cock.

She was disappointed. She didn't know what she was doing wrong. She wished he'd just tell her. As she knelt down beside the bed she was reminded of last night and it made her gag before she'd even put his cock in her mouth. But this wasn't Snowman, this was the man she loved and so she overcame it quickly. She had to. Besides, she knew she was good at this. She could feel his thighs tighten, his calf muscles tense and his toes curl. He was relieved. He could feel the tightness around the base of his cock that signalled impending orgasm.

'That's good, mmm yes, that's it.'

She grows in confidence, getting lost in satisfying her man. She squeezes his balls instinctively and he groans, one leg lifted from the floor.

'Yes, yes, yes!'

He feels his cock throb, the cheeks of his arse tighten and his head tilts back as he explodes into her mouth. She carries on sucking, drinking him dry and he flops his head forward to check out his image in the mirror. He gives himself a wink as he pulls her head away from his dick. He closes his eyes, leans his head back again and smiles before collapsing backwards onto the bed.

'Was that good?'

'Fucking amazing, darling.'

She stands up and walks over to her window to grab her music box and her stash of cigarettes. She takes them out and offers him one but he opens one eye, closes it and shakes his head. She looks at herself in the mirror in front of the door, her figure brushed with sweat, the edge of her mouth red and wet. She wipes it with her duvet and climbs next to her man, leaning on one elbow, the hand holding the cigarette across his chest. She looks at him. She knows she loves him, she has never been so sure of anything in her life other than the fact that he loves her too. But she needs to hear it, needs to hear him tell her. She knows she should wait, that he'll tell her when he's ready, that if she pushes him it could piss him off and push him away, but her impatience has her mind form the question, the question she is dying to hear answered.

'Billy?'

Billy shoots upright and Marie turns around sharply. That was what she wanted to say but that wasn't her voice.

'What the fuck!'

It is David's.

'You fucking n –'

'David, no!'

'David mate, it isn't –'

David picks up the mirror by the door and brings it crashing down on Billy's naked body. It smashes on his shoulder and he screams in pain. Marie tries to jump on her brother but he throws her off and grabs Billy by the hair and begins to pound his head into the wall. Billy's arms thrash but he can offer little resistance as his face is crushed into a poster of Usher, blood pouring from his nose and smeared across his shoulder and arm. Marie gets up and grabs her music box from the window ledge. She raises it above her head and breaks it across David's crown. He grunts in recognition, turns around and grabs her wrists, forcing her out of the door and out onto the landing. He throws her into his bedroom and fastens the padlock on the door so she cannot escape. Foolishly, Billy has grabbed his clothes and tried to make a dash for it but David grabs him and throws him down the stairs. Both men are making noises, shouting unintelligible utterances as David jogs down the stairs before laying a boot into Billy's crumpled body at the bottom. Billy coughs blood and curls into a ball as David kicks and screams, 'You fucking pervert, you fucking nonce, she's my fucking sister, my fucking baby sister!'

Next door, Chris hears the commotion coming from his house and runs out of Mr Buckley's front room with apologies. He runs through the kitchen and out into the yard, leaving Mr Buckley's back gate swinging as he opens his own just in time to see Billy, naked – penis still semi-erect – come tumbling out of the back door, covered in snot and blood and clutching a pile of clothes. Billy half-runs past the stunned Chris and out into the street, not stopping until he disappears onto the main road, shooting across without looking to see if traffic is coming, cars screeching and beeping as he gallops, hobbling and crying.

The figure of David disappears into the kitchen as the back door swings off its hinges in the aftermath of events. Chris approaches the door and stops.

Zeb stands outside Snowman's house. He is a little out of breath after jogging all the way. He has knocked and rang and is now shouting.

'Snow! Snow! It's Zeb. Open the door, you dickhead!'

Snowman is sat on his grandmother's bed, crying. They are tears of happiness. Happiness at the memories he has, memories triggered by the smell of her things through his numb nostrils. His snot is sour as he sniffs up to clear his nose.

'Snow! Answer the fucking door. It's important. I've got news. About Graham –.'

He'd forgotten about Graham. The coke and the nostalgia, being here with his grandmother's things had soothed away his worries but that name brings it all rushing back and he stands up to attention.

'You've got ten seconds, Snow, and I'm going. One, two –.'

Zeb stands outside, counting. He is sure Snowman is here – where else would he go? – and he needs him. Only Snowman could make him feel better.

'Seven, eight....'

Snowman hurtles down the stairs, almost falling as he leaps for the door latch and opens it on ten.

'What? What's up?'

Zeb looks at Snowman aghast.

'Well? Tell me! What do you know? What do you know?'

Zeb says nothing. It is then that Snowman realises what is wrong. He is wearing his dead grandmother's clothes.

16.30

Chris is brewing up. His sister has stopped banging on the door upstairs and he imagines her sitting with her back to the door, sobbing, just like a character from Hollyoaks. He can hear his brother crying in the living room and so he is making the tea extra strong so that David can get himself straightened and not have to face the embarrassment of being seen in such a state.

Chris' tea bag floats towards the top of the cup, orange-brown leaking through the perforations and swirling in the hot water. In David's cup, a stained spoon pins the teabag to the bottom of the mug – his favourite mug, his Knight Rider mug. When he hears the snivelling stop, the cough and clearing of the throat, the mumbles of pulling himself together, Chris sighs the fridge door open and takes out the milk with relief. He adds the milk and with the spoon squeezes the last of the life out of the teabags and plops them in the stainless-steel sink. He takes out the sugar bowl, dips in the damp spoon and stirs two sugars into his tea and three into David's. Brown spots dampen the white crystals in the sugar bowl.

The commotion of minutes ago has scared Squire out into the yard, and he's staying. Chris picks up the two brews and pushes the living room door open. He passes the Knight Rider mug to David.

'Cheers.'

Snowman takes the cup of tea from Zeb. He has changed out of his grandmother's clothes and into an old Adidas T-shirt and shorts. Zeb sits on the settee, forty-five degrees to Snowman, slurps the tip of the brew and then places it on a coaster on one of the tables taken from its nest. He remembers Tash's parting words and looks at his friend. He takes out his phone and hits the write message page:

wont b out 2nite. busy

He searches out Tash's number and presses send before turning his phone off.

A strange feeling wraps itself around his shoulders; warm, clay-coloured, and Zeb at last recognises this feeling as compassion. He looks at his friend Snowman sat in the chair, sniffing continuously and trying to shake off the shame.

'It's alright, mate. I won't say a word.'

Zeb's show of mercy lifts Snowman's head.

'Fancy a game of Pro Evo?'

'Yeah, that'd be great, cheers.'

Chris goes back into the kitchen to fetch a cigarette for his brother. He brings it back in with an ashtray and David lights it, his fingers shaking like Mr Buckley's. He doesn't ask him what happened. He knows, and having to explain it again would be too much.

It was having to explain everything that led David to be like this. The shame of explanation. The shame of finding his own father dead in the yard after falling off the roof trying to put up some Christmas lights. It made Dad sound like such a fool. Nobody could completely repress the laughter that such a death invoked and still David had to inform everyone because all of a sudden he was man of the house.

'How was the christening?'

'Nice, you know. I think. I had to go.'

'St Peter's, was it?'

'Yeah.'

David takes a long pull on his cigarette. All thoughts of revenge have left his mind. Fuck Cod-Eye, fuck Billy, fuck Graham. He's been so busy making sure his stock stayed high with the likes of them that he has devalued himself. His mother, his brother, his fiancée, his sister. While he was concentrating on being a man he allowed that to happen to his sister. Well, no more. Chris can see it in his eyes. It is a defeated look, but an honourable defeat. David stands up.

'I'm just going to get something from the car.'

Chris follows his brother out into the kitchen to collect the third brew – his sister's. He takes it upstairs and leaves it by the door to his sister's room before going in. He picks up the mirror from the floor and collects all the broken shards of glass he can see. He takes the bloodstained Usher poster from the wall and puts it in the bin with the glass. He picks up the broken music box from the bed and thinks of putting it back on the window ledge, thinks it might be repairable, but he remembers what Mr Buckley said about things passing and puts it in the bin with the rest of the rubbish. But some things he can't let drift, some things are too good to pass.

He puts his hand in his pocket and takes out his phone, flashing up the write message screen. He shakes his head and goes back to the phone book and brings up Keeley's number. There is no hesitation, he's not scared anymore – scared of hoping. He presses call and puts the phone to his ear.

'Hello.'

'Keeley?'

'Hiya, Chris. What's up?'

'What are you doing now?'

'What?'

'Now. Are you doing anything special?'

'No. Why?'

'Can you get down to the woods?'

'The woods, yeah.'

'The entrance by the factory. Meet me there in ten minutes. I've got something to show you.'

'What is it?'

'It's a surprise. Meet me there, yeah?'

'Okay.'

'Nice one. See you in ten.'

He puts his phone back into his pocket, takes his sister's dressing gown from the hook on the back of the door, and collects her slippers from under the dressing table. He walks out of the room, folds her dressing gown over the banister on the landing and opens the padlock with his free hand.

'Marie?'

She doesn't answer. He holds the dressing gown through the gap in the door and she takes it. She puts it on.

'Come in.'

Billy walks into the hallway, bruised, blood still crusted around his nose. Beth doesn't ask what happened. Joey runs to his dad and jumps into his arms and Billy winces. He thinks he might have broken a rib.

'Better get you a cup of tea.'

Beth goes into the kitchen and starts to brew up. She looks skywards and takes a piece of extra absorbent kitchen towel, levelling its edges with her eyelids and dabbing the moisture so as to not smudge her mascara. He's going to have to go. This is the end. But he's not going until he's fixed up her new bookshelf.

She squeezes out the teabag with a spoon and puts it in the swing bin before taking a deep breath and going back into the front room. Billy is sat with Joey on his lap. The Ikea bits are still spread out across the laminate floor on their dust sheet. Beth hands Billy the tea.

'There we go.'

Kish collects his belt and his shoelaces and mobile phone from the officer staffing the desk at the front of the station.

'Thanks.'

His mother is in the waiting area. She won't look at him. He sits next to her on the bench and begins to re-lace his Air Force Ones. They sit in complete silence as he does up his laces.

When he has finished, his mother stands and he follows her out to the front of the station. His father is sat waiting in his taxi, his black turban visible from the other side of the road. There is little traffic on the Main Road and so they walk across. Kish opens the car door for his mother and she ignores him. His father doesn't say a word. Pound coins are all over the car.

He'd only been in the cell for a short time. Questioning didn't take too long. He told them everything – where he got the jackets, Graham's plans, his Uncle's shop. He didn't tell them Zeb was with him and they charged him with receiving stolen goods. His Uncle refused to press charges.

They told him Graham was being kept for further questioning, that they could keep him for twenty-four hours before they charged him and that he would be going to jail. They told Kish next time he would too.

He takes out his phone and punches in a message:

wont b out 2nite. grounded. sorry xxxKish

Graham punches the cell wall. He has been stripped of his

golden armour. He runs his hot palms over his hair and cries.

Chantelle pulls the straighteners through her hair and okays the message she has just received on her phone. She smiles. Three kisses.

Chris kisses his sister's forehead. She sits on David's bed in her dressing gown.

'You better put these on. There still might be glass on the carpet.'

'Is Mum back yet?'

'No. Where's she gone?'

'Town. Shopping.'

'Shopping? What for?'

'Clothes. She's got a date tonight.'

'Fuck off.'

Marie smiles.

'Honest. Old Tommy from the chip shop. He's taking her to Don Juan's tonight.'

Twenty minutes ago Chris wouldn't know what to feel at hearing this news. He'd certainly feel a little angry.

'Brilliant. That's fucking great.'

But now he just feels happy.

'Come on. Let's go downstairs.'

Chris takes his sister's tea and leads her out of his room and down the stairs. He walks into the front room first. David is sat holding a piece of cloth wrapped around something. Marie walks in slowly. David says nothing so Chris breaks the silence.

'What's that?'

He ushers his sister into a seat and hands her the cup of tea.

'Something Graham asked me to get from Tantasia.'

He opens up the cloth to reveal its contents. Chris' eyes widen. It is Mr Buckley's scales.

'They're Mr Buckley's!'

'Eh?'

'I swear, next door: Mr Buckley's. They're his scales.'

David looks at the scales.

'You best give them back to him, then.'

He hands the scales to Chris and sits back down, cradling his tea.

'Do you know where Mum is?'

'No, but Marie does.'

David takes a large swig and looks at his sister.

'She's shopping in town. She's got a date.'

Tea spurts from David's nose and all three of them start laughing. All laughing together.

Jean holds the tea in its plastic tumbler and sits back down next to her son's bed. His collapse in Saturn Amusements was due to a concussion caused by yesterday's fall. Jean nudged in the jackpot and made Jenny get out of her buggy before placing Paul in it. She wheeled him around to the taxi rank and threw her winnings at the turbaned driver, ordering him to get her and her children to A&E. When they arrived, they asked Jean about what happened and said he'd be okay but they'd have to keep him in for observation. Jean thought of ringing Barbara but then decided against it. She'd just done the right thing and she'd done it on her own.

Paul is awake now but groggy, his head bandaged properly and a drip in his tiny hand. Jenny is quiet in her buggy, watching the injured people in the other beds. Jean takes a sip of her tea and looks at her daughter. She's glad she didn't ring Barbara.

Barbara bursts through the front door, laden with shopping bags. David stubs out his cigarette and Marie gets up to give her a hand with the bags.

'What's all this about you going out tonight?'

David has a smirk on his face and Barbara glares at Marie for telling him.

'Just a meal. With a friend.'

Marie corrects her mother and winks at David: 'Not just a friend, though, David, a man friend.'

'A man friend! You old slapper!'

'Oh give over, David. It's only Old Tommy.'

'The dirty old man. Must be putting Viagra in his batter.' Barbara glows crimson and Marie laughs, holding the bags aloft.

'Come on upstairs, then. Let's see what you've got.'

David listens to their excited voices as they leave the room and head upstairs. It's nice to hear his mum so happy. It's nice to see his sister so happy. Just one more thing to do to make sure everybody is happy. He takes out his phone and puts in Tina's number by heart.

'Cross my heart Mr Buckley. Said he found it in a skip by Frank's Food and Booze.'

Mr Buckley looks at Chris and then at his scales.

'Is everything alright next door?'

'Oh. That. Yes. Just the dog. Squire had a mad half hour. Listen; mad rush, see you later, yeah?'

'See you. And thanks, Christopher.'

Chris checks his phone for the time. He begins to jog towards the woods; down past David's Garage, the dented corrugated door unlocked but untouched. He comes out at the zebra crossing – the multistorey car park to his right and opposite that the bowling green. He does a double take, making sure everything is okay, but there are no bodies on the bowling green and no people perched on the car park.

Chris heads down between the Trouble and Strife and McDonald's, checking himself in the windows of both. Maybe he should have changed. He's wearing his silver cap and blue school jacket. He's even got on his old Rockports. Fuck it. He's late, no time for that.

Chris darts past the Central Gardens. Two toddlers sit the wrong way around on a bench, legs dangling through the back and arms gripping imaginary steering wheels as they sound the engine of a racing car. Their mothers sit on another bench smoking cigarettes a catching up on who shagged who last night while their children imagine.

Chris cuts through the Archer Centre. The security guards are still moody and the kids are still giving them the run around but as he rushes past the card shops he remembers something – it's his birthday tomorrow.

Chris comes out of the back of the Centre and through to the bus station. The shelters are still painted with who loves who but the other messages flash by him as he sprints towards the main road, the bingo hall behind him making someone rich for the day. He crosses the main road and turns up past the detergent factory – the provider of Summer Snow.

Chris stops at the entrance to the woods, ready to catch the bride's bouquet. He puts his hands on his knees and breathes heavily, wiping the sweat from underneath his cap and then putting it back on. He stands in front of the entrance wall, legs at ease, one hand on his hip, his cap peak pulled back and his other hand shielding his eyes as he searches the road for a sign of her.

Chris is going to take her to the Field, the Field of Dandelions. He's going to watch her face as she looks at the blanket in front of her. He's going to instinctively know when she wants to run amongst those snowy heads and he isn't going to put his hand on her shoulder, he's going to take her hand and run with her, watch the feathers fly, see time disappear around them until only they are left.

Chris is looking for Keeley, and here she comes.